The car had nothing to do with the shooter

That meant there had been a third party involved.

Bolan placed the rifle across the hood of the Ford, drew the Desert Eagle then walked around the far side of the vehicle. The ground was covered in footprints, and rivulets of dried blood ran down the door panel. As he followed the trail of drops, the deposits of blood became heavier.

The Executioner opened the trunk and peered inside. The body lay in a pool of blood, the gaping wound in the man's throat still glistening.

Carson was dead. The unknown shooter was dead.

Somebody was playing for keeps.

Don Pendleton's Mack Bolan®

The Judas Project

A GOLD EAGLE BOOK FROM

WORLDWIDE®

TORONTO • NEW YORK • LONDON
AMSTERDAM • PARIS • SYDNEY • HAMBURG
STOCKHOLM • ATHENS • TOKYO • MILAN
MADRID • WARSAW • BUDAPEST • AUCKLAND

First edition September 2008

ISBN-13: 978-0-373-61525-4
ISBN-10:   0-373-61525-6

Special thanks and acknowledgment to
Mike Linaker for his contribution to this work.

THE JUDAS PROJECT

Life does not give itself to one who tries to keep
all its advantages at once. I have often thought
morality may perhaps consist solely in the
courage of making a choice.

—Léon Blum
1872–1950

Where is the morality in making the wrong choice?
Where is the morality in betraying your country?
I'm not concerned about redemption. I'm concerned
about justice.

—Mack Bolan

PROLOGUE

Lubyanskaya Square, Moscow

From the terrace of the Loft Café overlooking Lubyanskaya Square, Mischa Krushen could see the former Lubyanka KGB headquarters, now the FSB, where he had worked alongside the other members of the Unit. Those had been busy, heady days, when the Soviet juggernaut had been in full flight. Then life had had a definite purpose. They were safeguarding the status quo, working against the enemies of the state and orchestrating policy against them. For the Unit that had meant working every conceivable angle to bring disorder and chaos against the United States of America. They had an open mandate. Nothing, *nothing*, was barred: blackmail, out-and-out coercion, the use of terror and even death. It was all fair game to the Unit. It was the ultimate level in state covert action against America.

With the breakup of the Soviet Union many things changed. They didn't happen overnight, and behind-the-scenes power struggles and interdirectorate rivalries resulted in bloodless, and not-so-bloodless, coups. There were unexpected nighttime strikes, when dazed victims were hauled out of bed and driven to lonely spots. Many grievances were settled in that way. A single pistol shot to the back of the head cleared the way for new positions to be created. The culling lasted a short time, but when the smoke cleared there were new faces to be seen behind desks. Questions were posed, but seldom asked. Political maneuvering at the top seeped down through the ranks, affecting all aspects of government activity. The breaking away of Soviet satellite states simply added to the confusion. There was a hectic period when no one knew friend from enemy, and there was a great deal of closing ranks. The faithful remained together, watching one another's backs, and there were survivors. When the tidal flow receded and a kind of sanity returned, the time was ripe for new alliances and a rekindling of old ones. On the surface the New Russia showed a fresh face, embracing its hard-won freedom from the Soviet yoke. In the background the old guard drew into the shadows, watching and waiting, shaking heads in mistrust of free enterprise and the "me" culture, seeing values shrink and greed rear its ugly head in the form of the Russian *mafiya,* drugs, prostitution and the loss of military power. The early years of freedom, eagerly lapped up by a population long-starved of the consumer life, overshadowed the machinations of the political and the guardians of Russia's security.

The KGB became the Federal'naya Sluzhba Bezopasnosti, the FSB. The Federal Security Service had a fresh face that masked much of its KGB origins, and hidden within its many layers, the Unit still existed. It was employed in much the same way as it had been in previous years. There were still enemies to deal with. Conspiracies to uncover. Policies to carry out. Long-dormant projects to be dusted off and brought into the cold light of the new day.

Which brought Mischa Krushen to his vantage point, drinking a latte while he waited for his section chief to join him.

The day was chill, a searching breeze swirling across the square. It had the sharp bite that threatened snow. Krushen felt it against his face. He was well protected in a heavy overcoat and fur hat. He glanced up as he heard a chair being moved and saw General Yuri Berienko sitting down on the far side of the table.

Berienko had to have been in his late sixties now, his broad, Slavic features as severe as they had always been. Berienko seldom smiled. He viewed life and the world as serious matters, and especially the condition of his Russia since the disintegration of the union. Old guard he may have been, but his undying loyalty to the old Soviet Union was possibly even stronger than it had been when he had served it in the military. As a young commander in Afghanistan, his units held the records for the most favorable successes ever. His zeal and his ruthless attitude toward the enemy had never been bettered. He literally took no prisoners.

On his return to Moscow after the war he was to take up a command position within the KGB, where he helped to create and staff the Unit. He ran it as if it had been one of his military squads. He brought in men who had served with him in Afghanistan, men who were loyal to the state, but covertly more loyal to General Berienko. Under his control the Unit thrived. It held its mandate proudly, carried out its missions with unerring success and anyone who stood in the glare of its spotlight knew they were facing a formidable enemy.

Looking across the table at his commander, Krushen admitted to a degree of trepidation. As it should have been, he had always regarded Berienko with reverence and not a little fear. Krushen understood that was the way it had to be. He cleared his throat.

"General. Unusual to see you out of the office."

Berienko barely nodded. Like Krushen he was wearing a thick overcoat, the collar turned up. On his head he wore a black, wide-brimmed fedora. The thought crossed Krushen's mind that this was one of the few times he had seen the man out of uniform. It had been a well-kept joke within the Unit that Berienko most likely slept in his uniform and probably at attention.

"You know why I asked to meet you?" Berienko asked.

"Only that it had something to do with the Unit."

"Specifically Black Judas."

Berienko unbuttoned his coat, reaching inside to take out a thick cigar. The Cuban cigars were probably the only vice Berienko allowed himself. He lit the cigar with a battered old lighter he had carried around with him for years. When he was satisfied the cigar was well lit he turned his attention back to Krushen.

"Someone is trying to infiltrate Black Judas. I want you to find out who and put a stop to it. The last thing we need is some outside party attempting to access the project."

"Do you know who is behind it?"

Berienko studied the end of his cigar. "I have my suspicions."

"I would place Federov at the head of any list I had," Krushen said. "There is more to him than just a watchdog. We know how ambitious he is. He makes no secret of his desire to become even more powerful than he already is."

"Discretion is required here, Mischa. The Unit might still exist but I have people watching every move I make. You understand the situation as well as I do, Mischa. If Federov could gather enough evidence, he would have us removed. The man is just waiting for his chance."

Krushen understood that. Karl Federov was in charge of an oversight directorate, charged to monitor sections of the FSB. He was fanatically ambitious, a man who viewed everyone around him as a potential threat to himself and what he wanted. Krushen had run-ins with the man on a regular basis. He found it difficult to hide his contempt for Federov.

"Doesn't he realize the Unit is still an important asset? That the work we do is for the good of the country?" Krushen shook his head. "I begin to wonder whether Federov is as loyal as he makes out."

"His loyalty is to himself. Mischa, you must look beyond your mistrust of Federov. The man works for Alekzander Mishkin. Both of us know that Mishkin also has ambitions that go far beyond his present position. He is a minister in the Security Directorate, but he wants more. He has his eye on becoming president one day. Mishkin placed Federov to oversee the FSB so he had eyes and ears there. And the ploy is paying off.

"Look how many have died. The department is culling itself by weeding out those who even hint at any disloyalty toward Mishkin and his cronies. Assassinations. Accidents. Mysterious poisonings. There are times, Mischa, when I wish I was back in Afghanistan fighting those tribesmen. At least that was good, clean combat. You knew who the enemy was then. Now it is like battling in the dark with my hands tied behind my back. I trust no one inside that building," Berienko said, staring across the square at the monolithic yellow structure, "except you and the Unit. Mischa, we must do what we can to protect Black Judas. I want you to gather your people and look into this. Do whatever it takes. There is no place for being squeamish. Understand what is at stake here. Go where you need to, even America, which may be necessary to protect Black Judas. We need to secure our people there. I will try to find out who is betraying us here in Russia. And who, between Federov and Mishkin, is the greater threat to us."

"You can rely on me, General."

"Nothing on paper, Mischa. That is why I suggested this meeting. You can use any of the hidden accounts to fund your operation. Cash money is no problem. I'll wager that fact hasn't escaped Federov. That we have secret accounts available. It is well known Federov likes money. So beware. And make deals with only those you can really trust."

"Contact?"

"Nothing official. My own cell number only. I will call only on *your* cell. Let us hope no one has discovered those. Keep calls to the minimum. If I discover anything that might assist, I will inform you." Berienko toyed with his cigar, deep in thought. "The committee is meeting later today. We need to satisfy them we have everything under control. Be there, Mischa, but keep this meeting between ourselves."

Krushen picked up his cup of coffee. It had started to cool. As he drank, he found himself staring out across the square to Lubyanka. A slight shiver ran through him. He was sure it was only the cold, but for a fleeting moment he felt as if the building was watching him.

He lingered over his coffee, trying to put off the time

when he would have to return to his department office and take up his work. His concerns had not been eased by Berienko's remarks, but there was little he could do about that.

KARL FEDEROV AND his companion were driving alongside the Moscow River, the Ivan the Great Bell Tower and the Kremlin beyond the red brick wall on their left. The river had that gray, choppy look to it that mirrored Federov's mood. He had picked up Chenin at the last intersection. The man was hunched in the corner of the rear seat as if he were trying to make himself invisible.

"No one can see in through these tinted windows, Yan."

"So you say." Chenin stared at the back of the BMW's driver. "Can he hear what we are saying?"

"I am unlikely to employ a driver who is deaf, dumb and blind, Yan. Of course, he can hear. Now let's get this done."

"Krushen met General Berienko this morning at the Loft Café. They spoke for about twenty minutes before Berienko left. They looked as if they were deep in conversation. And Berienko out of uniform is enough to create suspicion. I'm sure this all has to do with them working toward activating their Black Judas project."

Federov managed a thin smile at that information. "I knew that pair was up to something. Good. Maintain a watch on Krushen. I can keep the general under observation once he is inside the building. Be careful. If Krushen even suspects you are watching him, I'll be arranging a section funeral for you."

Chenin's eyes widened with alarm. "Not exactly the most comforting thing to be telling me."

"Think of it as your sacrifice for the good of Russia."

"What about Mishkin?"

"I know his game, Yan. Mishkin has his eye on the premiership. He believes I am obeying his orders to the letter, and so I am. But only part of the truth reaches him. I tell him enough to make it seem he has the upper hand. Do whatever you need to gather information from Krushen."

They drove to the next intersection and Chenin got out. The moment the door closed, the black BMW glided away.

"Well, Kyril, what do you think our comrade will be doing after that conversation?"

Federov's driver found it difficult to keep the humor out of his reply. "Hurrying home to change his undershorts I should imagine, Colonel."

"I believe you may be right, Kyril."

"Where to now?"

"A slow drive back to Lubyanka. Take your time, Kyril. I'm in no hurry to return to that damn mausoleum. In fact you can drive to Kirov's apartment. I need to bring him up-to-date."

LEOPOLD BULANIN REPLACED the receiver, smiling to himself at the conversation he had just had with Mischa Krushen. He reached out and ran a hand across the smooth surface of the digital recorder that monitored every call he received. Bulanin had always believed in insurance, in one form or another. And the digital kind was the most lucrative of all. Of course it might never need to be used, but just in case matters got out of hand, it paid to be prepared.

He had recently accepted a contract from Krushen that required him to provide extra men to keep a check on some people who might pose a threat to the status quo.

Captain Pieter Tchenko was an investigative Moscow cop who had been running an investigation that was getting too close to Krushen and the FSB. Krushen wanted the cop out of the picture in case he started making waves, and he was not overly concerned how the task was done. He also wanted to know if Tchenko had any data that might point fingers at Krushen and his department. Despite the FSB's reputation when it came to stamping out such interference, Krushen wanted the matter resolved by an outside source. Mainly because he didn't entirely trust all those who worked with and around him. It was not the first time he had used outside help.

Yan Chenin, who worked for Krushen, was showing signs of becoming a little nervous, and the man needed watching. Bulanin was constantly amused at the complexity of business that came out of Lubyanka. The building had always been host to rampant paranoia. Even now, since the demise of the KGB, the place reeked of subterfuge. Bulanin suspected that everyone who worked in Lubyanka had to have a permanently stiff neck from constantly looking over their shoulders.

Thankfully he was a plain and simple businessman. His police file, because he had read a copy provided by a friendly cop, had him down as a criminal. A racketeer. A member of the Russian *mafiya*. Bulanin didn't care what they called him. He was successful, extremely wealthy and his association with people like Mischa Krushen meant solid, important connections.

He glanced again at his digital recorder.

And he always had his insurance to maintain those connections.

Bulanin reached for his cell phone, deciding that the first on his to-do list was the local cop, Tchenko. He would be the easiest to deal with, and anyway, Bulanin did not like cops. They were bad for business.

CHAPTER ONE

General Berienko spoke at some length, his commanding presence dominating the shadowed conference room and the men gathered around the large table. Seated next to the general, Mischa Krushen absorbed everything the man had to say, aware of a degree of unease coming from the group. They were all individuals with varying degrees of influence and power, each one committed to the older values of what had been the Soviet Union and distrustful of the way things were going in the New Russia. Each had a deep-rooted suspicion concerning America, watching the imperialistic moves the U.S. was making across the globe, and fearful that if it was allowed to continue, even Russia might be swept aside by the American monolith. Thoughts of armed confrontation with America was not to be considered within the near future. The downgrading of the once mighty Soviet war machine had removed its sting. It no longer had the mass of machines and men. The fracturing of the Soviet Empire had weakened its threat. It would take some considerable time to build up military superiority to its earlier strength.

When Berienko finished, he indicated that it was

Krushen's turn. A rumble of agitation rose from the group as it assessed what Berienko had said and Krushen allowed the moment to pass. He considered his options before he spoke, knowing that the men seated around the table were as committed as he was to Black Judas, but were still nervous as to the outcome if the project was brought into play.

"America has grown fat and greedy since the fall of the Soviet Union. It has reached out and used our demise to swell its wealth and influence. It has done it under the guise of helping Russia reconstruct. Admirable on the surface but by no means a selfless act. The Americans do nothing for nothing. Somewhere there is always the catch. There are those who do it by stealth. They employ others, often Russians themselves, to broker their deals for them. It allows them to infiltrate under a smoke screen. They manipulate or they buy or they bribe. They offer us their gifts like they did to the Indian tribes in their own country. Blankets and beads, trinkets to bedazzle while they stole land and slaughtered the buffalo. Now they do it with fast-food franchises. Burgers, and coffee in paper cups. And the people clamor for more, because they are blind to the larger picture. And all the while the deals go on behind closed doors. For Russian money and oil. Anything the Americans can add to their treasure chest. Nothing is done to halt this greed. Our so-called leaders do little except pretend concern, so we need to make things happen, and soon."

"Mischa, as much as we love the sound of your voice, is there a point to all this?"

The speaker was a stoop-shouldered man with a shock of white hair framing his lined, old face. He was Georgi

Bella, a Georgian with a fearsome reputation. He was old-guard KGB, and still a force to be reckoned with.

"With respect, Georgi, I am coming to the point. America wants to dominate. It is as simple as that. Look at the way they made war on Iraq. To get rid of Hussein? His demise was a bonus, something to add to the main prize. First they destroy the country and then return with their people and get money to rebuild. Again this was just a ploy to detract from the main prize. The oil. America would like nothing better than to get its hands on *our* oil, and they will try every trick in the book to achieve that. They want Middle Eastern oil, as well. To control it. To feed their greedy population and to maintain their war machine. In quiet rooms negotiations go on. Contracts are signed and deals are negotiated. All done behind the scenes by means of manipulation and coercion. The Americans are very good at this kind of thing. They have a sure ingredient that gets them what they want."

"What is that? Fried chicken in a box and bottles of cola?" someone said.

A ripple of laughter followed. Krushen allowed it to flow, easing the mood for a moment.

"Money," he said as the laughter settled down. "America lives and breathes on its fabulous wealth. It is what keeps the country alive. They have so much, yet they crave even more, and what it brings them. Power. Influence. If they can't get what they want by flexing their military muscle, they use money. It makes them believe nothing is impossible for them. But I think it is also what makes them vulnerable. America exists on a knife edge of uncertainty. If Wall Street draws breath, the country panics. At even the hint of a financial problem, shares tumble. The interest rate fluctuates. Millions can be lost in an instant."

"All very well, but how does it help us?" Bella asked.

"By understanding America's vulnerability, we have something to attack. Not with missiles. But by going for the financial heart. By destroying the U.S.A.'s financial power base."

"Black Judas?" Bella asked.

Krushen smiled and tapped the file resting on the table in front of him.

"Exactly. By using this," he said. He picked up the file and let the assembly see it. "We activate Black Judas and put it into operation. It is the right time. America is vulnerable at this moment. The dollar is weak. Hit the U.S. financial base now and we can throw the economy into recession. Use the skills of the Black Judas team to bring America to her knees, then take advantage of that weakness to gain control of the financial markets."

"You make it sound too easy," Bella said.

"It won't be easy, but the rewards could be incredible."

Bella nodded. "That is the part I am interested in. *If* it works."

"The team we put in place will make sure it works. The day the project goes into operation, the knowledge these men will have gained becomes vital."

"You are talking about individuals who have been in place for almost seven years," Bella said. "How do we know they have stayed loyal? Or were matters like this not included in your master plan?"

"All those things and more were considered, Georgi. An operation such as Black Judas required much planning. Failsafes were built in. Six men. Three teams of two. We spread them across the American continent. Each team carried codes that would allow it to access Black Judas and bring it online. In reality all we needed were two men to survive. Each one carrying one half of the access code. Their codes will be combined and Black Judas brought online."

Bella nodded. "And have you had these men watched? Are they all still alive?"

"Yes. We have a man in place, a handler responsible for an American turncoat. He also oversees the Black Judas people from a discreet distance. Since they became model U.S. citizens, they have kept up with technology advances and are highly proficient with all forms of computer skills. Probably to such a degree they could walk into any IT environment and make the staff look like kindergarten underachievers."

"And once this project is activated," Bella persisted, "what do *we* achieve?"

"Hopefully great things as far as we are concerned—crippling and widespread breakdowns within the U.S. financial world, meltdown of their administrative databases. For example, their welfare program would crash. Cash benefits that are paid to applicants would vanish. Bank accounts would disappear from computer systems. Even federal accounts would be affected. On Wall Street a virus would engage and spread throughout the entire system, wiping out transactions and losing monies and stock details.

"Our programmers have been upgrading and inserting current data into the Black Judas core for months. Even as we speak they are feeding in even more information, all collected via our own systems, which are extremely versatile. Our team is constantly checking American systems, preparing the way for the day we give the go-ahead. They are permanently monitoring the safeguards and backups that the American institutions maintain to protect their financial world. Taken to the next level, we could conceivably hack into their utility companies and put them out of action. We could turn off America's lights and plunge it into darkness."

"How soon will Black Judas become active?"

"Within the next few weeks," Krushen said. "Final protocols are being written as we speak. Once these have been fed into the core, the project will become viable. Within days of the activation codes being sent out, Black Judas will go online."

What Krushen did not relay to the committee was the information that had reached him from America that there was some kind of operation taking place aimed at dislodging the sleepers. He had the feeling it had something to do with Karl Federov, but until he could prove it he preferred to keep the details to himself. There were incidents that had taken place that concerned Krushen because they involved Black Judas. He had used his power and influence to keep them under wraps, not wanting to alarm anyone. Some members of the committee might panic if they were brought into the picture. Krushen found it easier to simply deal with the matters and say nothing to anyone who did not need to know.

KARL FEDEROV STOOD at the window, his hands thrust deep in the pockets of his thick overcoat. The concrete apron was awash with rain, a chill wind blowing it in rippling waves across the area. The airstrip had once been a Russian airforce base. It had been home to a squadron of SU-27 fighter planes, each armed with a GSh-30-1 cannon and carrying AA R27 missiles. This base had been one of many that encircled Moscow. Now, like many others, it had been closed because of rising costs and military cutbacks. All, Federov thought with some bitterness, in the name of democracy and freedom. He almost laughed out loud at the falsity of the words.

Freedom.

Democracy.

That foolishness was responsible for the breakup of the Soviet Empire and the emasculating of its powerful military might. The Russia he once knew had become another nation ruled by greed and hypocrisy and all the depravity that could grip a nation. Looking deeper, he could see that little had really changed within the isolated corridors of power. Those in control became stronger and increasingly wealthy. The never-ending struggles to stay in positions of power still existed. Those who had reached the higher levels were constantly having to fight off the ambitions of challengers. Mistrust, divided loyalties, plots and counterplots were the order of the day. It was the time of the wolf, a time when each individual had to ensure his own life and expectations were considered above everything else.

Karl Federov was one of those individuals and had already realized the potential riches Black Judas offered to someone willing to reach out and take an offered opportunity. The potential wealth to be gained by utilizing the Black Judas project would be staggering.

Alekzander Mishkin, Federov's boss, was no exception. The Security Directorate minister had ambitious plans of his own. He was not content remaining in his current position. Mishkin wanted to rise, to attain greater stature. His ministerial appointment had empowered him with wide-reaching authority. It was that authority and the ability to access restricted information that had resulted in Federov discovering the Black Judas file.

Federov had unearthed the secret of the project by sheer good luck. He had been going through old files, long forgotten in one of the basement storage sections in Lubyanka. He had almost passed over the sealed document file. Ready to put it aside, he had paused, something about the package rousing his interest, especially when he saw that it had been filed incorrectly and the stamp on the flap of the cover indicated it had been designated as ultrasensitive. Federov laid the file on the desk, aware that he had discovered something special. When he broke the seal and opened the file and saw the Black Judas legend on the first sheet, he *knew* he had found something special.

His first thoughts were concerned with how and why the file had been misplaced, but he dismissed the reasoning. Important files had been lost before, mistakenly shelved by some harassed, overworked documents clerk, moved around within the bulk of other files until it became forgotten. The staggering number of files held within Lubyanka's vaults, the bulk still typewritten and photocopied in the old-fashioned way of the ponderous machine that was the state security system, left itself open to mistakes.

Federov spent the next hour going through the stack of documents and photographs. He quickly realized he had before him the entire Black Judas project, from the overseers to the actual operatives who would be living their manufactured lives in America. The six-man sleeper team, awaiting the day when the call would come to activate the operation. Federov was not a man given to excitable expressions. By the time he realized the potential of the documents in front of him, his head was swimming with almost childish delight and he had a smile on his face that was entirely out of context with his surroundings.

He considered his options.

The first involved his superior Alekzander Mishkin. The discovery of Black Judas would realize Mishkin's dream of becoming even more important than he already was. He would seize the moment and use it to forward his own career. Taking control of the project and removing it from General Berienko's control would allow Mishkin to die a happy man. Once Federov handed over the details of Black Judas, any control he had would be taken away from him. Mishkin would become hands-on, wanting to be in charge of every aspect of the project. Federov would be given the task of overseeing the Unit's demise.

Federov found he didn't like that idea in any way. He sat and stared at the Black Judas file, lighting yet another cigarette. The ashtray on the desk was already full of half-smoked stubs. Pushing through his ordered thoughts was an alternative, one that even Federov found exciting, scary, full of risks, but if he managed to pull it off it would ensure *his* future way beyond his wildest dreams.

Understanding the way Black Judas worked had planted a rebellious thought in Federov's mind. It was based on the "what if" concept. What if *he* took control of the project and employed it to benefit himself rather than Mishkin? The potential yield from Black Judas was limitless. Instead of destroying the American economy, the project could be diverted to manipulating the financial world for Federov's gain. The more he considered, the stronger his feelings became.

He could do this. He had control of men, and the finances to fund those men. He thought of his life and things others had that he was denied. Black Judas could change all that.

Federov sobered up, aware of the magnitude of what he was considering. One of the stumbling blocks was Alekzander Mishkin. It was through Mishkin that Federov commanded his power. He would need the protection of Mishkin's position while he engineered Black Judas. To do that he would need to bring Mishkin into the loop. He would need to inform Mishkin about Black Judas, but not give him full details. Federov's mind began to work feverishly. While he considered how to gain Mishkin's approval, Federov was extracting sheets of data from the file, making swift notes on how he could work the information into a saleable item for Minister Mishkin. It took him another couple of hours to create his alternative file. By the time he made his way from the basement, back to his secure office, Federov had it all clear in his mind.

He was going to need time to make copies of the file and transfer data onto a CD through his own computer system. He would create two versions. One version would be of the complete file for himself. The other would be an abridged version, which he would present to Mishkin, with apologies that he needed more time to search for additional details. The minister would be pleased with what Federov had supposedly uncovered, unaware there was more. His gratitude would allow Federov to ask for whatever he needed in personnel and special dispensations. These considerations would let Federov pursue his own agenda, while keeping Mishkin dangling.

Federov spent the next few days transferring the Black Judas files onto his personal computer in his apartment. He scanned the documents and the photographs, building up a full dossier for himself, then edited the information into a presentable form for Mishkin. He made copies of both editions, deleted the data from his computer and shredded the original files. He took his time, not wanting to make any errors by rushing the process. Federov had a personal safe in the wall of his apartment. He placed one of his CDs there. The other copy he deposited in his safe-deposit box at his bank.

Later that same morning he presented himself at Minister Mishkin's office where he spoke in private, detailing what he had found, then presented Mishkin with the two copies of the Black Judas file.

Federov could still recall the expression on Mishkin's face as he had read through the data on his computer monitor. His enthusiasm spilled over to the point where he was almost drooling. Mishkin had finally turned away from the screen, staring across at Federov. He did not speak for a while. Federov could see the gleam in his eyes, almost hear the thoughts turning over and over inside his head.

"Who else has seen this, Karl?"

"No one. I did all the checking myself. Kept no written notes. The files I found were removed from the archives so no one else might stumble across them. I scanned everything I located into a computer and saved it to a CD. Once I'd done that I wiped everything from the computer and destroyed the originals. You have the only copies."

Which actually was not strictly true.

Mishkin was not the only one with high ambition, and Karl Federov was well placed to be able to use information he had found to his own advantage. Mishkin might yet find out he was not as clever as he imagined—not with Karl Federov working against him and not for nationalistic reasons.

"Black Judas," Mishkin had said. "That project has been guarded for so long, and deniability has been so strongly maintained, even I suspected it was nothing but KGB legend. But it does exist and now the FSB has picked up the baton and is sitting on the damned thing. Why haven't they activated the sleepers? What are they waiting for?"

"Chenin believes the final countdown is under way. Once the last details are established, the activation codes will be issued to the teams in America."

"Karl, we have to gain control of that project. If we do, we can write our own ticket."

Federov nodded in agreement, but for a different reason. *His* personal reasons. "I agree. The Unit will resist, though. They are still powerful, and we have to make sure we obtain every piece of information about Black Judas before they are eliminated. That's why I need to keep searching for additional data."

Mishkin had slapped his hand on the desk. "Damn Krushen's pack of rabid hounds. If I could get away with it, I would have them up against a wall tomorrow. A swift volley from a squad of our security men would solve that problem. Unfortunately those days are gone. We need to be cautious, however. There are too many unfriendly eyes and ears out there."

"Leave it to me."

"Anything you want, Karl, just ask."

This was working out better than he had ever imagined. Here was Minister Mishkin offering to give him anything Federov wanted. How about your job, Mishkin? Federov cleared his throat. "I have no problem gathering my main team. But if we really want this to work, I need the best."

Something registered in Mishkin's eyes as he had

glanced across the desk. He suddenly grasped what Federov was intending.

"My God, man, are you sure?"

"Can you think of anyone better to deal with Krushen and his people?"

"I see your reasoning—but…"

"We need him, Minister."

Mishkin still hesitated. He understood Federov's request. His urgent need to use the one man capable of dealing with Mischa Krushen on his own terms. The problem was that the man Federov intended to bring on board presented his own problems.

"Minister, you want this to succeed? Then give me what I want. Give me Viktor Kirov."

CHAPTER TWO

The Russian air-force transport landed on time, despite the inclement weather. Karl Federov watched it taxi along the runway, then turn toward the hangar. He remained where he was as the mobile steps were pushed into place in front of the opened door. A tight group of five men emerged from the plane and descended the steps. Four were carrying submachine guns. The fifth, walking slightly ahead, his shoulders hunched against the bitter rain, barely glanced at the men who had provided the steps as he proceeded in the direction of the hangar.

Someone opened the access door and the group moved inside, away from the rain. They made their way to the office where Federov waited, only now turning from the window. The man they were escorting held his hands in front of him, lifting them when he recognized Federov. Steel manacles circled his wrists. The man held them out to Federov.

"Take them off," Federov said.

"We were told—"

"To bring him to me and leave him in my charge. You have done that. Give me the key, then you can climb back into your aircraft and leave. You have carried out your orders. He is no longer your responsibility."

The man in charge of the detail still protested. "Do you realize who he is?"

The manacled man glanced at Federov, a faint smile edging his lips. He was tall, with broad shoulders. His head was shaved, the smooth skull glistening from the rain. He had lost some weight since Federov had seen him last and his face was pale, a little gaunt. Federov saw the big hands flexing. He knew exactly what the man was thinking, what he would do if he was not covered by the SMGs. Whatever else, Federov thought, they have not subdued his personality.

"Yes," Federov said. "I know exactly who this man is. His name is Viktor Kirov and he is my friend." Federov's nostrils flared slightly as he allowed his anger to rise. "Now get out of here," he yelled, "before I show you what my authority allows me to do."

The leader of the escort detail took a key from his pocket. He handed it to Federov without another word, turned and led his men from the office. Federov watched them leave the hangar and return to the plane. His own men had returned to the building and remained there as Federov closed the office door. He crossed to the waiting man and removed the manacles, tossing them onto the desk that stood against the far wall.

Viktor Kirov rubbed each wrist where the manacles had chafed at his flesh. He remained where he was, watching as Federov unscrewed the top of a large steel flask and poured hot coffee into a plastic mug. He held it out to Kirov.

"Not the celebration I would have wished for, Viktor, but welcome home, my friend."

Kirov took the mug, savoring the smell of the coffee. After he had tasted it, he nodded slightly. "An improvement on that cabbage water they gave us to drink and called tea."

If Federov felt any awkwardness, he hid it well. "Once we get to Moscow, I promise you something even better. I have arranged to have an apartment placed at your disposal. The wardrobe has new clothes in it and the refrigerator is well stocked."

"Will I find a young woman in my bed, as well?"

"That can also be arranged. I suspect you might have a little tension that requires relieving."

"A little? My God, Karl, have you forgotten how long I've been locked up? Three long, lonely years. Just make sure whoever you send has stamina. She will need it."

They both laughed.

Kirov watched as Federov drank his own coffee, his hands wrapped around the mug. "Are you cold, Karl?"

"Yes."

"Compared to my cell this is almost tropical. There even the rats wore overcoats."

"Dammit, Viktor, I only wish this opportunity had come sooner. You should not have spent so long in that place."

"I'm not going to argue that point," Kirov said. "Karl, I know that if there had been any other way, you would have worked something out. I heard how you fought to have me transferred to a better prison. You have been more than a friend, Karl. More than anyone had a right to expect. For that I thank you."

Federov nodded. "Drink your coffee, then we can get out of this place. We have a long drive back to the city."

"Plenty of time to talk, eh?"

"Yes."

"Good. Then you can tell me who I have to kill for you first."

For the first time since he had entered the office Viktor Kirov's eyes glistened with enthusiasm. Seeing the expression on his friend's face, Karl Federov smiled.

He had his man, the one individual who would help his cause and who would do exactly what Federov wanted without argument, or regret.

Kirov was thirty-two years old. The last three had been spent in a bleak, isolated prison run by the FSB and overseen by guards who were little better than some of the inmates. These were political dissidents, men, and some women, who posed a threat to the regime, as well as recidivists and terrorists, or possible terrorists. The government played no favors. If someone was an embarrassment, dangerous, with agendas that might create an outcry, then the isolationist regime in the prison would either kill or cure. Once the subject was out of the public eye, it became easier to handle.

Viktor Kirov was a special case. He had been trained by the very people who finally locked him away. Kirov was a natural-born killer, a man who had no conscience when he was given his orders. It didn't matter who the victim was. Man. Woman. Child. Kirov handled them all with the same cold detachment. His training had come from the best, and Kirov surpassed every one of his instructors. His supreme test came when he was given the order to kill one of the other applicants on the training course. The man had failed to reach anything like the required standard. His dissatisfaction turned him sour, and he began blaming everyone at the training academy for his poor achievements. His grievances were looked on with disapproval. He managed to alienate everyone around him. His vehement lack of control drew the attention of the academy director, a man who despised those who showed weakness. The director solved his problem easily. He chose the best pupil from the course to carry out his order.

He chose Viktor Kirov.

He was confident he had picked the right man. Kirov's performance during the course had been exceptional. The director, who prided himself on his ability to know his trainees, had reached the conclusion that Viktor Kirov was head and shoulders above the rest. Kirov was an individual. Something of a loner. A borderline sociopath. And his instructors had reported that Kirov had that rare quality capable of making him an excellent assassin. There was a cold streak within him, a propensity for violence that he kept close to the surface, contained and controlled until it was needed.

Three days after the failed trainee had quit the academy, the director asked Kirov into his office. He told Kirov what he wanted in no uncertain terms, explaining that he would not allow the man to spread malicious rumors about the academy. An example had to be made. Kirov understood what was being asked of him and accepted the mission without hesitation. The director offered assistance, but Kirov declined.

Two days later there was a small report in the press that a young man had been found dead in a back ally. His neck had been broken during an attempted robbery. No one had seen or heard a thing. The case was never solved and became just another statistic.

The director found the man's wallet on his desk a day later.

Kirov was immediately recruited into a special section

of the FSB and over the next few years his particular talents were well used. He became his section's chief assassin, traveling extensively to carry out wet work for his employers. Europe, Africa, even the U.S.A. played host to Viktor Kirov. He was never caught. He was that good. Perhaps too good. He began to enjoy his work too much. His masters tried to rein him in, but all that achieved was to make him strike out at them. He began to kill off the books. He turned rogue, killing anyone sent to bring him in.

In the end he *was* caught. His secret trial was swift, and the verdict all too obvious. He was sentenced to thirty years in one of the department prisons located in the bleak extremes of eastern Russia, a dark, harsh place where the worst of the worst were confined. Not executed, but placed in solitary exile in case the long-term needs of the state might one day require their dubious talents.

Kirov was one of those instances. He had been created and trained by the state as a killer. There was always the need for such skills. So Kirov was hidden away so he might reflect on his aberrations and consider his future.

Karl Federov had been Kirov's only true friend. Over a number of years an unspoken bond had developed between the two men. Neither could explain it, nor ever tried. During Kirov's good years in the section, he and Federov spent social times together. Drinking. The occasional female. It was an odd matching, but it worked for them both. Each accepted the other without question.

When Kirov was detained after his rogue episode, Karl Federov was the only one who spoke in his defense. He used his influence in attempts to have Kirov freed. Nothing came of it. In the end even Kirov advised his friend to give up, realizing he was going to be locked up. The day he was taken away Kirov's last request was to be allowed to speak to Federov, thanking him for his loyalty. For his part Federov said he would get Kirov out of his cell one day.

And now he had.

Kirov would be the ace up his sleeve, Federov's own secret weapon to be aimed and guided and allowed to use his unique talents against those who stood in Federov's path as he homed in on Black Judas.

A few nights after Kirov had come on board, Federov drove them around the city while he explained his intentions. Kirov listened in silence until Federov completed his announcement about Black Judas. He had smiled, then actually laughed out loud.

"Karl, you have become even more devious than before I went to prison."

"Does that mean you are in?" Federov asked.

"Of course. Did you think I would pass up the opportunity to screw the bastards who locked me away? I owe my loyalty to you, Karl, and no one else. In the whole of Russia there was only one man on my side. Karl Federov. My friend." Kirov peered through the sleet-covered windshield of the car, pointing to neon-lit signs that indicated a bar. "We can use this Black Judas to take back what those bastards owe us. Karl, let's go and celebrate. Then in the morning we can start to fuck the Kremlin."

Federov parked the car outside a nightclub. As he led the way inside he laid a hand on Kirov's shoulder.

"By the way, Viktor, I have a passport and visa for you."

"Am I going somewhere again?"

"Yes. This time your trip will be much more comfortable and pleasant. The U.S.A. You will go as a member of the Russian diplomatic service. Using the information we have from the Black Judas files, I want you to start tracking down the sleeper teams and eliminating them."

"Didn't you explain that these men carry the codes needed to operate the system?"

"Three teams of two men. Only one pair is actually required to activate the project. Now that we know where they are located, we can dispense with four out of the six. It reduces the chances of Krushen gaining control. If we take charge of the surviving team, we have the upper hand."

"It sounds good when you say it, Karl. Let's hope it works that way."

"Have I ever let you down, Viktor? Given you reason to doubt me?"

"I have to admit that has never happened. In fact you are the only person I know who can be trusted."

Federov nodded. "Let's drink to that, my friend. To you and me and Black Judas."

CHAPTER THREE

Stony Man Farm, Virginia

Aaron Kurtzman waited until his team was assembled before he laid out the information he had been gathering.

They were all there: Carmen Delahunt, a red-haired, ex-FBI agent; Huntington Wethers, a tall, pipe-smoking academic, a thoughtful black man who was a former professor of cybernetics; and Akira Tokaido, a sharp, young computer hacker who listened to hot music piped through the earbuds of his MP3 player.

Kurtzman's cyberteam, some of the best IT specialists in the world, were the SOG's eyes and ears. They manned the databanks and, aided by Kurtzman's programs, had the ability to get into the databases of existing agencies, extracting what they needed to push forward their backup capabilities for Stony Man's combat teams. Kurtzman's cybergenius was the driving force that enabled the team to create its unique qualities and advance them day by day. He was versed in computer science to a degree that reached near perfection. If he couldn't solve a problem with existing programs, he would write a new one to address the problem and get around it. He pushed himself and his team to the limits, constantly aware that when the SOG teams needed help, they needed it ASAP, not in a few days. His unshakable loyalty was legend, and his ability to come up with the goods on time was not open to debate.

"As we have no ongoing missions at the moment, and the teams are on R and R, I need you to look at something I'm going to transfer to each of you. Analyze the data, make up your own minds. I want to see if you get the same feeling I do. No bullshit. Honest opinions. I got the nod on this from a guy I know. He picked this up on one of his database searches and felt it worth further checking. I've done some, but I want to hear your views."

Kurtzman worked his keyboard and transferred the file to each workstation. As their monitors flashed into life, the members of the team swung their chairs around and got to work. Kurtzman wheeled himself across the room to his infamous coffeepot and helped himself to a fresh brew, then returned to his own workstation and began to widen his search parameters.

When mission controller Barbara Price walked into the Computer Room several hours later, she was surprised to see the team so focused on their tasks, as the threat board was just about clear.

"What's up, Aaron?"

Kurtzman eased his chair around. "Team collaboration," he said. "I need confirmation on something that could be important."

"As in Stony Man important?"

Carmen Delahunt looked around. "The way this is panning out, it could be."

"Hal know about this?"

"Uh-uh," Kurtzman said. "No point calling him until we're sure."

"Well, you've got me interested. Am I allowed to join the inner circle yet?"

Kurtzman's bearded face broke into a wide smile. "If the team's ready to give its verdict, you might as well come on board. Extra input on this is going to be welcome."

"Carmen," Wethers said, "tell her what we have."

Delahunt held up the printout she was holding. "Okay, basics first. We have three dead people. All male. All in their thirties. One in Grand Rapids. The other two came from Spokane. They all died within a couple of days of each other. Coroners' verdicts all stated the same cause of death. They were all murdered. Given a lethal injection of a poison that was difficult to pin down until requests for very thorough toxicology reports were requested. The tox reports identified the poison as an extremely potent strain that hasn't been seen for some years."

"It's been used before?" Price asked.

Delahunt nodded. "It was a favored means of execution from the days of the KGB. Back in the day no one could get much information about it, but some years ago a sample was obtained and it was checked out thoroughly. So much so that we now have a complete breakdown of the substance and it can be recognized. The last known instance of it being used was three years ago in Brussels when a former KGB agent was found dead in his apartment. It was suspected he was killed because he was in the process of negotiating a book deal where he was about to expose the old KGB and name names."

"So three men are dead and you're saying some cold-war KGB poison was used?" Price held up her hands. "Am I missing something here?"

"Yes," Wethers said. "Look at my notes." He handed Price a clipboard. On a sheet of paper he had written each man's particulars.

Price read the details. "Three ordinary American citizens killed by lethal injection? Why would anyone…wait a second. Why is the name Leon Grishnov written in brackets after Harry Jenks's?"

"Nothing gets by Barbara Price," Kurtzman said. "Go ahead, Hunt, you found it."

"There was a recurring shred of evidence that came up on all three autopsy reports. Each dead man had characteristicly Slavic facial bone structure. Not second generation that might suggest the men had been born here from Russian parentage. So we dug a little deeper, went into ex-Soviet medical databases. Military as well as civilian. The next problem arose when I realized they were not as extensive as I expected. I kept coming up empty until I ran across some dental records and we got a match."

"One lucky strike," Tokaido said. "The X-rays taken by one of our coroners matched the Russian ones."

"Harry Jenks is Leon Grishnov. Once we had that," Wethers said, "I concentrated on the guy and hit lucky again. He was in the military, trained as an infiltration specialist and designated as Spetznaz. The last entry in his record has him reassigned to special duty. After that there are no more records of him. It was as if he vanished from the face of the earth."

"We're widening our searches," Kurtzman said. "Might be we'll pick something up on the other two vics. Akira spotted something and is looking into it."

Tokaido tapped his keyboard and brought up an enlarged image. "I got this from the autopsy photographic records. From both cities where the deaths occurred. Had to do some cleaning up and sharpening."

"Is that a tattoo?" Price asked.

"Yeah. Each guy had one on the left shoulder. It's no larger than a quarter but very detailed. I had to focus in real close to make any sense out of it. Even when it was made clear, none of us could understand what it meant. So I sent them to one of our Russian contacts. I figured if the guys were Russian the tattoos might also have some Russian symbols."

"That's smart thinking."

"Has the contact come up with anything yet?" Price asked.

Kurtzman shook his head. "Lena did report it looked vaguely familiar but she needs a little more time." He turned his full attention on Price. "What do you think?"

"I worry when I hear KGB and Spetznaz. And especially what you found out about a Russian taking on the identity of a U.S. citizen."

"Okay, we know the old KGB was disbanded and the FSB took its place," Wethers said. "We also know that there are still ex-KGB around, some of them hard-liners in place in Lubyanka and who still have some influence. Right now we don't have a line on what we might have stumbled on. My vote is we keep digging."

"Could these men have been sleepers?" Price asked. "Put in place as part of some operation that might have been forgotten about?"

"That's a possibility," Kurtzman said. "Don't dismiss the thought about a forgotten operation. Though, we know some sleepers have stayed in place for a lot of years before they got the signal to go ahead with their planned mission."

"So why have they been killed? If the mission has been

wiped, why terminate the operatives? That part doesn't make sense to me," Price stated.

"I have to admit I can't figure that one myself," Kurtzman admitted. "Unless someone has decided to clean house and remove all traces of a redundant operation."

Price ran her gaze over Wethers's notes again, then reached a decision. "Okay, let's run with it, Aaron. Stay with day-to-day protocols, but see what you can figure out on these three dead people. I'll update Hal when he gets back, and I think Mack should sit in on any meetings. We could be needing his special input."

MACK BOLAN COMPLETED his reading of the file presented by Hal Brognola. He glanced around the War Room conference table.

"It points to something that needs checking out," he said. "There are too many facts to be labeled coincidence."

"It's the way we all saw it," Price said. "I was on board as soon as Aaron showed me the initial data he'd pulled together and got the team's backup."

Bolan tapped the file. "Priority is to assess what a possible operation might consist of. We have to work on the assumption that whatever was planned could still be online, just waiting for someone to issue the green light."

"We're digging deep trying to get a handle on it," Kurtzman said. "One problem is, we have no idea how covert this might be. We don't even have the luxury of a name for the damn thing."

Akira Tokaido opened a folder. "I may have something for you on that," he said, sliding photos of the tattoos found on the dead men.

"They tell you something?" Price asked.

Tokaido nodded. "The writing in the tattoo design turned out to be an obscure Cyrillic alphabet." He picked up one of the remotes that controlled the wall-mounted monitors and clicked on a screen. "On the left are the original three tattoos. Worked into the entwined snakes-and-scorpions design are number and letter sequences. Two of the tattoos have the same number-letter sequence. The third is different. Two different sequences come from the dead men from Spokane. The remaining one is Grand Rapids. If you look on the right, here, I've laid out all three sequences, this time in English."

They all studied the sequences. Even in English the lines didn't make much sense.

"Computer codes?" Bolan asked.

"I don't think so," Kurtzman said. "Not the sort of configuration that makes any sense. We'll run them but I can't see them giving us much."

"Maybe a number-letter code," Delahunt said. "I can check them against the FBI code-breaker data, but they don't seem to have anything I can get a hook on."

"Lena Orlov did find something that might offer us a starting point," Tokaido said. He highlighted a curving banner that sat over the main design. It was identical on each tattoo. "In English it means Black Judas."

"Great work," Brognola said. "We all understand Judas. The disciple who betrayed Jesus. Give anyone a thought?"

"Not immediately," Delahunt admitted.

No one else had any flashes of inspiration, so they spent some time going over what they had, pushing theories back and forth.

"Did Akira's suggestion about the three dead men being into computing go any further?" Bolan asked.

"Yes. He did find out they were all familiar with the latest technology. Systems. Security advances. They took every IT course they could log onto. These guys were heavily into it. You have an idea?"

"Pretty loose at the moment," Bolan stated. "We have three dead men. It's becoming more than likely they were foreign agents sent to the U.S. to assimilate into society and stay low. Each has a tattoo that appears to contain some number-letter sequence, meaning unknown at the moment. Our guys were all into finance-based employment and also heavily into computer knowledge, which in today's climate isn't suspect in itself, but could be."

"Don't forget Judas," Tokaido prompted.

"My next piece of the puzzle. Judas walked with all the other disciples. Passed himself off as one of them, while all the time he was working against them. Just what a sleeper does. Then Judas broke his trust and betrayed those who saw him as a good guy."

"Okay," Price said. "The Judas analogy works fine. But where is the betrayal here? Were our sleepers here to betray someone? Set him up as an assassination target?"

"Think about that."

"Why so many men?" Price asked. "An assassination wouldn't need that many, would it?"

"Good point," Bolan said. "And a hit against a current figure doesn't gel with a sleeper put in place for a long period. People and situations change over the years. Your assassin is more likely to be inserted in the short term."

"So no individual hit?"

Bolan shook his head. "Not someone. I'm thinking something. This looks like a complicated operation. A killing is a relatively simple matter. A target. A weapon. An operator. I believe these guys were going after something bigger, and not a bomb or a bioweapon."

"Striker, even *my* head is starting to spin," Brognola said. "Is there a payoff here?"

"Speculation at the moment. Theorizing. But I'm looking at the special interest in computers and the financial backgrounds all these guys had. And then Black Judas. I remember one of Katz's favorite words when he was building scenarios—extrapolation, making an educated guess at a possible conclusion once facts were brought together. In this case I'm linking Black Judas to Black Monday. I think we all remember that day in '87 when the stock market went haywire."

"Okay," Brognola said, pushing to his feet. He took a moment to consider what he was about to authorize. "I believe we have enough to initiate an initial probe."

"More than enough," Kurtzman said.

"Okay, people. I need to bring the Man up to speed. He's going to grumble about the possible effects on U.S.-Russian relations. I'll have to put the emphasis on possible illegal Russian presence within our borders. I guess that should convince him we have enough to look into this. Press the Go button, Barb. We need to be on the starting blocks. You ready to move out, Striker?"

Bolan picked up his copy of the file. "Give me an hour to run through this again and I'll suit up."

"Any thoughts where you might be heading?" Price inquired.

"Spokane first, then Grand Rapids. See if I can pick anything up from the crime scenes. Liaise with the local P.D."

"I'll set up flights," Price said, "and arrange for rentals at each airport."

"If you get to talk to the cops, check out whether they got hold of the victims' computers," Kurtzman said. "If they have them, I could do with downloading whatever's stored. Might add to our information."

"You'll be going in under Justice Department cover," Brognola added. "I'll call ahead and tell them we would appreciate their help. Aaron, what do you need?"

"Internet link is all. I can go in and pull out what I need from that."

"If they know we're downloading data, the cops might start asking questions," Bolan said. "Cooperation is one thing. Downloading from a victim's computer might hit their suspicion button."

"Tell them all you need is ten minutes to have a look at their e-mails," Kurtzman said. "My program can worm inside and download without even showing on screen once you get me Internet access. Nothing will be deleted and they won't know." He grinned broadly. "Sneaky, am I not?"

"You have no competition," Bolan said. "Okay, Hal, set it up."

CHAPTER FOUR

Natasha Tchenko had flown from Moscow to Heathrow Airport, in the UK, where she had been met by a cousin she hadn't seen for many years. She spent almost a week in London, and carried out the first part of her plan by tracking down one of the men she had been looking for. She had gotten his name from the hired thug who had attacked her in the basement garage under her apartment. Before she had rendered him unconscious she had extracted the name of the man who had given him instructions on how to find her. She kept that part to herself, planning to deal with Ilya Malenkov her own way. All she had told people was that she needed a long vacation to get over the sudden deaths of her family. Her main goal remained *her* secret. If she had even hinted at what she hoped to achieve, she would not have been able to proceed.

It was in London that the first moves in the tracking of her family's killers started. Using the information she had gained, she located Malenkov.

ILYA MALENKOV had paused at the entrance to the house, his feelings of uncertainty rising again. He half turned to look back over his shoulder, expecting to see someone watching. Apart from a couple of pedestrians at the far end, the street was deserted. The only movements close by were leaves from the trees blowing along the sidewalk. Even though he felt a little foolish, Malenkov took his time checking out the area until he was satisfied his feelings had proved false. Only then did he push open the door and step inside. Closing the door behind him he felt the silence of the house wrap itself around him. It still amazed him that despite being in one of the busiest cities in the world, here inside this house it was so quiet, removed from the frantic pace of London.

Malenkov shrugged out of his topcoat and hung it on one of the hooks in the narrow hallway. He felt the chill in the house and realized he had forgotten again to put on the heating before he went out. He moved along the hall to the door that led into the kitchen. As he pushed it open, his world went dark and silent around him as something slammed across the back of his skull....

HIS FIRST IMPRESSION WAS of bitter cold. Not just the chill he had felt earlier, but a persuasive cold that pervaded his whole body. The air he breathed in held a dampness that went with the smell of mildew. Malenkov tried to move, then realized he was unable. His wrists and ankles were bound and when he forced open his eyes he saw he was tied to the arms and legs of a wooden chair.

He realized he was completely naked, as well, his body pale and so chilled he was shivering. Now he could feel a sickly ache across the back of his skull. The clammy feel of drying blood that had run down the back of his neck. Someone had struck him as he had entered the kitchen, then dragged him down to the cellar beneath the house. He saw bare brick walls and felt the boarded floor beneath his naked feet. A single bulb hung from an electric cord, throwing pale light on the stacked boxes and other household items that had been stored in the cellar and pushed against the damp walls.

He squinted his eyes and tried to ignore the pain in his skull as he attempted to understand what was happening. Who had done this to him?

And why?

Malenkov believed it could be down to Karl Federov. He would do anything to discredit Krushen's authority.

Once the search for Black Judas had been activated, all interested parties would be alerted. Any information gained would be fair game for the others. But Malenkov was surprised at how easily his location had been discovered. The London safehouse had always been just that. Safe. It was a jumping-off point where agents could travel from London to distant points, away from Moscow. Despite the stepped-up security in the UK capital, it was still a freer place than back in Russia. A cosmopolitan city, where almost every nationality from around the globe moved back and forth, London was still one of the easier cities to maintain a safehouse. And they had always been so careful. The address and location had never been committed to any database. It had been rented through a number of anonymous aides, making sure none knew any of the others personally, nor had any more contact than via dead-drop mailings. Malenkov reconsidered that, admitting that nothing in reality was ever completely risk-free. Somewhere along the line, someone might have let something slip that had been picked up by a third party. Also, there was no dis-

counting the possibility of betrayal by one of their own.
Again that was something not unheard of.

In the final analysis it came down to the fact that the
safehouse had been compromised. At this juncture of
Malenkov's life the who and the why didn't really matter.

Especially in regard to himself.

What did matter was whether he was going to emerge
alive from this situation.

He heard movement off to his right. As he turned his
head, a dark shape loomed from the shadows. A figure
stood over him, silhouetted against the light from the suspended bulb. There was a sudden blur of movement and
he took a hard blow to the side of his face. The force
twisted his head, blood welling from a gash in his cheek.
The blow dazed him for long seconds, and Malenkov let
his head fall forward. Blood dripped onto his naked chest.
He picked up more movement and braced himself for more
blows. Nothing happened.

"What the hell do you want from me?"

"It speaks," a voice said from behind in Russian.

The sudden sound startled Malenkov, and what added
more surprise was that it was a woman's voice. Young, too,
from the tone. He was reminded of his naked condition.

The voice's owner moved to stand in front of him, easing aside so that the light from the bulb fell across her. She
was young, he saw. Midtwenties and very attractive,
though the expression on her face hardened her features.
Black hair framed a strong, well-defined face. Her eyes
were cold, devoid of any emotion. She wore dark, slim-
fitting pants and a black turtleneck sweater. A long, dark
topcoat completed her outfit. Malenkov saw the dark shape
of a handgun tucked in her waist belt and recognized it as

his own. She had to have found it in the drawer where he kept it upstairs. Now she took her time deliberately looking him over, her gaze lingering, a wry smile edging her lips. Malenkov felt an embarrassed flush color his face.

"Who are you? Dammit, woman, do you realize who you're messing with?"

"No one very big," she said. "Just a small scrap of lowlife."

"A dangerous mistake," Malenkov said. "I have no idea what this is all about, but you are playing games with the wrong kind of people."

"Believe me, Malenkov, I am not playing games."

Malenkov struggled against his bonds. His face darkened even more as he failed to loosen the ropes. Added to his frustration was the fact that the woman apparently had no immediate fear of anything he might say.

"Get me out of here, you bitch!" he yelled. "This will bring you more trouble than you can imagine. One word from me and I could have your family wiped out."

He saw her stiffen, recognized the fierce look in her eyes as she fought back some deep emotion.

"But you already did that, Malenkov. You and your sick comrades. My family all died at your hands, you pig. It's why you're tied to that chair. So I can let you feel what my mother and father and my young brother felt before you vermin finally killed them all. It wasn't all that long ago, so you must still recall the name. Tchenko. My father was Captain Pieter Tchenko. You do remember? Yes, I thought you would. So you see, your threats don't worry me. There's nothing left you can take away from me." She reached inside her coat and took out a gleaming steel-bladed knife, holding it so light rippled along the smooth metal. "Today is your turn. I ask questions, you answer. Each time you lie, I use the knife."

Malenkov realized from the start that she was not just trying to scare him. She made him aware of this by making a token cut across the soft flesh of his stomach. Deep enough to make him bleed and feel the pain. Not enough to incapacitate him. As the warm rivulets of his blood settled in his groin, Malenkov realized he needed to make a swift decision.

Refuse to answer the woman's questions and suffer further living pain, or tell her what she wanted and accept the bullet through the back of his skull that would end his life far quicker. He was under no illusion. One way or another, he was going to die today. The only question was whether he gave up the names of his partners and sent this woman after them, or tried to protect them and suffered by the knife in her hand. It was not much of a trade-off either way.

In the end Malenkov found out he was not so much of a man as he had anticipated. He gave up names and locations. He told her everything he knew. But not before Natasha Tchenko made him suffer because of his early resistance. Her use of the knife was crude, and Malenkov spilled a great deal of blood on the cellar floor. Whatever his resolve, it faded quickly, his pleas for mercy falling on deaf ears. So he gave her what he could, asking for her forgiveness. He did that with no sense of shame. Only because the pain he was enduring had to stop.

It did stop.

Suddenly and without warning. He experienced a sudden powerful impact to the back of his head, and before he even had time to realize what it was, the bullet from the gun in Natasha Tchenko's hand ripped into his skull and reduced his brain to mush.

Tchenko returned to the main part of the house and made her way into the living room where she had finished her search earlier while waiting for Malenkov. She had found the laptop he had stored in a cupboard. Now she connected it to the power and ran the modem cable to the telephone socket. Once on the Net, she opened the link and tapped in her own password to access the OCD's central computer database and ran a check on Malenkov. She had to utilize different strings before she pinned down his file. Her first attempts at getting deeper into the files were blocked. She had to employ her not inconsiderable computer skills to get around the blocks.

Interestingly she found herself in the FSB database and managed to extract data files before she was closed down. Despite her repeated efforts, Tchenko was unable to get back into the FSB computer. She had been locked out once her intrusion had been discovered and knew that a trace would already be in operation to find out where she had been working from. It would confuse Moscow when they learned she had been hacking in from an FSB link. She picked up a flash drive from the table beside the laptop and placed it in the USB port, quickly downloading the data she had saved. With the flash drive in her shoulder bag, Tchenko composed a short e-mail and mailed it to her OCD boss, Commander Valentine Seminov. She cleared the computer, making certain it was disconnected from the Internet, then pulled the modem and power plug.

Minutes later Tchenko let herself out of the house's rear door. She walked along the cracked stone path, through the untended garden and out through the gate. The alley at the rear took her almost to the end of the street, where she rejoined the sidewalk, checking the area. No one saw her leave the house, as no one had noticed her original entry to the building. It was that time of day when the majority of people were at work. Tchenko picked up a taxi shortly after reaching the main road. She rode it into the city and made her way to the river. Here she bought a ticket and boarded one of the Thames's excursion boats. Partway through the trip, alone, she leaned on the stern rail, waiting for her moment, then calmly eased the pistol from her coat. It was wrapped in a duster she had picked up in the kitchen and had used to wipe the weapon clean. Now she let the gun slip from her grasp and watched it hit the dark water and vanish. She repeated the move with the knife, then remained at the stern until the boat turned and started its return journey. Only then did she move away from the stern to wander along the deck, her thoughts racing ahead as she planned her next move, which would see her arranging a flight to the U.S. where she would carry on her search for the other men responsible for the deaths of her family.

THREE DAYS LATER, in the air over the Atlantic, Natasha Tchenko huddled in her seat, grateful at least that no one was sitting beside her, and refused to even admit that what she was doing bordered on the impossible. In her mind it was clear and direct.

She was going to America to find the people responsible for the deaths of her family.

And when she did find them she was going to kill them all…or as many as she could.

Ilya Malenkov had furnished her with a mix of information and, combined with what she had gleaned from the computer, it was enough to give Tchenko a starting point.

Malenkov, an FSB agent, had been part of the team responsible for the slaughter of her family. The initial hunt had been orchestrated by Leopold Bulanin. Bulanin was a Moscow racketeer, an opportunist who would involve himself in any venture that offered a profit. He was a careful man, who covered his tracks well and managed to stay ahead of the law through high contacts and bribery. From Malenkov's confession Tchenko learned of Bulanin's involvement with the search for information her father had gathered on the FSB's involvement with something he called Black Judas. Pieter Tchenko's investigation had brought the covert team of FSB and gangsters on his trail. Though she didn't know whether her father had given up the information he had collected, her family had still been murdered. Coming to terms with that was proving difficult for Natasha Tchenko, and she was not even sure that if she actually completed her mission her pain would be ended. All she could do now was go through the motions, pushing the memories to the back of her mind while she conducted her search.

She had names and locations.

The e-mail to Seminov pinpointed the names she had extracted from Malenkov. Her hope was that it might kick-start another investigation into the connection between the FSB, Krushen and Leopold Bulanin.

Her starting point was the city of Grand Rapids, Michigan, where Malenkov had told her the Russian team led by Mischa Krushen had just moved. Once she had her flight arranged, she had asked the London travel agent to book her into a hotel there. It would give her a base, somewhere she could work out of. She knew she was going in cold, with little advance information about her enemies. When she was on undercover operations for OCD, there was always a pre-ops period to study the opposition to learn about their habits and their propensity for violence, whether the undercover operative might be known to the target. It was standard procedure, necessary so that the undercover agent had less chance of facing the unexpected. It didn't guarantee total safety. There was no such thing in undercover work.

This time Natasha Tchenko was walking in blind. All she had were sketchy pictures of the men she was stalking. She had read up on what OCD had on the suspects. It gave her some physical images, but little else. But she knew they were dangerous individuals, used to working in the shadows. If it hadn't been for Commander Seminov's generosity, she might never have been able to look at their thin files.

It was late afternoon when she finally checked into the hotel. She went directly to her room, undressed and relaxed under a hot shower. After she had dried herself she fell into bed and slept through until the following morning from sheer exhaustion.

TCHENKO AWOKE from a deep and troubled sleep with a shocked gasp bursting from her lips and sweat coursing down her face. Panting for breath that seemed to have difficulty forcing itself from her lungs, she stared across the hotel room, barely aware that sunlight was ghosting through the curtains. The bedsheets were tangled around her lower body, almost imprisoning her legs, and she kicked them free with frantic actions until they slid to the floor. In a protective response she pulled her arms around her body, lowering her head, and fought back the tears threatening to flood her eyes. She remained in this position until her emotions calmed and she was back in control. Only then did she uncoil and slowly swing her legs off the bed, pushing to her feet where she remained motionless. She fought to eliminate the dark horrors flooding her mind, concentrating on reminding herself who she was and why she was here....

Her name was Natasha Tchenko. She was twenty-six years old, and was a Russian cop with four years served in the OCD in Moscow. At this present time she was on extended leave in the United States of America.

She had come to America to find the men responsible for the slaughter of her family, and when she found them she intended to pass sentence and execute them.

As the departing fragments of the dream drifted from her conscious thoughts—the same dream that came to her unbidden and unwanted most nights—Tchenko crossed the room and parted one of the curtains enough for her to stare out at the morning.

The dream was the same as always, seen from her perspective and reliving that dreadful moment when she had walked into the Moscow apartment to find her cruelly murdered family: her father and mother, throats crudely slit, blood pooling thickly into the carpet; her fourteen-year-old brother, Karel, his adolescent body naked and disemboweled, the glistening viscera trailing in soft coils across the floor.

The visions returned to her in the long, dark nights when her very soul cried for release, when she fought her silent battle to be released from those images, yet felt herself paralyzed and helpless as only the victim of a sleeping nightmare can feel. There was no escape until the nightmare scenario had played itself out and she would burst from that soundless torment, as if floating up from the deep, escaping into reality, her naked body bathed in sweat, gasping for breath.

The woman turned from the window and crossed to the bathroom where she stepped into the shower and turned on the cold water. As it struck her flesh she gasped against the chill, but stood until she became used to the hissing stream. She reached for the soap, lathering herself until she had washed away the sweat and with it the remaining shadows of her nightmare. When she stepped from the shower, she crossed to the sink. Her image stared back at her from the mirror. Thick dark hair framed a strong, not unattractive face. True, she needed a little sun to remove the pale skin and the emergence of shadows under her bright, deep brown eyes. She stroked fingers across the firm, high cheekbones, flexed her full, generous mouth.

"Tasha Tchenko," she said to her image, "you are a mess. Do something about it."

She called room service and ordered breakfast. While she waited for it to arrive she turned on the TV and flicked through endless channels until she found a news program that felt a little less frenetic than most. She sat in one of the comfortable leather chairs and immersed herself in the news summary. When her breakfast arrived she handed the smiling bellman a tip, then settled down to scrambled eggs, crispy bacon and toast. She helped herself to a cup of coffee. Immersed in her food she almost missed the item on the TV. She leaned forward so as not to miss a word of the report, turning up the sound.

It concerned a death. A murder, in fact. Nothing unusual in that. Most TV news reports back home in Moscow carried such items every day. East or West, people still indulged in killing each other on a regular basis.

This crime caught Tchenko's attention because the photograph displayed on the screen, taken from the dead man's passport, identified him as one Jarek Ovid. That was not his real name. She knew him as Oleg Risovich. He was a member of the FSB, working under Mischa Krushen. She listened to the report with growing interest. It appeared that Risovich had been attacked and stabbed to death in a downtown area known for its drug dealing. If Risovich had been trying to do some business, he most likely would have been going against Krushen's agenda. Krushen would not be pleased about that. He would want to remain in the background, not draw any unwanted attention to himself or his people.

Tchenko picked up the local telephone directory and searched for the Grand Rapids Police Department's address.

CHAPTER FIVE

Mack Bolan picked up his rental car from the agency and headed for the city. His task here was relatively simple—liaise with the Grand Rapids P.D. and take a look at the computers the police had seized as evidence. It was normal procedure for the police to check personal and business computers following unexplained homicides. Vital information could be stored on hard drives, something that could point to the reason why the victim had been murdered.

The call from Hal Brognola, explaining to the G.R.P.D. that the Justice Department needed some cooperation, had fixed the visit for Justice Department Special Agent Matt Cooper. All Bolan needed was to have access to the victims' computers and a modem so that he could set things up for Aaron Kurtzman to download the contents of the hard drives. The operation would be completed without any outward sign and the original data would still be left intact.

Bolan had already completed the first part of his assignment by visiting the police in Spokane, where he had performed the same routine on the laptop owned by Harry Jenks—Leon Grishnov. He had also carried out the same routine on the one from the bank where Jenks had been employed. Stony Man was already analyzing that data.

Clad in a smart gray suit, white shirt and a dark blue tie, Bolan approached the desk sergeant. He showed his Justice Department credentials and asked for the cop whose name he had been given by Brognola. He was shown to the squad room and introduced to the homicide detective in charge of the double investigation.

Homicide Detective Rick Hollander was in his midthirties, fit, but looked as if he had just emerged from a war zone. The guy looked weary, a little pissed off, struggling with the myriad complications that together make up the working life of a police officer.

"What I hate the most is the paperwork. It just never stops coming. Fresh forms to fill in. New rules to follow. And I keep asking myself, why did I want to be a cop? You know what else? I can't remember."

Bolan grinned, sympathizing with the cop. "Paperwork? Tell me about it. It's all I get to do most days. A field trip like this is heaven."

Hollander led Bolan across the squad room to his office. He showed Bolan the table that held the computers that had belonged to the two victims.

"Both plugged in and connected to phone lines. Anything else you need, Agent Cooper?"

"That's fine," Bolan said gratefully. "Hollander, thanks for your cooperation. I know you're busy and probably figure I'm a pain in the ass, so I appreciate your help."

Hollander grinned. "Hey, we're supposed to be helping each other these days. Right?" He jerked a thumb in the direction of the computers. "Knock yourself out, pal. I'll go get you copies of the case files I was told you need."

He left Bolan alone, closing the door behind him. There were two units on the table, a desktop computer and a laptop. Bolan set up the connection that allowed Kurtzman to access the first computer. While the download took place Bolan sat in front of the monitor, going through the motions of checking it out, jotting notations into a notepad. When the signal came through that the download was complete, Bolan made the second connection. Once the two machines had sent their data to Stony Man, Bolan used his cell to contact Kurtzman.

"We done?"

"My man, you have performed sterling work here today. Have the rest of it off."

"As generous as always."

Bolan switched off the computers and slipped the notepad into the pocket of his gray suit.

RICK HOLLANDER THREADED his way back across the busy squad room, a buff folder in his hand. One of his fellow officers waylaid him, discussing an ongoing case. As he listened, Hollander noticed Agent Cooper, back in the noisy squad room, watching Detective Steve Cross who was in a conversation with a striking young woman. Cooper seemed to be taking particular notice of the woman. Not that he could be blamed for that. She was, Hollander saw, a looker. Very attractive, with dark hair and a supple figure that couldn't be hidden beneath her slacks and jacket.

What Hollander was not aware of was the reason Bolan had taken an interest in the dark-haired beauty. She and the police detective were close enough for Bolan to have picked up on their conversation.

Bolan heard the words *Commander Seminov.*

And *OCD*.

He had turned his attention on the woman, just as Hollander appeared in front of him, holding up the file.

"Hot off the copier," he said.

"Good," Bolan said, neatly sidestepping the cop.

"I thought you said this was urgent."

"Thanks. It is. Keep hold of it for me."

In that moment the squad room erupted in a burst of shouting and general mayhem as a group of suspects decided they had taken enough time and decided to cause trouble. Fists flew and bodies were shoved back and forth. Desks were pushed across the floor, chairs thrown. Bolan was caught in the human swell, and the last glimpse of the dark-haired woman was of her being hustled out the door and into the corridor. By the time he shoved his way through the melee she was gone and so was the cop who had been talking to her. Bolan stood, glancing up and down the corridor, wondering who she was and why she had been at the precinct.

It was at least a good ten minutes later before the squad room was restored to what was considered normal. Bolan spotted Hollander, still clutching the file and nursing a bruised cheek, leaning against a desk. He made his way over to the detective.

"You okay, Hollander?"

"All in a day's work." He held up the file again and Bolan took it. "I thought you'd run out on me."

Bolan grinned. "Sorry. That woman talking to one of your detectives. You know who she is?"

"No, but we can find out. What's the interest? You figure on dating her?"

"Nothing as easy as that. I think she might be connected to an ongoing investigation."

"How so?"

"Something I overheard her say. It meant something."

"Oh? You sure it wasn't 'Hey, I'm available and I have an inheritance'?"

"For a cop you have one hell of an imagination."

"Yeah? Cooper, I'm not sure whether to take that as a compliment or a put-down."

"Believe me, it was a compliment."

"I made copies of everything we have on our two vics. Right now you're as up-to-date as we are."

"I'll leave my cell-phone number," Bolan said. "If anything else crops up, I'd appreciate a call."

Hollander turned and beckoned to the cop who had been talking to the young woman. When he came over Hollander introduced him to Bolan as Steve Cross, explaining that Bolan was a Justice Department agent. Bolan shook the young man's hand.

"Some kind of Fed, huh?"

"Something like that."

"Steve, Agent Cooper would like to get a line on that young woman you were talking to."

Cross rubbed a hand across the back of his neck, a grin forming. "Who wouldn't? You know her, Cooper?"

"Not personally, but I recognized a couple of things she said—OCD and Commander Seminov."

"Still think she's part of your investigation?" Hollander asked.

"I'm going to check that angle," Bolan said.

"Turns out she's a Moscow cop," Cross explained. "Showed me her ID and said if I needed confirmation all

I needed to do was to call this guy in Moscow. He's her boss. By the way, her name is Natasha Tchenko."

"What was her reason for calling here?"

"She saw a TV report about a drug-related homicide we're dealing with. Said she might know the guy from Russia. Said she'd be grateful for any information we could give her. Said it was in-line with an investigation she was working on and she would give us feedback."

Bolan found the information interesting, wondering what an attractive female Russian cop was doing in the U.S. with a connection to a murdered man.

"How did you leave it?"

"I told her we'd need to check out her credentials before we could pass along anything. Said I'd get back to her."

"Did she leave you a contact?"

"Cell phone and the hotel she was staying at."

"Can you let me have that information?"

"Sure." Cross wrote the details on a sheet and handed it to Bolan. "Hey, Agent Cooper, if you see her, tell her I said hello."

Bolan patted the young cop on the shoulder. "I'll do that, Cross. In the meantime try to stay cool. And thanks for the assist. Both of you."

"No problem," Hollander said. He handed Bolan a business card. "That's my cell number. Anything you need, you call."

BOLAN SAT IN HIS CAR outside the Grand Rapids P.D., ready to talk to Commander Valentine Seminov of the Moscow Organized Crime Department. He had contacted Kurtzman on his cell and a solid connection had been made via Stony Man, then routed to Bolan's cell.

"So how are you, my friend?" Valentine Seminov asked.

"Surviving. Have you brought down the crime figures in Moscow yet?"

"Ha. I see your sense of humor is as weird as ever. So, *Matt Cooper,* how can OCD help you this time?"

"A cynical attitude, Valentine. Maybe I'm just calling out of the goodness of my heart."

Seminov's throaty laughter rattled the telephone in Bolan's hand. "How remiss of me not to realize that."

"Natasha Tchenko."

The line appeared to go dead for a long few seconds before Seminov spoke again. When he did, all traces of humor had vanished.

"Is she safe?"

"As far as I know right now."

"You have spoken to her?"

"No. Only seen her once from a distance. She disappeared before I could get to her. She was in a police station asking questions. Identified herself as a cop working out of OCD in Moscow. Gave your name as a reference."

"Damn. I told her not to…"

"Valentine, I need to know why she's here and what it is she's after."

"Is it involved in something you're investigating?"

"Right at this minute all I can say is it could be."

"Are you sitting down?"

"Why?"

"Because this may take a little time."

"Go ahead."

"Tchenko *is* one of my officers. A very qualified member of the OCD. Determined. Single-minded. Resourceful. And stubborn. Like someone else I know."

Seminov detailed Tchenko's background. She came from a family with a long history of law enforcement. It seemed to be in the family genes. Her father had been a captain in the civil police, stationed in Moscow. "Had been" were the operative words. Tchenko's family—father, mother and her teenage brother—had all been murdered a couple of months back. Her father, Captain Pieter Tchenko, had been handling a case that had delved deep into matters that had moved far beyond his normal investigations. He had, it seemed, stumbled onto a deeply covert operation involving the FSB and former associates of the old KGB. When his inquiries started exposing names, Tchenko was asked to back off. When he continued his investigation, he was officially ordered by his superiors to let the matter drop. The case had been referred to internal FSB jurisdiction. Word came through that Tchenko was putting his life at risk if he did not back off. It had been the wrong thing to say to Pieter Tchenko. While he considered his options, something happened that forced his hand. His wife received a telephone call promising extreme violence if he did not walk away. The same evening Tchenko himself was tailed as he drove home and someone fired on his car with an automatic weapon. A second phone call, just after he got home, told him that next time the bullets would not miss. The physical and verbal threats simply increased Tchenko's determination. He upped his pressure on his contacts and concentrated his searches into the background of his investigation.

Less than a week later his Moscow home was broken into by hooded men. Tchenko, his wife and his son were tied to chairs and subjected to savage beatings. Worse was to come. Tchenko's son underwent a terrible attack by one of the invaders who tortured him with a knife and finally eviscerated him. The house was ransacked as the invaders searched the place for any files of evidence Tchenko might have put together. When they found nothing, Tchenko was shot twice in the head. The same happened to his wife.

"Natasha was on an OCD investigation at the time, out of the city," Seminov concluded. "She came back to Moscow to find her family slaughtered. Then she had to identify the bodies officially."

"Had she been aware of what was happening?"

"Yes. She and her father were very close. They discussed work all the time. She knew about the threats. She also knew that Pieter Tchenko would never give in."

"How did she take it?"

"That was the odd thing. She was calm. Even when we went to identify the bodies. I knew she was grieving but she refused to let it out. Not one tear showed, Cooper."

"Valentine, are you sure the killings were connected to the investigation? Couldn't they have been caused by a crime that went wrong?"

"We considered that but I don't believe so. From the way the family had been beaten and tortured it was obvious the raiders were looking for something. It was all very methodical. These people knew their business. They were more than street criminals. Oh, one more thing. Two days later Tchenko's office was found to have been searched, too. And the small dacha they owned outside the city. These people were searching for something."

"And Natasha?"

"She told me that on the day of the funeral she was followed to her apartment. Being Natasha she turned the tables and waylaid him in the basement parking garage. He went for her so she defended herself and broke an arm and gave him a good thrashing. We brought him in and questioned him for some time. He refused to talk until I threatened him. He broke down soon after and admitted he had been hired to follow Natasha and get her alone in her apartment. It seemed he was looking for data her father might have left with her."

"Who was he?"

"An ex-soldier. Hired by a *voice* on the telephone. That is how he described it to us. Even threats from Natasha couldn't get any more from him. We arrested him but by the next morning I had instructions from above to release him. I suspected OCD had been put under pressure from Lubyanskaya Square. My superiors told me not to make any protests and to let it go. Two days later that ex-soldier was pulled out of the Moscow River. His throat had been cut. Explain that if you will. I have a theory that when he attacked Natasha at her apartment she got something out of him. She never gave me any indication she had, but I think this is what she must be following up."

"Silencing that suspect could have been his employers covering their tracks. Making sure he couldn't be picked up again."

Seminov grunted.

"There is something going on here that is driving me crazy, Cooper. It has me by the throat and won't go away until I find out what is happening. This has the oily hand of the FSB involved. A shady deal."

"You watch your back, Valentine."

"I wish you were here to do that for me, Cooper."

"Was any data retrieved from Tchenko's investigation?"

"Nothing yet," Seminov said.

"Let's talk about Natasha Tchenko some more," Bolan said.

"I saw how restless she was so I insisted she take an extended leave. It was as much for her own state of mind as to get her out of the way for a while. Maybe I should have become suspicious when she accepted my suggestion so readily. I reminded her that she was not authorized to look into the case of her father's death. I should have known better. A day after she left I telephoned to see how she was and there was no reply, just a message saying she was taking a break, going to stay with family in London and she'd be in touch when she got back. Now you have told me where she has gone, Cooper, I can't prove why she went to the United States. But my guess is it has something to do with what happened to her family. As I said, I believe she learned something from that thug who attacked her."

"When I meet her I'll ask."

"You can tell her I'm mad at her, too." Seminov paused, clearing his throat. "But don't tell her I was worried. I like that young woman. She is a good cop. Intelligent. Capable of becoming a high-ranking officer. I would hate for anything bad to happen to her. Cooper, one more thing. I think you should hear about it. I did receive an e-mail from Natasha some days after she left Moscow. There were names she had learned about that only increased my curiosity. Enough to keep me looking. But I have to stay low key. You understand? In the e-mail she mentions a name. Mischa Krushen. He is FSB, and from what Natasha e-mailed he has some covert connection to a man in Moscow called Leopold Bulanin. Bulanin is a racketeer. His greasy hands are in everything illegal. The e-mail got me thinking. And I am still mad at being told to drop my investigation into Pieter Tchenko's death. I do not enjoy being made to back off."

"The more people make a fuss over something usually means they have a reason not to have it dragged into the open."

"We think alike, my friend."

"Valentine, I'll be in touch once I have some answers."

"Good. If I turn anything up here I will pass it along. You be careful, too. If there is a connection to the FSB, and maybe former KGB thugs—we need to be cautious. There is nothing nice about them. These are bad people."

"Hell, Valentine, if there weren't any bad people, you and I would be out of a job."

"That is very true. If I find anything I will let you know."

"I owe you, Valentine."

"Again? One day, Cooper, I will collect." Seminov's booming laugh echoed down the line. "Take care, Cooper. I have a feeling these people have something to hide and will do anything to keep their secrets."

"Remember that when you start poking around again."

"Of course. I am always careful."

"I remember that, Valentine. Goodbye, my friend."

Bolan ended the call, started the car and headed across the city in the direction of the hotel where Natasha Tchenko was staying. His conversation with Seminov had alerted him to the fact the young woman could be pitting herself against extremely dangerous opponents. It crossed his mind that *they* might be watching her and could decide to take some kind of offensive action.

CHAPTER SIX

He parked outside the hotel and went inside. At the desk he asked for Natasha Tchenko's room. The clerk was unhelpful until Bolan flashed his Justice Department badge. After that the clerk was only too eager to help. Bolan took the elevator to the third floor and made his way to the Russian agent's room.

He stood at the door, about to knock, when he noticed scuff marks in the pile of the carpet. Bolan crouched. The pile had been disturbed by twin trails of deep indentations. The pile had not had time to return to its normal position, so the marks were fresh. They could easily have been made by the shoe heels of someone being dragged away from the room. Bolan was about to move when he picked up sound from inside the room. He rose to his feet, opening his jacket and taking out the Beretta 93-R. He checked the selector switch and set it to single shot.

He tapped on the door.

"Room service, miss. Your coffee and sandwiches."

Bolan heard movement as someone approached the door. He heard the interior lock being released and the door was pulled ajar. A lean male face peered at him, scanning Bolan's clothing.

"You are not room service."

The accent was Russian. Bolan drove his full weight at the door, pushing the guy backward. He stepped inside, heeling the door shut behind him, then followed through as the surprised guy went for the handgun tucked behind his belt.

Bolan back-fisted the guy across the side of the jaw, following with a solid kick that slammed into his opponent's exposed stomach. The man grunted, still trying to pull his handgun free. The Executioner caught a handful of his shirtfront and hauled the guy close, then slammed the Beretta across the side of his skull. The Russian stumbled to his knees, his handgun slipping from his grasp. Bolan kicked it out of sight under the bed, then planted a foot against the guy's rear, shoving hard. The Russian skidded across the carpet, burning the side of his face on the pile. Bolan knelt astride him, one knee hard in the guy's spine. He caught a handful of the thick black hair and hauled the man's head up and back. The cold muzzle of the 9 mm pistol ground into the Russian's flesh, just behind his right eye.

The Russian cursed in his own tongue.

"You're in America, talk English."

"Who the fuck are you?"

"I see you have a good grasp of the language," Bolan said. "See how good you are answering questions?"

The man stiffened as Bolan pushed down harder with his knee.

"What?"

"The woman. Where did they take her?"

"I do not know." The guy twisted his head around to

speak. Bolan saw blood running down his face where the Beretta had landed.

"Start to remember. I'm not going to spend too much time on this."

The Russian bucked violently, dislodging Bolan, and they rolled across the carpet, each trying for the advantage. The Russian seemed oblivious to the gun in Bolan's hand as he twisted and squirmed in his attempt to break clear. He managed to get clear, but instead of making a break he threw himself back at Bolan, arching above him, reaching out with both hands. His move was badly mistimed, giving Bolan the opportunity to draw up both legs, then slam his feet against the guy's lower body. The big American put his full strength into shoving the man away. The force of the move lifted the Russian off his feet and launched him backward across the room. The outer wall brought him to a bone-crunching stop. The Russian's breath exploded from his lips as the back of his skull impacted against the wall.

Bolan gained his feet and bent over the Russian. The man was barely conscious, breath gusting roughly from his lungs.

He searched the Russian's pockets and found nothing of great interest until he came across a folded piece of paper that looked as if it had been torn from a pad. On it was a telephone number and some writing in Russian.

Bolan took out his cell phone and speed-dialed Aaron Kurtzman's direct line. After a series of relay cutouts, Kurtzman picked up.

"Bear, I want a telephone number trace fast. I think it's a Grand Rapids local number." He read off the number. "I'll stay on the line."

While he waited Bolan crossed to the bed and retrieved

the gun the Russian had dropped. It was a Glock. He checked the mag and found it full. He tucked the pistol in his belt.

"Got your location," Kurtzman announced.

"Go ahead."

"It's an old office building in downtown Grand Rapids." Kurtzman gave him the address. "Hey, do you have a navigation system in your rental?"

"Yes."

"Write down these coordinates. Feed them into the unit and it should guide you direct to the address."

Bolan wrote the numbers on a pad he found on the bedside cabinet.

"Thanks, Bear. Tell Hal I'll update him when I get the time."

Bolan cut the connection, then punched in the number for Rick Hollander. When the detective came on the line, Bolan didn't give him time to ask questions.

"Natasha Tchenko's hotel. Her room. You'll find a guy there. I suggest you call an ambulance. Make sure he stays under guard."

He cut off instantly, left the room and made his way down to the hotel lobby. Outside he climbed into the rental, tapped in the reference numbers Kurtzman had supplied and watched as the navigation system adjusted its display. The map showed where he was and the route he needed to take to locate the address.

"God bless technology," Bolan muttered as he pulled into the flow of traffic.

RUNDOWN AND DESOLATE. Broken windows. The frontage littered and graffiti covered. The building exuded despair.

Even the For Rent sign had quit trying, sagging loosely from the wall.

Bolan parked a couple of hundred yards down the street from the entrance to the basement parking garage. He eased out of the vehicle and made his way across to the down ramp. There was no time for an extended recon of the place. If the men who had taken Natasha Tchenko were anything like the one back at the hotel, finesse would not be a job requirement. From what he had already learned about these people they had little regard for human life.

The Executioner walked slowly down the ramp, spotting a couple of cars parked close to the access doors. The garage was shadowed, the air musty and damp. Water dripped somewhere, and the concrete under his feet was dusty. Sound echoed. He pushed through the doors and into the building proper. He made for the stairs next to the bank of elevators, noticing the scuff marks in the accumulated dust. As he catfooted to the next landing, Bolan eased the Beretta from its shoulder holster and moved the fire selector to 3-round-burst mode. He pushed open the door and stepped into the corridor beyond.

A number of doors lined the corridor, and his attention was drawn to scuff marks in the dust leading to one. Bolan pressed against the wall to one side and reached for the doorknob. He turned it slowly, keeping the bulk of his body away from the flimsy wood panels. The second he felt the door free itself from the latch he paused, lowering into a crouch. He slowly began to push the door open from floor level.

The crackle of autofire confirmed he had chosen the right room. The upper panel of the door was torn to shreds by the volley of 9 mm slugs passing through it. The angle of the shots told Bolan the shooter inside the room was standing directly in-line with the door. When the firing stopped, he hit the door with his left shoulder, driving it back against the inner wall. The shooter stood in front of him. Bolan's arm was stretched forward and he hit his adversary with a 9 mm trio, chest high, the slugs coring in to puncture the heart. The guy stepped back, his expression revealing shock before he toppled to the floor.

The Executioner sensed someone at the far side of the room, partially concealed in shadow. The gunner swung his weapon toward Bolan, who turned on his heels, dropping to a crouch. The move put him below his opponent's muzzle. As the man attempted to correct his aim, Bolan hit him with a triburst. The guy grunted under the impact, stumbling back, striking the wall and losing all coordination. Bolan, still crouching, angled the Beretta's muzzle up and laid a second burst that slammed the guy's head back against the wall, leaving a red smear when the target dropped.

The room, once a large office, appeared empty until Bolan saw the dark-haired figure slumped in a chair, hands bound to the frame behind her. He double-checked the room, making sure there were no other entrances or exits, then crossed to stand over the captive, slipping the Beretta back in its holster. He recognized Natasha Tchenko immediately. Her clothing was crumpled and dusty, her hair untidy and she had a raw bruise around the left side of her mouth. As Bolan appeared in front of her she looked up, her eyes locking on his. "You were at the police station," she said. "Looking for me?"

"Not then, Miss Tchenko. But I have been since."

"Are you a policeman?"

Bolan stepped to the rear of the chair and crouched to loosen the electrical cord that held her immobile. As it fell away he saw the red marks it had made in her flesh.

"You didn't answer my question," she said, and pushed to her feet. She would have keeled over if Bolan hadn't noticed her sway and grabbed her. "Hey, let go."

Bolan ignored her demand and maintained his firm grip. "You want to fall down? Or are we going to start off right?"

Tchenko let herself lean against him for a moment, her breath warm against his cheek. Then he felt her body firm up and she gently eased out of his grip, reaching up to run her hands through her hair. "I must look a mess."

Bolan smiled. "No, you don't."

"Who are you?"

"A friend. On the same trail as you are."

"You are looking for Krushen?"

Bolan nodded. "And the others working with him. Plus a few unknowns. The problem is, they know you're here searching for them. These people have good intel."

Tchenko impatiently brushed at the dust on her clothing. Cop or not, she was still a woman and couldn't avoid concern over her appearance. "Shouldn't we get away from here? They told me others would come to question me."

"I have a car outside." Bolan turned and crossed to the first dead guy. He bent over and searched him, finding a SIG-Sauer P-226 pistol inside the guy's jacket. He took it and the extra clip from one of the pockets. "You might feel better with this," he said, handing the weapon to the woman.

She took the pistol, checked it, then tucked it behind her belt, beneath her jacket. "You obviously know my name. What do I call you?"

"Cooper. Matt to my friends."

He led the way back down to the parking garage, walking with Tchenko across the dirty concrete. She stared at him assessingly.

Bolan led her out onto the street, to where his rental was parked. He fired up the engine and moved off.

"Where are we going?" Tchenko asked.

"Somewhere we can talk and give you time to take stock. There's no point going back to your hotel if they know where you're staying. By now it's likely to be crawling with cops, as well."

"Are you sure *you're* not a cop? You act like one."

"According to Commander Seminov, you're a good one. He sends his regards by the way."

"You have spoken to him?"

Bolan nodded. "He told me all about you."

"I wish I could have heard that conversation."

"He's good and mad at you. But he says you're good at your job, and Valentine doesn't lie."

"You must know the commander well."

"We've worked together a few times. He's concerned about you."

"I know what I'm doing." Her tone was suddenly sharp and defensive. Bolan was on fragile ground now. "Don't even think about talking me out of it. It is not your business."

Bolan didn't say any more on the subject. He wanted to save any arguments until they were out of the public eye. Beside him Tchenko had moved to the far side of her seat, leaning hard against the door. She stared out the window, refusing to meet his gaze. He left her to it. Bolan understood her feelings. She was still fighting the loss of her family. He could sympathize with her. He had gone through the same loss when his own family had died, filling him with thoughts of revenge. The hurt was a hard thing to handle and the loss itself never went away completely. Even now, after all the years, Mack Bolan still missed his family.

As he drove, Bolan contacted Stony Man again and asked the mission controller to make a hotel reservation for him.

He got a return call ten minutes later. "Suite at the Amway Grand Plaza," Barbara Price told him.

Bolan thanked her and hung up.

It had just started to rain and a chill breeze was cutting along the street, sharpening the air. Bolan climbed out of the rental and handed the keys to the parking valet, then took the parking slip. He took his bags from the trunk and waited for Tchenko to follow him inside the hotel. He identified himself at the desk. The receptionist asked him to fill in the registration card, smiling across the desk.

"Your suite is ready for you, Mr. Cooper," she said. "If you need anything just call the desk and ask for Shelly." She absently touched the metal name tag on her jacket.

"How about a large pot of fresh coffee and a plate of sandwiches, Shelly?"

"I'll arrange that. What kind of filling in the sandwiches?"

Bolan grinned. "Why don't you surprise me?"

"I'll do my best, Mr. Cooper."

Bolan took the key card, picked up his bags and led the way to the elevators. They emerged on their floor and made their way along the subdued, dimly-lit corridor.

"This is better than the hotel I was staying in," Tchenko commented.

"I'll be reminded about that when I hand in the bill."

He opened the suite door and they stepped inside. Bolan closed and secured the door.

Tchenko stood in the center of the room, staring absently at the decor, hands at her sides. "Very nice."

One of Bolan's bags contained his combat gear and weapons. He showed the contents to her.

"I'll stow this in the wardrobe so you'll know where it is if things go bad."

"Are you expecting trouble?"

"I always expect trouble," Bolan stated. He took out the Glock he'd confiscated from the Russian in her room. "Sometimes the opposition contributes. Always handy."

"And the money?" she asked, seeing the wedge of cash in a plastic wrapper that was tucked into the side pocket.

"Money talks in anyone's language. Can be useful."

Tchenko's response was negative. Her mood had changed abruptly, leaving her pensive.

"Coffee shouldn't be long," Bolan said, getting no further response. "This is going to be hard if we don't talk."

"What do you want me to say? I *am* grateful for what you did back there. Yes, you saved my life. I can only thank you once. But it doesn't mean I have to explain myself to you. Or to Commander Seminov. I'm sure he told you every detail of what has happened. But this is my business, something I have to take care of because no one can understand what has happened to me." Her voice was hard now. "None of you can understand what I have lost. How I felt when I saw what had been done to them."

"Yes, I can. Only too well. Right now you have blind anger directing you. Making you take unnecessary risks while you race around trying to get at the ones who took your family away. That anger is going to get *you* killed.

And if that happens your family will have died for nothing. What do you want to do? Chase around and shoot at every shadow? Jump off buildings, letting everyone know who you are? Let Krushen see every move you make? That would suit him. Make it easy for him to take you down. I thought the plan was for you to deal with him?"

She rounded on him, her face flushed with anger, her eyes burning with the all-consuming fires of rage keeping her on her feet. Bolan saw her body tense up, as if she was about to hurl herself at him.

"How can you know what I'm feeling? To see your dead family that way? Life taken away by some animals, and to know those people are still walking around. At night I see them in my dreams. And I see my father and mother and my brother, too. Dead and bloody. And when I wake in the morning all I think about is how I can make it right. The only way is to make sure Krushen and his people do not get way with it. And you say you understand how I feel, Cooper? That is an insult."

Bolan turned to face her, his expression passive, his voice gentle when he spoke. He did understand. His problem was to make her realize without sounding as if he was patronizing her. The last thing he would ever do was play down the terrible thing that had happened to her family and what it had done to her.

"Before you jump in and tear my head off, yes, I do understand what you're going through. You lost your family. They died because of what others did. And that's exactly how mine died. They were innocent victims, too. I had to make things right for them. The first thing I learned was to stay in control. So let the rage go. It doesn't diminish the loss, but it lets you control it, gives you the clarity to look beyond the madness and concentrate on what you have to do. You want to settle for your family? I have no quarrel there. All I'm suggesting is you lay it out and study what has to be done. Take a piece here and there. Work on *their* weaknesses and use those weaknesses against them. Do that and there's a better chance you'll come through in one piece. Go at it head-on, and you'll miss the main chance and offer them an opportunity to catch you blind. If you die going in hog wild, your family doesn't get their chance."

Right then she reached under her jacket and dragged out the SIG, and in her anger she pointed it at Bolan, struggling with the emotions that were bubbling beneath her tough outer shell. The muzzle trembled as she stared across the weapon at Bolan's face, searching for answers to the turmoil inside her. She wanted someone to strike out at. Someone to punish for her loss.

"They slaughtered them, Cooper. Tied them up. Tortured them and slaughtered them."

"Natasha, your family would want you to find peace."

Bolan watched as she absorbed his words, the frustration still etched across her face. It showed in the taut set of her jaw. The way her brows arched above angry eyes. White creases formed at the corners of her lips as she fought back the torrent of words that threatened to unleash themselves on him. He sensed, even felt, the turmoil fighting inside her. He understood because he *had* gone through the same thing. His own emotions had hauled him back and forth, demanding vengeance, yet at the same time cautioning for a reasoned response.

He watched as she turned and slumped against the wall, her shoulders hunched as she struggled with her inner demons. Her breasts rose and fell rapidly, the breath ragged, expelled in tight gasps. He began to realize that this was most probably the first time she had allowed real grief to emerge. The hand gripping the pistol slackened, the barrel drooping toward the floor as her simmering emotions came rushing out of her, draining away the pent-up rage. He heard a soft, almost childlike sigh and for the first time her eyes glistened with repressed tears. Bolan didn't say a word. He simply reached out one big hand and she eased away from the wall and allowed him to pull her into his arms. He felt her head against his chest, heard the pistol drop to the floor just before the wrenching tears came and she gave in to her long-held emotions.

CHAPTER SEVEN

"The traveler wants to come home."

As the quiet statement burrowed into his consciousness, he felt his fingers close tightly around the telephone
receiver, knuckles popping under the exertion. Only six
words, but having the impact of a bullet driving through
his brain. For a moment he was lost, his world spiraling
around him. He was staring out through the living-room
window, across the neat lawn to the peaceful aspect of the
houses across the street.

The words had always been there, pushed far to the
back of his mind, yet he had always known that one day
they might be spoken to him and his life could change if
he allowed them to influence him.

"Did you hear me?" the caller said.

He cleared his throat, aware it had gone dry. "Yes. I
heard."

"And you understand?"

"Of course I understand." This time a little sharpness entered his tone.

The caller had to have recognized his defiance. There
was a hesitation before he spoke again. "So?"

He failed to grasp what was expected of him for a moment, then his distant training clicked in and he knew he needed to respond.

"The traveler will be welcome."

"Good. Expect another call soon. We need to meet very soon. Things have happened."

The caller cut the connection and he was left holding the phone, the tension in his fingers curled around the receiver starting to hurt.

"I said, hey, sleepyhead, there's coffee here."

The voice cut through his reflective mood and he turned to see his wife standing at his side, holding out a mug of steaming coffee. She was looking at him with a puzzled expression on her pretty face.

"Is everything all right? Was it a bad-news call?"

He looked at the receiver, then snapped back to reality. He dropped it back on the base. "No. Just an impatient client needing advice."

"Don't they know you're allowed days off, too?"

"I scheduled him for midweek." He took the coffee. "Thanks, honey. You off to the mall now?"

"Oh, yes," she said, smiling.

Even in soft, faded jeans and T-shirt, her dark hair framing her face, she looked ravishing. Turning, she picked up her jacket and purse, then leaned across to kiss his cheek.

"See you later," he said. "Hey, you be careful."

"I will. Just stop fussing, okay?"

She was gone moments later, the front door clicking shut behind her. He stood and watched her appear outside, walking to the red Suburban parked beside his own BMW. She waved at him from behind the wheel, then reversed onto the quiet street and was gone.

In America he was Thomas Carson. He ran his own financial consultancy business, employing ten people. The house he lived in had been paid for two years ago. His wife, Megan, was a successful Realtor. It was through her job they had met, when he was looking for a home to buy. In every respect Carson was a success. He worked and lived the American dream.

In the reality of his past he was Boris Yolentov, Russian born and a sleeper agent placed within American society as a member of the Black Judas project. Along with his five other team members his initial brief had been to become a model citizen, building his life and honing the IT skills that would be used once the project had been activated.

"The traveler wants to come home."

The phrase that told him Black Judas was soon to become a reality. Though he was unsure what had been meant by "things have happened."

As far as he was concerned, Black Judas had lost its credibility. His response to his caller, the expected phrase, had been through sheer reflex, and delivered because if he had not given the correct answer suspicion would have been aroused. His caller would be expecting him to set into motion the first moves in the predetermined Black Judas scenario, which would allow him some clear time to make *his* own moves. His get-out clause. Something he had been planning over the past two years. Thomas Carson, because that was who he considered himself now, had not simply been playacting the American dream. He had come to embrace it within the first three years of coming to America. He enjoyed the freedom, the wealth, the trappings that went with it all, and he wanted no more part in the project that had been named Black Judas. Once he had opted out,

Carson accepted certain restraints that would be placed on him with that decision.

The Unit would view his defection as a traitorous act against Mother Russia. More than that, he would be immediately placed under a death sentence. He had no doubt about that. Anyone who decided to step away from the operation, denying allegiance to his country and betraying his comrades, would be hunted down and exterminated with extreme prejudice. He took that on board with the same cool deliberation that had generated his defection. Every decision, every alternate move, had an equal response, and that had to be considered and accepted before any move ahead could be taken. Thomas Carson absorbed the consequences of his decision and carried on regardless.

He'd made his arrangements. Carefully and by degrees. He had a flair for business, and his company, of which he had full control, was extremely successful. So money was no problem. He diverted cash amounts, via a personal computer that was separate from the company IT system into an account established in the Cayman Islands. Another in a Swiss bank. Under a new name. The same name he used to rent an apartment in Miami. His business trips to the city allowed him to furnish and stock the place. The place was looked after by the rental service company. All he had to do was to phone ahead and whatever he wanted would be delivered and ready whenever he showed up, which became regular. He established his credentials, using the identity he had created for his Florida persona.

Carson's main regret would be leaving his wife, abandoning her after three years. But his own survival left him no choice. If he remained, the Unit would find him. Its objective was the activation of Black Judas. Nothing else mattered. They would use his wife to force him to carry out the scheme. Disappearing was his only option. He would simply walk away, give no clue to his whereabouts. He had been trained in evasion. Now he would put that training to good use.

As he moved through the house, eyeing the possessions he would be abandoning, he consoled himself with the knowledge he could easily replace them if he decided to. Material things were not life, but simply the attachments that came with it.

In the bedroom he pulled an expensive leather overnight bag from the clothes closet and dropped it on the bed. Back in the closet he reached to the far back of the shelf and pulled out the box he had hidden there. Inside was a SIG-Sauer P-226 pistol and three full clips in addition to the one already in the weapon. He had purchased the gun two years earlier and had never touched it, except to regularly service and oil it. He dropped the box into the bag, covering it with a couple of towels and shirts. He added pants, socks, underwear and a sweater.

Back in the living room he wrote a brief note for his wife: "Gone to gym. See you later."

That would cover his absence for a couple of hours. By the time she started to get anxious he would be long gone. He left the note propped against a coffee mug on the breakfast bar in the kitchen.

The last thing he did before leaving was to pick up the phone and tap in a number he knew by heart. He got the message that the person he had called was not available. He left a quick message.

"The traveler has made his call."

There was nothing else to say. His contacted man would

understand, and would need to make his own decision about what to do.

Carrying the overnight bag, he picked up an expensive leather jacket, left the house and climbed into his car, driving away from the house he would never see again. He experienced a slight regret that lingered until he turned the corner at the end of the street and then it all faded behind him.

He drove to a bank on the far side of the city where he had opened an account, using a different name and credentials. He also had a safe-deposit box there. Correspondence from the bank was delivered to a post-office box number. At the bank he accessed his safe-deposit box. Alone in the small cubicle he emptied the contents of the box into his overnight bag. There was more than ten thousand dollars in cash, a disposable cell phone and charger, a notebook that held names and telephone numbers of contacts he had made. These people could supply him with necessary documents he might need. The Unit had been extremely thorough when it came to providing backup for deep-cover operatives.

There were also details of individuals from the Unit he had previously had contact with. Carson had always held the conviction that it was wise to know his enemies, but to know his supposed friends even better. Policies and sides had a nasty habit of changing, so it was prudent to play the game with a healthy dose of skepticism. His long-held belief had been engendered by his fiery but loving grandfather who had drilled into the young boy his own personal dictum: "Enemies are the ones who yesterday said they would never betray you, and called you friend. But the world tilts and even whole nations change. Your life is all you truly own. Never let them take it from you. In the end all you can do is protect yourself. Never trust anyone to do it for you."

So it was that he became part of the Unit and absorbed everything they taught him. He watched as he learned his craft, observing how his superiors were always looking over their own shoulders. Even after the fall of the old Soviet Union the paranoia remained. The internecine struggles continued. The sparring for individual power and position. In effect little had changed within government levels. It was each for his own, using others as pawns. The political chessboard had changed its colors and called itself something different, but in reality the game was still being played by the old rules.

Carson walked out of the bank, exchanging pleasantries with the odd staff member. Back in his car he drove to a nearby multilevel parking garage. He left his car in a corner slot and made his way back to street level. He picked up a taxi and asked for the rail station where he bought a ticket on the first available train going west. He had a thirty-minute wait, so he located a coffee stand and sat out his time. When the train departure was announced he waited until the passengers had formed a crowd, then merged with them as they pushed through the barrier. Once on board he located his window seat and sat down, his overnight bag on the floor at his feet. The car he was in was only half-occupied when the train pulled out, so Carson didn't have to share.

This was the way Thomas Carson traveled, crisscrossing the country, switching from train to coach and back, until his anonymous journey reached its destination in Miami. He caught a taxi for the last leg of his trip, reaching his ocean-view apartment. When he finally closed the door and crossed to stand at the panoramic window, taking in the view, he felt safe.

The feeling was bound not to last long.

CHAPTER EIGHT

Aaron Kurtzman's update clarified what had happened. A man called Thomas Carson had left a message on the answering machine belonging to Roger Bailey. Carson, unaware the man was already dead, had left a brief message that had all the hallmarks of a run signal. Kurtzman had worked his computer investigation into Carson's background and when he tied the search pattern into the one he had used earlier, he came up with Carson's real identity. The searching had also revealed Russian backgrounds for the two dead men from Spokane.

Carson was Boris Yolentov. Another Russian. His profession in the U.S. had him down as a financial adviser. One more connection to the other dead men. Kurtzman's check into Carson flagged a report from Grand Rapids P.D. from his wife, saying her husband had vanished. It appeared that Carson had simply walked out on his wife and home, and presumably his former life. His car had been located abandoned in a parking garage. There had been no signs of a struggle. The police had checked out Carson's background. There was no electronic trail to follow, which suggested he had opted to slip into a new identity, possibly using a different bank account where he had been storing cash in readiness for such a day to occur. If he had done that, it had to have been because he had become disenchanted with the prospect of following orders and initiating the project he had been sent to America to take part in. That the years since his insertion had made him forget his former role. Carson liked his assumed identity and the life it offered him. He had abandoned his Boris Yolentov self and moved on.

That was fine for him. Bolan was concerned with the woman Carson had left behind. If his Russian masters were looking for him—which they undoubtedly would be—that could leave her in danger. She most probably had no idea where her husband had gone. His handlers wouldn't know that. They would be very insistent she tell them what she knew, and they wouldn't be very gentle when it came to extracting such information.

Completing the call, Bolan tapped the address into his navigation system and while it worked out a route he used his cell phone to contact Detective Rick Hollander. The local police would have a better knowledge of the neighborhood and would be able to reach Carson's home address ahead of him. If they showed up and the man's wife was there alone, then they could take her into protective custody. If the alternative existed, they might be able to intervene if matters got out of hand. Bolan had the same intentions, but he was not going to risk Megan Carson's life if there was a viable alternative to him showing up.

He finished the call and placed the cell phone on the seat while he negotiated his way through the heavy traffic, following the navigation system's instructions.

As he turned onto the wide, pleasant street, he saw cars

at the curb outside Carson's address, doors left open. Someone was down on the tended lawn, and an armed figure was in the act of turning toward the fallen man. It took seconds before Bolan realized the man on the ground was Detective Rick Hollander. He jammed his foot down hard on the gas pedal and sent the rental hurtling in the direction of the armed man, distracting the guy from his intended purpose. Bolan's car hit the curb, clearing the sidewalk and dropping hard on its suspension. As it slewed across the lawn fronting the house, Bolan freed the door and slammed on the brake. He came out of the car as it rocked to a stop, his Beretta in his hand. He tracked in on the guy with the SMG now turned in his direction, the triggerman hesitating in a moment of confusion at what was happening.

Bolan didn't wait any longer than it took to acquire his target. The 93-R, set for tribursts, crackled briefly. Bloody flecks blew out of the target's shoulder. The guy stumbled, crabbing sideways as he tried to regain his balance. His weapon snapped out a shot that went high over Bolan's head. He corrected his own aim, this time placing his burst directly over the other guy's heart. The armed guy went down without a sound, his SMG spilling from his fingers.

Turning for the house, Bolan saw Rick Hollander pushing up off the ground, struggling to support himself, blood covering the front of his shirt.

"They got Steve," Hollander said, almost choking on his words. "Jesus…"

"Stay there," Bolan snapped as he went by the man. "Call it in."

He hit the front porch at a run, anger clawing at his gut when he saw Hollander's partner, Steve Cross, sprawled just to one side of the front door. His upper chest and throat had been torn and shredded by a shotgun blast. Blood had run across the porch boards in thick pools.

A woman yelled in an odd mix of anger and fear. Her cry was cut off by the sound of a hard blow. The woman grunted, stunned, and as Bolan pushed his way through the front door he took in the scene.

The young woman was slumping to her knees, one side of her face bloody, eyes glazed following the blow that had rendered her helpless.

A second armed man was standing over her, his face flushed with anger, the heavy pistol in his hand raised for a second blow. He sensed Bolan's presence as the Executioner came in through the door and halted the upswing of his gun hand, making a desperate attempt to pull his weapon back in-line. Bolan swung the Beretta in a two-fisted grip and hit the guy with a pair of tribursts that spun the target, blood and shreds of clothing trailing after him. He went down on his knees, his exposed skull blowing apart as Bolan hit him with another burst. The dead guy flopped facedown.

Still in his combat crouch, Bolan swung the Beretta in an arc, covering the room and beyond. There was no movement, or sound. Bolan saw a cutoff shotgun leaning against the wall just inside the door.

Bolan stood up, still keeping the Beretta on track. He prowled the room, checking the arch that led into the spotless kitchen. He saw that the kitchen door was locked. No one had come or gone via that entrance. The house was silent around him. He checked each downstairs room. Nothing. Bolan moved to the stairs, going up rapidly and scanning each room. No intruders. As he returned to the living room, he picked up the rising wail of police sirens. They were coming from both directions.

Bolan knelt beside Megan Carson, checking her pulse. The side of her face where she had been struck was already starting to bruise, and there was a shallow split in the flesh oozing blood. Even as he reached to stroke her hair back from the wound she uttered a low moan and started to move, uncoordinated, her hands trying to push away unseen threats.

A police cruiser came to a rubber-burning stop at the curb, uniformed officers moving quickly to advance on the scene. Bolan heard Hollander calling to them. One officer knelt beside him while his partner moved on to the porch, staring down at Steve Cross's body. He stepped inside the house, picking up on Bolan and Megan Carson, the dead perp.

"Cooper?"

Bolan nodded. "Is there medical help coming? The lady needs some, and I'm not sure how bad Hollander is hit."

"On its way," the cop said.

"Scene's clear," Bolan told him.

The cop kept his gun in his hand. "What the hell happened here?"

"We'll get to that later. Stay with Mrs. Carson. I need to check on Hollander."

"Sure."

Outside Bolan crouched over Hollander. He was pale and still losing blood. The cop with him had a pressure pad pressed to the wound. Hollander caught Bolan's eye. His own gaze was still focused.

"They hit us real fast," he said. "Took Steve with a sawed-off. I got off one round before I was hit." He paused.

"I came closer than I ever want to. If you hadn't turned up when you did, that mother was going to finish the job. I owe you, Cooper."

"Least I could do after sending you here. Hollander, I'm sorry about your partner."

A white-and-orange ambulance swept into view. Paramedics jumped out and opened the rear doors, grabbing equipment and approaching.

"Bullet wound here," Bolan said. "Lady inside had a nasty bang on the head. Two DOA inside."

The medics nodded. While one ran inside the house, the other knelt beside Hollander and took over. He checked the detective, making an assessment, then got on his radio to base, telling them they would be arriving with a gunshot wound.

Bolan stepped back. The medics had the scene secured now. There was nothing more he could do. He glanced toward the house, thinking about Megan Carson.

When he stepped inside, the paramedic was gently binding her head wound. Megan glanced up as Bolan entered. She was perched on the edge of a leather couch.

"She needs to be checked out," the medic said in a tone that suggested his diagnosis had already been kicked back at him.

"Not until I know what's going on," Megan insisted. "I won't go until then."

Her voice was shaky, but defiant.

Bolan glanced at the medic. The man shook his head.

"I need to ask a few questions while things are still clear in her mind," he said. "No more than twenty minutes, then the officers can drive her to the hospital. You have my word." He glanced at the door. "You need to get that cop the treatment he deserves."

"Just don't make it too long," the medic said. He gathered his kit and stepped out of the house.

Bolan stood over Megan. "Anything you want? Glass of water?"

"To be honest I'd prefer a double Scotch. But there's coffee ready in the kitchen. A mug of that will have to do."

"I'd better go check Hollander," the uniformed cop said.

"Thank you for your help," Megan said.

Bolan returned from the kitchen with two china mugs of black coffee. He handed one to Megan, then sat beside her on the couch.

"No heroics," he said. "If this gets too much for you, say so. Okay?"

"Okay." She sipped the coffee. "Please tell me what this is all about…"

"Matt Cooper."

She stored the name. "So, Mr. Cooper, who are you?"

"Justice Department."

His announcement widened her eyes. "My God, what has Tom been up to? First that armed man yelling at me. Demanding I tell them where he is. Now the Justice Department. I need to know, Agent Cooper."

"Plain Matt will do."

"Why has Tom run?" Megan asked. "I'd appreciate an explanation, Matt."

"Are you familiar with the term *sleeper agent?*"

"I understand the meaning…my God, are you going to tell me Tom is one?"

"The man you know as Thomas Carson is a Russian agent placed in this country as part of some long-term project. His real name is Boris Yolentov. From other events it looks as if that project is being activated. Your husband telephoned someone today and left a message telling this third party something had happened. What he didn't know was the third party was already dead. He'd been murdered. You reported Tom gone. It's either part of his programming, or his time here in the U.S. has rubbed off and he doesn't want to be part of the project."

"You mean, he's running to get away from whoever contacted him?"

"It's one possibility."

"Are you really sure about his Russian background?"

"Did Tom have a small tattoo on his left shoulder. Circular, with small letters and numbers?"

"Yes. He told me it was something he had done when he was in the service. Some team thing."

"As well as the man he contacted, there have been two other deaths. They were all identified as being Russian and they all had similar tattoos. Megan, do you have any idea where Tom might have gone?"

"No, but I think I have somewhere for you to start."

"Where?"

"Here in town. At the bank where he had a secret account. I know because I followed him there one day and saw him go through the door to the safe-deposit boxes."

"Something made you suspicious?"

"The first week of every month he would go out. Never told me where. He created suspicion and I started to believe he was seeing someone else. Before I confronted him I wanted to have some evidence. So one time I followed him. Parked across the street and followed him in. I watched where he went. I couldn't understand what he was up to. After he'd gone, I went to the counter and pretended that I thought I knew him. Told the girl his name.

She said that wasn't him and that his name was John Rennick. I made a joke about him having a double and got change for a fifty. By the time I came out Tom had driven off." She gave Bolan the location of the bank.

"Did you ask him about it?"

"No. To be truthful, I had no idea what to think. And I felt guilty because I'd followed him. I thought about it for days. I wanted to confront him, but I didn't know how. I guess I wanted everything to be okay. Time went by and I let it go. You see, life was good between us. Pretty dumb, huh?"

"You feel for people and you want to hold on to what you have."

"Matt, I have no idea what to do now."

"For now let the police look after you."

"Do you think those people will come back?"

"I won't pretend it might not happen. Protective custody will help."

To her credit Megan did not make a fuss. She realized the need for caution.

"All right."

"Megan, do you have a photo of Tom?"

"I can find you one. I wish I knew what was happening. Whoever he is, I still love him. If there's anything I can do to help…" She paused. "If he's caught, will he be tried as an enemy spy? I mean, aren't the Russian's supposed to be friendly now?"

"I'm only dealing with a possible security threat to this country. A lot would depend on what your husband does— or doesn't do to harm that security."

"If he is one of these sleepers and hasn't done anything yet?"

"I hope it works out, Megan."

She brought him a recent photograph. Bolan slipped it into his pocket, then beckoned the waiting police officer. They all walked outside. A vehicle from the coroner's office had arrived and Steve Cross's body had been placed in a gray body bag. Bolan watched the officer lead Megan to his cruiser. She got in the rear and the car slid away, easing through the throng of spectators and additional police vehicles.

Bolan called Stony Man on his cell phone. He detailed what had happened at the Carson house, asking for a full check on John Rennick. On the other end of the phone Brognola listened in silence until Bolan finished.

"This is getting out of hand. Is someone getting so desperate they have to conduct attacks in broad daylight?"

"It's looking that way. Hal, I'm going to call by the precinct again. I need to scan a photo of Carson. Get Aaron to run it through his databases under Rennick's ID to see if he can get a make. Have him check a local branch of the bank Carson was using to run a separate account. I'll forward the address on that. This is the one his wife didn't know about until she played detective and followed him. Could be he was preparing for something like today happening."

Brognola wrote down the bank details. "We'll see what we can come up with. Did you pick up the message Aaron sent you? He ran a trace on that number you asked for and got some feedback."

"Must have come through while I was busy here."

"He tried your room at the hotel, as well. Probably left the same message so you'd be sure to get it."

"I'll check my cell. Tell him thanks."

AN HOUR LATER Bolan walked into the lobby of the hotel. He had sent the photograph and details to Kurtzman from the police precinct, then swung by the hospital to check on Hollander. The cop was still undergoing surgery, but the prognosis was promising. Bolan made his way up to the room. He used his keycard to open the door.

"Natasha?"

He was greeted with silence. He had left her sleeping, getting her first proper rest in days. Closing the door, he drew the Beretta before he checked out the suite. It was empty. He checked the duffel bag he'd stored in the wardrobe. The Glock he'd taken from the guy at Tchenko's hotel was missing. She had not taken any of his own ordnance. He did notice that his cash backup had been disturbed. Five hundred dollars was missing.

"What the hell are you up to now, Natasha Tchenko?" he asked the silent room.

He saw the folded sheet of hotel stationery propped up against the room phone. It was from Tchenko, written in neat, clear handwriting.

Cooper, we are on the same journey, but taking different routes. Please do not be angry with me. You said you understood my feelings because you went through the same thing. In that case, wish me well. We may meet up again before this is over. I also borrowed some money. I will pay you back.
Natasha.

He read the note twice. The problem was he *did* understand what she was going through, so he had no right being angry with her. He channeled that into deep concern for her safety. He didn't doubt for a moment that she was a capable young woman. A trained, experienced police officer. But the people she was going up against were proving to be ruthless with little regard for anyone. They were offspring of the former Soviet Union, from a security branch renowned for its brutality and duplicity. If they were here in America, trying to resurrect some preconceived project aimed at damaging U.S. interests, they would fight to the last man in their attempt to bring Black Judas to life.

As far as Natasha Tchenko was concerned there wasn't a great deal he could do until she contacted him again. If she contacted him. She had stated it correctly. They were after the same thing, but for different reasons and by walking separate trails.

Tchenko was seeking justice for her family.

He was following his mission, and right now it was directing him toward John Rennick aka Thomas Carson aka Boris Yolentov. The man might have information that could increase his knowledge about Black Judas.

For the present Tchenko would have to work her own side of the street and Bolan his. And that meant a trip to Miami.

CHAPTER NINE

Washington, D.C.

In the beginning it had seemed like a game. He was courted by his new masters. They gave him money, opened doors for him, and in return he collected and passed information to them. They taught him how to access data without being found out and, impressed by his own success, he came to believe he was invincible. His new friends feted him, praised him for what he brought to them; they plied him with more money, gave him gifts and procured beautiful young women who would do whatever he wanted.

It never once occurred to him he was a traitor to his country, to America, the land of his birth. In his own eyes he was a businessman, giving his client what he wanted. Espionage, the selling of top-secret data and the stripping away of America's protection, none of that entered his thoughts. He was too busy playing the game, thrilled by the money, the gifts and especially the women. They were around him for one thing only. To perpetuate the myth that he, Lawrence Pennington, was playing an important part in the global extravaganza between the Americans and the

Russians. His indoctrination was subtle, a gradual eroding of any responsibility he might have had. He was made to feel important, taking part in a vital program that would help to defuse the decades-old struggle.

He lost track of how long he had been involved. He was too deeply committed now, completely overwhelmed by the treatment he received at the hands of his benefactors. They were, though he failed to realize it, playing him, casting their net wider with each request and then reeling him in with consummate ease. He gave them whatever they wanted, and all he asked for in reward was money and girls. The Russians, with their insight into the human condition, had assessed him early on and it became common knowledge that for money and sex, Pennington would do whatever they wanted. He was theirs by now. A puppet on a string, willing to dance to their tune.

His world turned cold when he read about an American caught spying for the Russians. There were so many parallels with his own circumstances for it not to be uncomfortable. The exposed man, *the traitor*, was reviled by everyone who wrote or spoke about him. Even his family disowned him. His trial was swift and without mercy, the man sentenced to prison without parole. He had been lucky not to have received the death penalty.

Pennington's lifestyle turned swiftly from paradise to hell. His concern affected him physically and mentally, and he found himself putting on a performance every day he went in to work. He was convinced he would be unmasked at any time, arrested and thrown into jail, or worse. His nights became dark and filled with dread. If he slept it was only to fall into hideous nightmares, and by the time the morning came he was exhausted. He realized he was going to give himself away if he continued to be haunted by what had become an obsession.

His handler went off-line. Pennington made his regular contact and found the man had disappeared. He knew something was wrong from the moment his call went unanswered. From day one his handler was never off station. He always answered Pennington's calls within moments. Now there was nothing. Only a dead line. Pennington tried to make contact over a couple of days. Each time he was greeted by silence, and after the fourth day he knew without a doubt that his contact was severed. Elation flooded through him, but the feeling lasted only for moments before being replaced with a chill of fear.

While his handler was around, Pennington had felt covered. Protected, if that was the right context in which to use the word. Now he had been cut free. He was off the leash. Yet that freedom left him feeling even more vulnerable than he ever had before. It was being faced by the unknown. Left to fend for himself, with no knowing who might be out there looking for him now, because he felt sure there would be someone.

On an impulse he made a final visit to the drop point where his handler would sometimes direct him to collect written instructions, or some small piece of equipment, correspondence or cash. It was a locker at Pennington's fitness club, a simple arrangement that had served them well over the years. The locker was empty, confirming Pennington's expectations.

Regardless of his actions in the past Pennington saw a chance to get out from under them. To escape his past and maybe build himself a safer future. He realized it was a straw he was reaching for, hoping it might save him from drowning, but he was not going to be getting any better offers.

He might have been correct in that assumption if Navotney, his controller, had not unexpectedly made phone contact, saying he needed to speak with Pennington. It was unusual for the Russian to break their routine and especially to demand a face-to-face meeting. They met rarely, normally exchanging information via the locker room drop point. Now Navotney was requesting a meeting. Pennington was intrigued and not a little nervous. Little had taken place between the two for some weeks, even before Navotney's silence. The Russian had not asked for any further data, and Pennington had taken it as respite from his previous activities. It had allowed him to breathe easier than he had for some months. He was aware of political maneuverings in Moscow. The media constantly reported inside factions vying for power. The Kremlin was going through one of its upheavals and while that went on outsiders, such as Pennington, were pushed aside until the internecine struggles calmed down.

Pennington used that period to consolidate his position. He saw his usefulness to the Russians coming to an end, and he decided it might be the time to move on, free himself from their hold over him. He was not foolish enough to believe it would be easy, maybe not possible at all, but he was at that stage in his life where he wanted to remove himself from the existence he had been forced to adopt because of his involvement with the Russians.

There was a way he could distance himself from his employment, offered when his department put forward a request for volunteers for early retirement. It was due to downsizing, that coy alternative to being made redundant.

Pennington put his name on the form. He was in his forties, had no family or ties, and the package being offered was generous. He saw it as an easy way out of his predicament. Leaving the department this way removed any suspicion that might have arisen if he had jumped ship on his own.

He kept the decision from Navotney, not wanting to force any overt action by the Russian. The lull in activity from his controller helped him through the process and as the department wanted the downsizing to take effect sooner rather than later, it meant Pennington had only a short wait. While the process was under way Pennington made his arrangements at home. He had always kept his affairs simple and up-to-date. He rented his Washington apartment, so there was no problem with having to sell. He decided to keep the lease for some months, even though he was going to move on. The money he had received from the Russians had been paid into a separate account in the Cayman Islands, which allowed Pennington to keep it secure. He would be able to access it from wherever he relocated to. Money was the least of his worries. His main concern was being able to disappear and set himself up at a new location.

Would the Russians be able to find him?

Want to find him?

His paranoia expanded. It started to intrude on his waking thoughts as well as haunting his sleep. The cliché of waking in a cold sweat became a reality. Pennington called himself a damn fool, a vain idiot who had believed his daring foray into the world of espionage was something he would look back on with a thrill. It was entirely possible now that it might end with a bitter taste in his mouth.

When Navotney made contact and arranged a meet,

there was little Pennington could do. He was still waiting for his notification from the Defense Department. Until it arrived he had to continue as if nothing was wrong. If Navotney asked him for some further data, Pennington would need to string him along. It wouldn't be easy. If Navotney suspected him of duplicity, the Russian could decide to settle matters himself. He would have people in the background he could call on to carry out some grim act. Pennington didn't fool himself about that. Navotney might appear friendly enough but he would show his true colors if there was a perceived threat to his own security.

The location of the meet, arranged out of the blue, in a deserted park on a windy night that rippled the surface of the nearby Potomac and sent chill rain scudding across the shadowed landscape did little to ease Pennington's sense of unease. He sat in his car, engine running to prime the heating system, trying to calm himself as he waited for Navotney to show up. The area was deserted at this time in the evening. The weather had made sure they were alone. No one with any sense was going to be frequenting the park when they could be indoors.

Exactly where I should be, Pennington told himself. This is not a good idea.

He glanced at his watch again.

Navotney was late, which was unusual. The Russian was punctual. He disliked being late for appointments. On all previous meetings Navotney had always been waiting for Pennington.

He saw movement at the edge of the trees to his left, the hunched figure of a man coming toward his car, clutching something to his chest. It was hard to see clearly through the rain-streaked glass. Pennington opened his door and began to climb out. Cold rain struck his face. He pulled his coat around him.

"Sergei?"

The approaching man raised his head at the sound of his name.

"I came to warn you, Lawrence. It's time to leave. I can't protect you from these people."

Navotney was having a problem speaking. As he closed in, Pennington saw the dark stains of blood on his coat. More ran from his mouth. He had some kind of leather attaché case tight against his chest.

"What people?"

Navotney was standing in front of him now. No more than a few feet away. In the pale light his face was bloody, his mouth twisted as he spoke.

"They're not my people. But they want the data I have." He clutched the case harder. "All the codes. They had all my codes. How to find me. And they knew about you. Tapped my phone so I had to take a chance and use a public phone to call you."

"What happened to you?" Pennington pointed to the blood.

"Traced me. Hit me with a car but I got away. Down an alley. I was sure you'd come. Pity it had to end like this. But go away, Lawrence. Get out of Washington. They will come after you. It's all over. I am cut off. On my own, so there's nothing I can do."

"You can get in the car," Pennington said. "I'll get you to a hospital."

Navotney shook his head. "Understand me. They will find you if you do not go now."

"I don't—"

"No time. Just go."

The roar of a powerful engine broke through the silence around them. The shadows blanched as strong headlights picked them out.

Navotney swore in Russian, then thrust the attaché case at Pennington. "Go, I'll hold them off," he yelled. His hand slid inside his coat and came back out clutching a heavy pistol. "Just fucking go, Lawrence. Or do you want to die?"

The Russian turned, facing the two dark shapes who had emerged from the vehicle. He raised the pistol and began to fire. Whatever else he might have been Sergei Navotney was a marksman. He took out one headlight with his first shot, then turned the muzzle at the advancing men before they could react. One went down, yelling in agony, toppling back against the parked vehicle. The second man opened fire with some kind of SMG, sending a stream of slugs in Navotney's direction.

Stepping back, a pained grunt bursting from his lips, his body shuddering from bullet hits, Navotney slammed his left hand against Pennington's shoulder and pushed him into the open door. He used both hands to grip his pistol as he engaged the distant shooter, catching him in the shoulder, the impact twisting the man around.

"Go!" Navotney screamed, pain and rage lending volume to his voice.

Pennington fell into his seat, the attaché case sliding to the floor on the other side of the car. He shut out the crackle of gunfire and concentrated on getting the car to move. Brake off, transmission in Drive. He trod on the gas pedal and felt the powerful vehicle lurch forward, tires spinning, then gripping. The car slewed to one side, dark sprays of dirt flying up from beneath the tires as he sent the vehicle surging across the grass. The forward motion swung the door shut, and the sounds of gunfire dropped to a faint level.

The last thing Pennington saw in his rearview mirror was Sergei Navotney moving toward the man with the SMG. The night was lit by the muzzle-flashes, and then even they were lost as his car cleared the grass and slid onto the paved road that took him toward the exit of the park and the highway beyond. He forced himself to ease off the gas as he cruised through the gates. The last thing he needed now was to be pulled over by some zealous traffic cop.

He knew Navotney was dead. Whoever it was who took his life would be following through and Lawrence would be next on their list. It took him some time to shake off the fear that was making him shake. He felt sick, too. Violence was something new in his life. The suddenness of it had shocked him, the way life changed so swiftly from a meeting into a shooting match. Pennington felt hot bile rise in his throat and he had to pull over to the side of the road, power down his window and lean out. He retched heavily, feeling the burning liquid rush from him and it forced him to remain there for a while until he had no more to give. He turned his face to the falling rain, letting it cool his flesh.

When he drove on, his mind was in a whirl of confusion. What the hell had happened back there?

Their ability to kill so casually stunned him. Nothing had prepared him for something like this. His life, despite the illicit thrills of his dealings with the Russians, had been normal. No overt violence. No use of firearms. But now he had been plunged into the brutal reality of a world he knew nothing about and it scared him to the point where he didn't know what to do.

He was only a block from his apartment when he slowed the car and pulled in against the curb.

What if they were at his apartment waiting for him? Navotney had said he would be next on their list. If they could locate the Russian, how easy would it have been for them to track down Pennington?

The worst thing was not knowing who *they* were.

Russian?

Or American agents from one of the security groups?

The thoughts filled his head, and Pennington could find no comfort from any of them.

Somehow he had to get into his apartment. There were things he needed before he could leave the city, documents that would establish his ownership of the Cayman Island bank accounts. Risk aside, there was no way Pennington was going to abandon the accounts. If he was moving on, he would need access to the substantial deposits. He sat for a while, working out how to gain access to his apartment if any of these mysterious individuals were around. He failed to come up with any clever solutions, admitting finally that his only option would be to walk in and hope he wasn't recognized. There was also the outside chance they hadn't yet staked out his apartment. That was a risky gamble, but one he was going to have to take.

He pushed the attaché case beneath the passenger seat, fastened his coat and turned up his collar. He pulled on a tweed cap he kept in the car, climbed out and keyed the lock. The rain was still falling, heavier now, the wind pushing it along the glistening sidewalk. He shoved his hands deep into his pockets and made his way along the block until he spotted the entrance to his apartment. There were only a few cars parked across the street. Pennington had no way of knowing who they belonged to so he ignored them, making his steady way to the apartment building entrance. Access was by a keypad. He tapped in his personal code and the doors slid open. He went in, feeling a degree of relief as the doors closed behind him. Pennington went to the elevator bank and called the closest car. He watched the floor lights wink on and off as the car descended. Inside he punched in his floor number, leaning back against the wall of the elevator, sweat beading on his face.

At his floor he stepped out and made his way to his apartment, using his key card to open the door. Once inside he secured the door, his hand reaching out to put on the light. He decided against it. No point advertising he was home. There was enough light coming in through the windows to guide him as he crossed the living room and went to the wall safe behind an Andy Warhol print. He had to pause a couple of times to steady his trembling fingers, but he managed to complete the combination. He opened the safe and reached inside.

"I knew if I waited long enough you would do that for me."

The voice came from close behind him. Pennington went rigid with shock. Damn, you, Lawrence, they let you walk right in. His next thought was that the accent was decidedly American. He had expected it to be Russian. Then why should it? He had worked for the Russians himself and wasn't he American?

"Just empty the safe. Put it all on the desk next to you."

Pennington heard the soft rustle of clothing as the man moved. Then the probe of a hard object nudged his spine. A cold jolt shivered through his body. He had expected the

man to be armed. The reality only struck home at the feel
of the muzzle against his body.

"Fuck with me, Lawrence, and I will shoot you."

Pennington recalled the actions of the men in the park
and did not for one second believe otherwise. His captor
pushed him toward the safe. The muzzle of the gun was
removed as the man stepped back a little.

He began to take out the contents of the safe, leaning
over to place them on the desktop. Documents. Stacks of
money. Plastic cards held together by a rubber band. His
thick notebook. As he touched the book, his hand brushed
the final object in the safe. Smooth and cold, the bur-
nished surface of the steel and the checkered texture of
the grips.

His insurance. His remaining chance of getting out of
his current situation. With a little luck.

The Glock Model 37 had been sitting in Pennington's
safe for twelve months. The only time he had removed it
was when he had gone to a local shooting range to practice. Buying the gun had been a deliberate act on his part,
a reassuring presence in uncertain times, on the advice of
colleagues and friends who had done the same. Protection
in case anything happened within the home. So Pennington had filled in the forms and eventually had been able to
purchase the weapon. He never expected to use it.

Situations changed.

Life turned around and allowed no other choices.

"That it, Lawrence?"

The voice was goading him a little now, the intruder enjoying his moment of power.

"Just a few personal items."

"Nothing personal tonight, pal. Just bring 'em out."

"All right, all right, just don't hurt me, please." Pennington didn't have to fake the fear in his voice as he spoke to reassure the gunman he was helpless. He just hoped it would convince the man.

Pennington's fingers closed around the Glock. He remembered the weapon's configuration. No safety lever to move. The Model 37 was fitted with Glock's safety action. The safety lock was only deactivated when the trigger was pulled and went back on when the trigger was released. So no mistakes, no pistol being put down in lethal condition.

Come on, Lawrence, remember.

Pick up the gun. Aim. Pull the trigger. The Glock had a 10-shot capacity—he knew one was already in the chamber.

He realized he had no chance for error.

This was his single way out. Make a mistake here and he would simply die a minute or so earlier than being shot by the man behind him. He knew the guy was going to shoot him. Just the way they had come after Sergei.

Pennington lifted the gun, drew his hand out of the safe, his action partially shielded by his own body. He dropped his hand almost to waist level as he turned away from the safe, the shadows concealing his move.

"What have you got there?"

Heart pumping, aware he was close to death and desperately not wanting that, Pennington snapped his arm up, extending the Glock in his hand, and pulled the trigger. He was shocked at the sound of the shot. It seemed to fill the room. His hand jerked up with the recoil he hadn't prepared himself for and he stumbled, knees weak with the fear gripping him.

The dark shape of the man before him seemed to dissolve, slipping into the gloom. He made a strange, garbled sound as he went to the hardwood floor. Something hard cracked against the wood. Pennington didn't know whether it was the back of the guy's skull, or the gun he had been holding.

Despite the mix of emotions flooding through him, Pennington managed to stay upright, his left hand resting on the edge of the desk. He sucked in deep breaths, desperate to calm himself for what lay ahead. If he was going to get out of the apartment, he needed to organize himself, complete what he had come for. He was aware of a dragging weight in his right hand.

The Glock.

The gun he had used to shoot someone. He forced the thoughts away. If he hadn't it would have been him on the floor right now.

Just remember that, Lawrence. He hadn't come to sell you cookies. The son of a bitch was going to kill you.

He could hear a low sound coming from where the man had fallen, a rasping, wet sound. And there was a scraping noise, too. He looked down at the dark bulk and saw one of the guy's shoes moving in erratic little jerks. Then it stopped.

I've killed a man, he thought. Taken a life.

CHAPTER TEN

It was close to midnight when Pennington stopped running. He turned in at a motel, killed the engine and went into the office. The man behind the desk glanced up from his TV.

"Rough night out there," he said pleasantly.

Pennington agreed. "I need a room. Can't drive any farther. I'll fall asleep at the wheel if I do."

"Take your pick. We're not too busy."

"Comfortable bed and a shower is all I need."

The man grinned. "Take number three. Best we got."

Pennington filled out the slip, paid and took the key.

"Early start in the morning?"

"Problem with that?"

"No. Just that the cleaner might wake you up if you ain't around by nine."

"No early start."

"Just hang the sign on the door handle and she'll leave you alone."

Pennington drove along the line and parked outside number three. He took his luggage and opened the door, dropped the bags, found the sign and hung it on the door. After locking the door he checked out the room. Clean and comfortable. King-size bed. Generous-size television. The adjoining bathroom was fine, too.

Pennington placed the Glock on the small stand beside the bed, took off his coat and sank into one of the low arm-chairs, using the remote to turn on the TV. He clicked through the channels and found a couple of news stations, confirming that there had been no reports about him or Navotney.

He spotted the coffeemaker and made himself a mug. Then the attaché case caught his eye. He had almost forgotten about it. Reaching out, he pulled the case to him, resting it on his lap. He clicked the catches, which were not locked. He raised the lid and saw a number of thick files inside. The uppermost file had a printed label on the front in Russian. There were also a number of computer CDs and a couple of solidly packed envelopes. He opened one. Inside were passports, driver's licenses, credit cards. The second envelope was stuffed with U.S. one hundred dollar bills. Pennington didn't count it. He just knew there was a large amount. The notes were not new and the few he checked did not have sequential numbers. He had no doubt they were genuine. He transferred the cash to his own carry-all.

Pennington removed the files and checked them out. The second one down had his name on the front. He opened it. The papers inside were mainly in Russian, though he did locate a few in English. He tried to read them but couldn't concentrate. He needed sleep. He put the file away. As he placed the other files back in the case, he read the label pasted on the slimmest one. It was in Russian that he was able to translate.

Two words.

Black Judas.

CHAPTER ELEVEN

Viktor Kirov lit another cigarette, inhaling deeply. It was a habit he had acquired in prison. One of the few comforts prisoners had been allowed. Then it had been packets of coarse tobacco and thin brown paper. Now it was packs of American cigarettes. The blend was weaker, not bland, but nowhere near as strong as the prison tobacco. He was convinced it had been laced with drugs to keep the inmates calm. He had accepted the possibility, because staying calm helped him to stay sane.

The sudden change in lifestyle made him uncomfortable. Kirov was still coming to terms with the hectic surroundings of America. His life had taken on a new perspective. No bare stone cell, with an open drain running along one wall. Now he was living in an apartment in Washington that offered him anything he wanted. Kirov wasn't complaining. He was simply overwhelmed by the availability of life's offerings. The simple things such as turning on a faucet and getting fresh, clean water; a large refrigerator that could hold enough food for a month; a soft, clean bed after a stone slab and a thin blanket—incidental things that meant a great deal to a man who had been deprived for three long years.

He kept his feelings close, not wanting to appear weak in front of his people. Kirov tried to concentrate on his mission, which crowded his mind most of the time. Only at times like this, when he was on his own in the apartment, did his anxieties push to the forefront of his thoughts.

He stood at a window, staring out across the capital city. Despite the rain the scene still looked impressive. Wherever he looked he was struck by the vastness of the country. There was a sense of freedom of space. America was a sprawling continent and its people had always made great use of that fact. They built on a grand scale. Always wide streets. Huge buildings. Open and with a sense of the limitless expanses around them. It gave them room to move, a freedom to express themselves and the lives they led. If Kirov had been a man given to petty jealousies, he might have sneered at the American way. He found their optimism refreshing. Not the stolid and often repressive attitudes of the Old Russia, with its dark buildings and claustrophobic atmosphere.

That did not deter him from his mission in the U.S. He was here to see to it that control of Black Judas was taken away from the Unit. He would achieve his goal and make it so that he and Federov could turn the project around to their own benefit. If they succeeded, the American lifestyle might easily become theirs and that prospect pleased Kirov.

To that end he had a dedicated crew under his control, men who were being paid handsomely for their skills and total lack of any moral hang-ups. His team consisted of both Russians and Americans. The Americans had an intimate knowledge of the place. The head man, Jake Waller, had military experience coupled with extensive contacts. Kirov had assessed him as someone who naturally challenged authority and got his excitement from creating chaos wherever he went. Ideal for what Kirov required. Waller's best quality was his lack of a need to question his orders. He received his instructions and acted on them instantly, directing his group of fellow Americans with consummate ease.

Their objective was to locate Sergei Navotney and an American named Lawrence Pennington.

Kirov despised Pennington's type. The man was a traitor to his own country. He had sold out, taking money and sexual favors, providing his Russian handler, Navotney, with sensitive American material. Kirov could never understand a man who turned his back on his own country and gave away her secrets. A man who could do that was never to be fully trusted. The concept though, was one that could not be ignored by the security services of any nation. The ability to gain sensitive defense material from a potential enemy had to be grasped with both hands. It went both ways. Russians had defected to the West, selling out in the same way Pennington had. They did it for different reasons. For material gain. Others from a misguided sense of responsibility—that the secrets they bartered would help to maintain the balance of peace. Reasons did not matter to Kirov. Traitors were traitors, no matter how they were dressed up.

The question of Kirov's involvement with Federov arose a number of times. Was their intended action treason? Or little more than a criminal act, albeit on a vast scale? Were they striking out against their own country? Was stealing money from America a treasonable act? Kirov could not accept that it was. They owed nothing to the people who were orchestrating the Black Judas project. General Berienko and his aide, Krushen, were attempting to activate the project so they could damage America through its financial institutions. In effect they were going to steal from America and gain an advantage for the good of Russia. It was well-known that Berienko and his group were of the old Soviet Union, men who refused to allow the cold-war mentality to fade away.

Black Judas was a child born from their ingrained opposition to anything American. They had been force fed the bleak rhetoric of the dinosaurs from the Stalin-Marx era, a way of life that had kept the masses under their boot heels and had fostered a pathological hatred of anything American. Even now they closed their eyes to the way Russia had emerged from the shadows into the light of day. Kirov would have been the first to accept that the New Russia was far from perfect, but the general state of the country was better than it had been before the fall. It had been the throwback mentality of the authorities that had trained him, then turned around and condemned him for carrying out his work. His reward for loyalty had been three years in prison, forgotten. It had been Federov who had negotiated his release, getting him out of that grim fortress.

Whatever happened Kirov would never forget that act. It would be with him until the day he died.

He heard his cell phone ring. Kirov retrieved the phone and took the call, recognizing Jake Waller's slow tones.

"Didn't go quite to plan, Mr. Kirov, but we're still on it. Navotney is dead, but he passed Pennington the damn case he was carrying before we could reach him."

"I told you he would have important data with him once he decided to run," Kirov said. "Where is Pennington now?"

"Sly old boy has slipped the coop," Waller said. "Hell, we lost Ric, as well. He was waiting in Pennington's apartment in case the son of a bitch showed up there. Guess he did at that. Don't know how it happened, but Pennington must have got the drop on Ric. My guy in Washington P.D. told me Ric took a slug in the head."

As good as his English was, Kirov still had problems with Waller's colloquial accent.

"He's gone?" Kirov maintained his steady tone. It would serve no purpose to express his anger at the failure of the team to take full control of Pennington. Waller still needed to push the pursuit, so there would be no profit in antagonizing him.

"We're on it. He slipped the city and headed out across country. I got ears and eyes on him. Now we know his vehicle ID we can pick him up through the inbuilt tracker. Don't you fret none, Mr. Kirov. That coon ain't about to lose this old hound."

"Keep me posted. Waller, we need that information."

Kirov cut the call. He put the cell phone down and lit a fresh cigarette. He sucked smoke deep into his lungs.

Setbacks were to be expected. No operation could guarantee total freedom from problems. The fluidity of such exercises allowed for things to turn awkward. The sensible thing was to view them as temporary. Once the matter became out of control, a small incident might grow all out of proportion.

Kirov's main concern was the material Sergei Navotney had passed to Pennington. He wanted that in his hands before Pennington did anything potentially harmful with it.

Such as handing it over to the American authorities. If Navotney had chosen to take material with him, it had to contain information that could be both helpful and at the same time harmful, depending on who got their hands on it. Navotney's long tenure as a handler within the U.S. meant he had sensitive material under his control. There would be details of his covert operations. Contacts and codes.

That would have been enough to cause concern. It had been expanded when Federov revealed that Navotney also had a connection with Black Judas. He had been designated as an overseer. Barely registered on the Black Judas roster, his name had come up during Federov's ongoing reading of the Black Judas files. Long established in America, Navotney had been trusted with information on the project and given instructions to maintain a low-profile observation of the sleepers. It was yet another fail-safe key put in place to ensure the smooth running of the inserted teams until, or if, they were to be activated. As far as Navotney would have been concerned, it was simply another phase of his American posting.

The attempt to take him out of the loop, failing in the first instance, had prompted Navotney to warn his protégé, Lawrence Pennington. Kirov's people had been monitoring Navotney's land-line and cell-phone calls. They had picked up his call to Pennington, arranging a meeting. The face-to-face meet had been a last-ditch move to persuade Pennington he should lose himself before he became targeted. Navotney would have seen the attack against himself as the beginning of a cull authorized by his superiors in Moscow. He could not have realized he was simply being targeted because of his knowledge of Black Judas's existence. Nor would he have been aware that those directing the assassination were working outside the box.

At a time when his life was being threatened Navotney's immediate thoughts would be to stay alive. Any questions could be asked later, if there was a later. Kirov had decided to cover Pennington's apartment as well as the meeting with Navotney. One of Waller's teams had made an early move on the man when he had left his apartment, prompted by the fact he had been carrying an attaché case. Figuring there might be sensitive material in the case and not wanting it to be lost, the team had made an abortive attempt at running Navotney down. The Russian had survived and had made his connection with Pennington despite being hurt. In the ensuing confrontation Navotney had shot it out with Waller's men. There had been injuries on both sides. Navotney had been killed but not before he had passed the attaché case to Pennington, who had then shown up back at his apartment. Against the odds, he had taken down Waller's waiting man and was on the run.

The cell phone rang. The caller ID informed him it was a call from Karl Federov in Moscow.

"Any further news?" Federov asked. "Have you located Pennington?"

"Not yet. The teams are on it."

"Krushen is in the United States. He has backup and they are going to do what they can to stall us."

"This is America," Kirov said. "Everything works on a challenge. It's good for business. Yes? Competition, Uncle Vanya."

Federov was silent for a moment. "I believe America is corrupting you with a sense of humor, my friend."

Kirov smiled. "How many of the family has he brought with him?"

"Enough, and he already has relatives there."

"I look forward to meeting them. Do you know where they are now?"

"Grand Rapids. I have also been informed of a third party looking for Krushen. I am e-mailing details to you now. Perhaps it's time for you to take charge in the field. Since our advance team dealt with the first half of the sleeper duo there, Krushen will be getting anxious."

"I have another team looking for him. We can terminate him and reduce Krushen's options."

"This American agent is becoming a nuisance, too. He needs to be watched."

"I understand."

"And watch out for this third party. She could cause problems."

"She? This is becoming interesting. What has Krushen been up to?"

"Check your e-mail. I will call later."

Kirov opened his laptop and accessed his e-mail program. Federov's message was waiting. He opened it and read the text, glancing at the photo image that came with it.

"Officer Tchenko, I look forward to meeting you. A great deal more than Mischa Krushen will."

"THE AMERICAN WHO INTERFERED at Carson's house. Our backup man followed him. He went to the police station, then to the hospital where they took the wounded cop. Then he drove to the airport and booked a ticket. I had Pushkin hack into the airline's system for the flight number. He is booked for Miami."

"Be a pity if he arrives," Kirov said.

"I managed to get a seat on the same flight for Chernov. Somehow I don't think our friend Cooper will arrive in Miami alive."

"Good."

CHAPTER TWELVE

Bolan settled in his seat and tuned out the sound of the other passengers as they filed along the aircraft. It was not a full flight. Many of the seats were still empty when the door was closed and secured.

He pulled the printout from his pocket and scanned the intel Kurtzman had sent him. As usual the Stony Man cybergenius had worked his electronic magic and gotten Bolan what he needed. Bolan's quarry, now John Rennick, had not escaped detection. His electronic trail led to Miami. His account in the Grand Rapids bank pointed the way to a second account in Florida. This showed that he had leased an apartment, which had been maintained for some months. The man also had a car available.

Rennick had been trained well in the art of evasion but unless an individual stayed completely off the grid, there were means of tracking them. That made Bolan consider the possibility of Rennick being picked up by the Russians. They had their own ways of locating missing people. The main problems were the methods they employed. An example was the way they had invaded Rennick's former home and involved his wife.

Twenty minutes later the airliner was en route for Miami, pushing its way through the gray cloud formation. Bolan left his seat and located the onboard satellite phone. He put his credit card into the slot and dialed the long number that would route him through the secure system to Stony Man. What he learned when he spoke to Barbara Price simply confirmed his suspicions about the opposition.

The vehicle transporting Megan Carson to a safe location had been hit en route. On a quiet stretch of road it had been surrounded and forced to stop. The police escort had been gunned down and Megan Carson abducted. There was no information regarding her current whereabouts.

"And there won't be," Bolan said. "They want her for one reason only. To find out where her husband is. Once they have that information Megan becomes a disposable item."

"God, Mack, that sounds so cold."

"It's the way these people operate. We've lost her. There's no way to sugarcoat the fact." Bolan was silent for a moment, his thoughts going back the few hours since he had spoken with the frightened young woman.

Protective custody will help.

Hadn't he told her that?

She had allowed herself to be comforted by his words. Another innocent caught up in some dark world she had no way of controlling. Possibly a life forfeited to the savages. He completed his call and returned to his seat, glad of the fact no one was beside him. He turned to stare out the window, his thoughts taking him on a backward walk through the killing ground, to the bleak places where the dead lay. Not the deserving dead. These were the unwilling victims of senseless brutality. The ones who were swept along with the currents of evil, washed into the bloody tides of senseless slaughter. Bolan had known many of them and sometimes felt they only suffered through their relationship with him. His own existence led him through the darklands, drawing others in through association. The merest contact had left others dead, their faces registering the surprise and pain when they were sucked into the maw of destruction. Bolan would mourn Megan later. And there would be payback.

The flight was due to land at Miami International at noon. Bolan rested as much as he could. They were an hour out when he got up to go to the washroom. Making his way along the aisle, he felt the aircraft shake slightly as it encountered an air pocket. The sensation lasted no more than a few seconds. He reached the rear section of the plane. Just beyond was the galley where the refreshments were prepared. As Bolan neared the washroom door, he sensed someone behind him. He glanced back, expecting to see one of the flight attendants. Instead he saw a man moving up behind him. The guy had a mass of thick, straw-colored hair. His pale eyes were fixed on a spot just over Bolan's shoulder. His right hand was held down by his leg, rigid, as if it was crippled and couldn't be moved.

When he was nearly beside Bolan, his left hand came up, fingers spread, reaching for the big American's right arm. It was all happening in the space of seconds, too fast for anyone in the passenger section to even notice because they were facing in the opposite direction. Bolan continued his turn, realizing there was something wrong here. The guy caught Bolan's arm, fingers gripping fiercely, and pulled Bolan in toward him. And suddenly his right arm came to life, swinging up from where it hung against his thigh. In the guy's hand was a stubby hypo.

The aircraft hit another pocket, easing through it in seconds. Bolan's attacker paused in midstride, hesitation etched across his face.

Bolan turned, pulling his arm from the other man's grip. He closed his fingers around the guy's wrist, holding the hypo away from himself, then drove up his right arm, delivering a powerful elbow smash to the side of the guy's face. It was powered by everything Bolan had; he was aware that he needed to put the guy down fast, avoiding the potential threat of the hypo. The guy grunted, his head snapping to one side as Bolan's blow landed. Straw Hair recovered quickly, muscles tensing in his arm as he attempted to break Bolan's grip on his wrist. He drove his right knee up at Bolan, slamming it into his thigh. The blow was hard. The Executioner fought against the effect, repeating his elbow smash, and saw blood smear across Straw Hair's lower jaw. The guy was cursing now, a low, monosyllabic stream of Russian words as he pushed Bolan back against the bulkhead. His left came out of nowhere and crunched against his adversary's cheek. The blow was repeated. Bolan jammed his free hand beneath Straw Hair's chin, shoving his hand back.

A slender figure dressed in the airline uniform appeared and stared at the struggling figures, then moved on through to the main cabin, approaching a single passenger seated near the rear. She bent over him. The man pushed up out of his seat and followed her back, dragging the curtain across the rear compartment as he reached under his coat to pull a pistol.

"Air marshal. Break it up. Now," he said, raising the weapon to cover Bolan and Straw Hair.

Bolan's attacker ignored the order.

"Stay away from that hypo," Bolan snapped.

Straw Hair increased his attack, punching and kicking as he tried to break free from Bolan's restraining hand. Swinging the guy around, Bolan planted his hand against the side of his opponent's face and slammed his head against the bulkhead, drawing more blood.

In the background he could hear the air marshal repeating his order, while in his mind he knew there was no way the struggle would cease on demand. He yanked Straw Hair in close, closing his other hand over the guy's arm and working it against the joint until the Russian yelled in agony. He felt the man yield a little and might have completed his move if the air marshal had not decided to move in, still threatening with his pistol.

Bolan increased his leverage on the arm. Straw Hair wailed as bone grated, then the forearm popped out of its socket. He lost his grip on the hypo and it dropped from his fingers, the needle point embedding itself in the floor covering.

The surge of pain galvanized Straw Hair. He lashed out with his left arm, the back of his hand connecting with the marshal's nose, snapping it. Blood spurted. The lawman froze as pain flared through him, and before he could reconnect Straw Hair had snatched his pistol from his hand, chopping it hard across the man's face. As the marshal stumbled aside, Straw Hair triggered two fast shots into his body, then turned the pistol on Bolan, who dropped to a crouch before launching himself at the flight attendant, looping his left arm around her slim waist, pulling her to the floor. They hit and rolled, the young woman gasping from shock. Bolan shielded her with his own body, clawing for the marshal's backup weapon.

He heard the sound of a shot as Straw Hair fired. The slug tore into the washroom door. Bolan raised the captured SIG-Sauer, and when he had Straw Hair in his sights, the Executioner triggered a single 9 mm round into the Russian's body. The man shuddered under the impact of the slug. His eyes wide with shock, he fell back.

Bolan released the flight attendant. She pushed her hands through her hair, tidying it as best she could. Her eyes caught Bolan's.

"I need to speak to the pilot to let him know what happened." She was staring at the bodies of the air marshal and the man Bolan had shot.

Bolan took out his Justice Department ID and showed it to her. "If he needs to speak to me, it's Cooper. Are you all right?"

"Thanks to you, Agent Cooper. I mean that."

Bolan indicated the bodies. "We should have them moved so the passengers don't have to see them."

She nodded. "Yes. I'll see to it."

Turning to go, she paused. "Thanks again, Agent Cooper."

Then she had gone through the curtain, leaving Bolan alone. He put away the SIG-Sauer. That was when he spotted the hypo. It was still in place, the needle buried in the floor covering. He retrieved it and examined the pale liquid in the body of the syringe. It had been close. If the plane hadn't gone through the air pocket, the contents of the syringe might have ended up in his body.

Too close, Bolan thought.

Too damn close.

BOLAN PICKED UP THE RENTAL Stony Man had booked for him and drove directly into Miami. He had been delayed for almost a half hour after the plane had landed, briefing the air marshal's office about the onboard incident. The syringe the Russian had tried to stick him with had been sent to the local FBI lab for analysis. Bolan had found a slim case in the dead man's coat. It held a card stating that the guy had been diabetic and the case held his insulin. All very neatly designed to avoid questioning.

In his car on the way into the city Bolan reviewed the events on the plane.

The attempted assassination told him the opposition had good intel. The abduction of Megan Carson proved that. And getting someone on his flight to Miami suggested they were well organized. There had to have been additional backup keeping watch on the Carson house. If that was true, they would have witnessed Bolan's involvement. He had been tailed when he left. They had to have had someone watching Megan Carson's movements to have been able to get to her.

For all he knew they could have a trace on his cell phone. Any business Bolan conducted that was concerned with the electronic information highway could lead to his actions being discovered. He had to consider the possibility. It could force him into the cold, cut off from backup where information could be siphoned off and used by the enemy. He accepted that. There had been a time during the early years of his campaigns when Bolan had existed in a solitary world. Then he depended on no one. There was no Stony Man. No satellite connections. He lived on his wits and on the combat skills he had honed on the stone of war. He tracked his enemies, dealt with them, and utilized their own weapons and finances to equip his continuous fight. He could do that again if the need arose.

Bolan's cell phone rang. He had to answer it. It was Barbara Price. There were no preliminaries. No light banter. She told him straight.

"We just heard that Megan Carson's body has been found. It looks like she was thrown out of a moving vehicle. Indications are she had been tortured before she died. Sorry, Mack."

"Sorry isn't enough."

"I know."

"I'll talk later," Bolan said and hung up.

The apartment building where Carson had his new home overlooked blue water and packed marinas. Bolan ran his rental car into the visitor parking lot and walked back to the entrance. Inside he crossed the lobby and checked the list of occupants displayed on a gold-blocked panel. "Rennick" was on the tenth floor. Bolan followed a young couple into one of the elevators and rode it to the floor he wanted. He stepped out into a corridor that had six apartment doors on each side. The one he sought was midway on the right. He tapped on the pale wood panel. The response took a little time.

"Who is it?"

"Agent Cooper. Justice Department. Open the door. Now."

"You can't…what's this about? How do I know you're who you say you are?"

"Open up and I'll show you my badge."

"This is a trick."

"Fine. I'll call Miami-Dade P.D. and we'll wait until they show."

Bolan stepped back from the door, ready to kick it open. He didn't want to resort to that because it would only draw attention and he needed time with Carson. Bolan drew the Beretta. The man's state of mind might cause him to do something desperate. He could be armed. In fact Bolan would have been surprised if the man wasn't.

The door clicked as the lock was turned. Bolan touched the handle and pushed, letting the door swing in. He stood to one side until he was able to see no one was pointing a weapon in his direction. Carson was standing back from the door, and he had the appearance of a man who had given up. His shoulders were slumped and his arms hung limp at his sides. When Bolan caught his gaze, he recognized defeat.

He stepped into the apartment, closing the door and locking it.

"You're a trusting man, Carson. Too trusting. I would have expected your training to have kept you sharp."

Even now Carson made a halfhearted attempt to bluff. "Sorry, I don't understand."

Bolan glanced around the well-appointed apartment.

"Comfortable," he said. "It should be for what it cost."

Carson raised his head. "What the fuck are you talking about?"

Bolan hit him, a brutal, hard-thrown right that caught the man across the side of his jaw, tumbling him backward. He didn't even have time to protest as the back of his legs caught a low foot stool. The Russian twisted and fell, landing hard. Bolan followed him and caught a handful of the man's expensive shirt. He hauled him upright, then swung him around and dumped him on the cream leather couch nearby. Carson slumped back, blood spilling from torn lips to mar the front of his shirt. He stared up at Bolan, real fear in his eyes when he read the expression on Bolan's face.

Carson touched his damaged jaw, feeling it starting to swell. "What the hell was that?"

"That was for two people who died because of you. A young cop and your wife, Megan."

If Bolan's intention had been to shock, he got it right. Carson's face drained of color as the words penetrated. He held Bolan's gaze as the words repeated themselves inside his head.

"Megan? She's dead? How?"

"Your friends took her, Yolentov. Your Russian friends. They needed to find you and she was their only lead. I'm guessing she told them about your John Rennick bank account. It wouldn't have taken them long to access that and to work out where you were. Just like I did."

"Megan knew?"

"She was smarter than you figured. She thought you were having some kind of affair, so she followed you to the bank and learned your new identity. Funny thing was, she still trusted you. Stayed with you and tried to forget what she'd learned. It got her killed in the end after you skipped town to save your own skin."

"I didn't mean for that to happen. I wanted to protect her from—"

"From your Russian friends? Walking out on her was a death sentence."

"She didn't deserve to die."

"Feeling sorry now? Who for? Your dead wife or yourself?"

Carson shook his head. He was lost for words. His world was crashing down around him, and he had no excuses, no way of talking himself out of his situation. Before he even had time to settle into his new life in Miami, the past had caught up with him.

"They called me on the phone, using the activation code.

I was supposed to follow the procedure. But I had finished with the project years ago. I wanted nothing to do with it. I had succeeded in America and made a great deal of money. Had a thriving business. But I knew the day would come, so I prepared by setting up the Rennick account and renting this place. The training I received for the operation was very good. All of us were into finance, computing. It was why we were selected. We were part of what was called the Unit, trained and based in Lubyanka. When they were satisfied with us, the Unit brought us here to America. They supplied everything. Identities. Documents. Money to start us out. We had a handler who remained in the background. He watched from a distance. Apart from that, we were on our own. Initial introductions via sympathetic Americans helped with jobs. We had to make our own luck and maintain our grasp of American financial business computing. That went toward being ready when the call came."

"To activate Black Judas?"

This time Carson was surprised. "You know about the project? It was supposed to be undetectable."

"It might have stayed that way if someone hadn't started killing off your team members. One was Roger Bailey. It was your call to Bailey that helped me trace you."

"He's dead? Stepan?"

"And two others in Spokane."

Carson dropped his head into his hands, his shoulders shaking. "What is happening?"

"It looks as if there are two groups involved. Your Black Judas handlers and a rogue team with their own plans for your project. Any ideas who?"

"I have no idea. Remember I've been here in America

for years. There has been no contact with Russia, or the Black Judas team in all that time."

"Until now?"

"When I was contacted, the man said something that puzzled me. After the identification phrase he said 'things have happened.' Maybe it had to do with what's been going on."

"How many of you were there?" Bolan asked. He figured this was the time to get Carson to open up.

"Six of us. Three teams of two."

"Two left. Unless they've already been located."

"It might not be the Unit trying to wipe us out. Maybe this other group."

Bolan shrugged. "Only way would be to talk with your people."

"I'm walking around with a target on my back here."

"Sympathy isn't on my list as far as you're concerned. Stopping Black Judas is."

Carson thought about that for a while. He was working on something inside his head, and Bolan didn't want to break that concentration. The man pushed to his feet and walked to the kitchen where he located a towel and soaked it in cold water, holding it against his jaw.

"What good would it do if I said I could bring them out in the open? The Unit."

"I won't know until you tell me how."

"There was a final plan we could initiate if the whole of Black Judas went sour. It was designed to get us out of the U.S. The three teams, or what might be left if things went wrong. A telephone number that would send an automatic abort signal to Moscow. Moscow would arrange for an evacuation team to pick us all up from an arranged place and take us home."

"You know where this pickup point is?"

"No. It was supposed to be changed every couple of years to maintain secrecy, but once the abort signal is sent, Moscow should come back with the current location."

Bolan indicated the nearby phone. There was no hesitation. Carson picked up the phone and punched in a long number sequence. It took some time before there was a pick-up at the other end. Carson acknowledged and began to speak in Russian. The call was brief. He replaced the handset.

"Now we wait," he said.

Carson crossed to a wet bar and splashed liquor into a heavy tumbler. He offered it to Bolan, who declined. The Russian emptied the glass, then refilled it. Bolan chose a deep leather armchair positioned so he was able to see the entire room and the door.

The phone rang after twenty minutes. Carson picked up and listened, spoke a few words and cut the call.

"Day after tomorrow. Twelve o'clock. An abandoned farm in Montana. They use it as a contact point."

CHAPTER THIRTEEN

Three miles from the rendezvous point Bolan climbed into the rear of the rented Jeep Cherokee and Carson took the wheel. The road they were on wound its way through a hilly, empty landscape. Since touching down at a small local airstrip and picking up the 4x4, they had been driving in a northerly direction, the elevation climbing gradually. In the far distance hazy mountains dominated the horizon. They passed a few isolated ranches. After an hour there was nothing. Just the land stretching out in all directions.

Bolan, clad in a blacksuit and combat boots, wore his Desert Eagle on his hip and the Beretta in its shoulder rig. On the floor of the Cherokee sat his duffel bag holding extra ammunition and weapons. Through Stony Man Bolan's weapons had been transported for pickup, waiting for him when he and Carson had touched down in Montana. The plan Bolan had was deceptively simple. Carson would make the rendezvous and allow Bolan to exit the Cherokee once he had moved to meet his contact. The Executioner had tried to dissuade the man from making the journey, but the Russian was adamant he needed to be there. If a strange face presented itself, the meet could go sour very quickly. Carson argued, correctly, that though *he* had no idea what his contact would look like, the reverse would be entirely different. His face was on file with the Unit. They knew him.

"I'll get you close," Carson had said. "After that it's up to you. You deal with them how you want."

"You want to walk into a setup? If it isn't your own people, they might shoot you on sight."

"My choice. Hell, Cooper, I don't have much of an option. Whichever way I go there's going to be someone on my heels. I put myself in this situation." He'd paused, shaking his head slowly. "I fucked up real bad and it got Megan killed.

"Sign ahead," Carson called over his shoulder. "LC Ranch. Half mile up this side road."

The 4x4 swung left, then hit uneven ground. Carson put it into a lower gear and headed along a rutted trail. Bolan drew himself tight against the rear passenger door behind Carson, the Beretta in his hand.

"I can see the ranch ahead," Carson reported. "They were right about it being abandoned. The whole place is falling apart. Overgrown. House. Barn. Double garage. Some outbuildings. Some kind of corral with the posts sagging. I see a car. Dark blue Ford. It's parked near the barn, and nobody's in sight."

"Drive by the car," Bolan said. "Make a turn and stop, facing it. Make it a good twenty feet. Try to park close to something so I can ease out when you do."

"Okay."

The Cherokee rolled across the ranch yard, then made a wide turn so it was facing the way they had come in. Carson slowed the vehicle, stopped and shut off the engine.

They sat in the surrounding silence. Gazing up through the window opposite, Bolan saw thin spirals of windblown dust ghosting by.

"I'm opening my door now," Carson said. "I parked next to an old water pump and trough."

Bolan heard the click as Carson eased his door free and pushed it slowly open. He waited until the Russian was standing outside the 4x4, his body blocking the rear door. Bolan followed suit, opening the rear door just enough so he could slide out, flattening on the ground and pushing the door shut before he slid partway under the vehicle. He heard the front door slam shut and saw Carson's shoes scuffing the dusty ground as he moved clear of the Cherokee.

Carson walked in the direction of the parked Ford, his eyes searching for his contact. He saw no one, heard no one.

"Here I am. As arranged," he called in Russian. "Do we need to play these childish games?"

Bolan checked the surroundings, the empty house, the outbuildings, large barn and the double garage, its open doors swinging gently in the wind. He considered the possibility of a setup, armed men waiting under cover for Carson. Maybe someone had a sniper rifle trained on him. Maybe there would not be any *contact*. Perhaps it had been nothing but a decoy plan to get Carson out here, away from the confines of a city where he could be dealt with quietly.

The way this meet had been staged it could go either way. Carson might face his man from the Unit and work his deal. Or the *other* side might be waiting to hand out their own kind of greeting.

Bolan decided it was time he dealt himself into the game. Someone was out there, waiting, and Carson had put himself in the open, making it easy for anyone to make his move.

Carson was near the parked car, looking around, bending to check if there was anyone inside. Satisfied the vehicle was empty, he straightened, raising his hands in a gesture of frustration.

And his head blew apart in a burst of bloody debris as a heavy-caliber rifle slug cored in through the back of his skull.

Before the twitching corpse hit the ground the hidden rifle was turned on the Cherokee, a stream of slugs shattering windows and tearing ragged holes in the bodywork. They followed Bolan as he rolled out from under the vehicle and worked his way to the rear. He ignored the rain of broken glass and the hot fragments of body steel.

Reaching the rear of the SUV Bolan worked around it until he could take a look at the shooter's vantage point. The man was in the partly open door to the barn's hayloft. Bolan made out the edge of the guy's body as he leaned around the edge of the frame, the long-barreled, heavy rifle sweeping the area. He saw the extended magazine under the weapon. Muzzle-flashes showed each time the shooter pulled the trigger. He was keeping up his steady fire, the big slugs hammering at the Cherokee.

Large capacity or not, Bolan decided, the guy had to run out of ammo sooner or later. His thought was followed by a pause in the firing. Bolan saw the weapon being raised as a hand reached to remove the magazine.

It was his chance.

Getting to his feet, he cut across open ground in the direction of the barn. Dust kicked up from beneath his feet as Bolan powered for the sanctuary of the barn's front wall where he would be directly beneath the shooter.

The sudden crackle of gunfire erupted from above Bolan. Divots of earth leaped at his heels as he launched himself across the remaining gap and slammed shoulder-first against the barn doors, then twisted to slip through the gap and into the shadowed maw of the cavernous structure.

Dust sifted down from overhead as the shooter changed his stance.

Bolan jerked away from the doors, aware of what was going to happen, milliseconds before the heavy boom of the rifle sounded as the shooter blasted slugs through the loft floor. The barn floor spit up geysers of trodden earth.

Ignoring the proximity of the shots, Bolan extended the Beretta, two-fisted, and began to place tribursts in and around where he guessed the shooter might be. He cleared the magazine, ejected it and snapped in a fresh one from his blacksuit pocket, firing again. Then he moved away from the front of the barn and located one of the wooden ladders leading to the loft. He went up fast, one hand gripping the Beretta, and as he reached the top he pushed himself up and over the edge of the floor and spread-eagled himself.

Raising his head, Bolan checked out the loft and the partly open doors. Dusty sunlight pushed in to dissipate the gloom. He picked out the shooter's figure, leaning against the wall. The guy wasn't moving. Light glanced off the barrel of the rifle still gripped in one hand, the muzzle sagging toward the loft floor. The rifle slid from loose fingers and dropped to the floor, followed by the slowly collapsing shooter. He pitched from his knees onto his face and fell on top of his weapon.

Bolan stood and cautiously made his way to where the shooter lay. He saw blood on the straw-littered floor and when he rolled the shooter over, he saw the bloody mess his slugs had made in the guy's chest and throat. There were ragged wood splinters in the shooter's flesh.

Opening the guy's coat, the Executioner checked his pockets and found a slim wallet—some cash, a couple of plastic cards. There was a cell phone in his pants' pocket. Bolan took the items and dropped them into a blacksuit pocket. He examined the rifle, which looked custom made. Large-caliber, auto-feed and, from what he could judge, the magazine could have held around thirty rounds. He spotted a leather bag lying near the loft doors. It held two more full magazines for the rifle and a loaded handgun with spare clips.

Bolan wondered who the shooter had been. From his equipment, no doubt he'd been a professional. The rifle was not something that could be picked up over the counter at a local gun store. This had been made by a specialist.

The shooter's cell phone rang. Bolan stared at it, then took the call. The voice had a foreign accent. Heavy.

Russian?

"Is it done?"

Bolan partly obscured the speaker with his hand. "Done."

"Any problems? This is a bad signal."

"No problems."

"Five minutes we pick you up."

"Okay."

Before the phone cut off Bolan picked up the background noise. It took him a minute before he realized that the caller had been in an aircraft, most likely a helicopter. The shooter's employer was coming in to extricate him from the kill zone. He glanced at the rifle in his hands.

Let them come, he thought. They could have a taste of their own medicine.

Bolan slung the leather bag onto his shoulder and made

his way from the loft to the barn floor. With the rifle in the crook of his arm Bolan crossed to where Carson lay. The man was on his back. The rifle slug had erupted from his head just above the bridge of his nose and had destroyed his face. A great deal of blood had fountained down to soak the man's front.

Bolan glanced at the abandoned Ford. Something was out of place. It took only a few moments for Bolan to figure out what it was.

The car.

If the shooter was being picked up by the incoming helicopter, why would he have driven to the rendezvous? It would have added to the logistical bill, and Bolan couldn't see the Russians allowing that to happen. They would want their man on the scene well ahead of time. So they would have dropped him off by chopper, then retreated, leaving the farm silent and deserted.

The car had nothing to do with the shooter.

That meant there had been a third party involved.

Had?

Bolan was thinking in the past tense.

He placed the rifle across the hood of the Ford, drew the Desert Eagle, then walked around to the far side of the vehicle. The key was still in the ignition, so he grabbed it. As he stood upright, he noticed the footprints in the dirt, then the dark drops where something had dripped. Long trails of dried blood ran down the door panel. As he followed the spot trail, the deposit of blood became heavier. Circling the Ford's rear, Bolan saw more blood smears on the bumper. He unlocked the trunk and peered inside. The body lay in a pool of blood, the gaping wound in the man's throat still glistening. There were a couple of stab wounds in the chest. The bloody knife had been dropped beside the body.

Carson was dead.

The unknown man was dead.

Somebody was playing for keeps.

Bolan picked up the sound of the approaching chopper, which was coming in from the north. He moved quickly, grabbing the rifle, staking himself out behind his own shot-up SUV and waiting for the bird to show itself.

He checked out the rifle, making sure he had the weapon's operation clear in his mind. He found there was little to memorize. The rifle had a simple mechanism when he analyzed it. No safety. A precision autoloader fed by a gas blowback system. The rifle was heavy but it had perfect balance, and Bolan felt he would be able to make the weapon perform as well as he needed.

The helicopter came into view, engine roaring and rotors clattering. It swung around in a wide circle and hovered above the car. Narrowing his eyes against the gritty dust sucked up by the rotor wash, Bolan picked out a pilot and a single passenger in the cockpit.

The cell phone in Bolan's pocket rang again. When he activated the phone, the speaker was suspicious. It showed in his tone.

"Where are you? This is not as arranged. Why?"

Bolan had no answer and he knew his subterfuge had been noticed. There was an angry curse from the caller. The chopper's engine powered up, and it began to rise. Bolan leaned across the hood of the Cherokee, angling the sniper's rifle up and triggered a burst of shots that hammered the chopper's fuselage, smoke curling from the engine cowling. Upping the angle Bolan went for the rotor assembly, jacking out repeated shots. The tone of the engine altered. A low, rising whine came from the machine as shards of metal spun out from the whirling rotor assembly. The helicopter slipped sideways, the tail starting to come around. One of the landing skids caught the garage roof, tearing off chunks of wood. The chopper hung for a moment, held by the trapped skid. The main fuselage tipped toward the garage, and the erratically spinning rotor blades ripped into the garage structure. Splintered wood flew in all directions. The rotors locked and the chopper sank with a ponderous sound, collapsing into the garage.

Bolan stepped out from behind the rental vehicle and raked the stricken chopper, the heavy slugs shattering the transparent canopy and lodging in the vulnerable flesh of the pilot and passenger. Blood spurted to splash the splintered Plexiglas. The chopper settled with a groan of tortured metal and creaking wood, coming to rest only a few feet off the ground. Bolan closed in, angling around so he could view the cockpit. He caught movement from the passenger, the guy slumped against the restraints of his safety harness. Hurt as he was, the guy still had fight enough to raise the SMG gripped in his bloody hands and track in on Bolan as the big American loomed into his field of vision. It was Bolan who hit his trigger first, raking the other with a number of high-powered slugs from his acquired rifle. The impact of the slugs drove the guy hard into the back of his seat, exploding out through his spine.

Bolan clambered across the tangle of splintered wood and metal struts until he was able to drag open the cockpit hatch. He checked out the dead passenger, going through his jacket and extracting a bloodstained wallet. Nothing except some cash. Peering at the dead man's face he failed to recognize him, but did register the Slavic bone structure and recalled the accent when the guy had called on the cell phone.

Russian.

Apart from the indications there was Russian influence at work, Bolan had the clear message two opposing factions were involved. A war between rival groups was bad enough. What raised his hackles was the fact they were using the streets of his own country to work out their differences.

He returned to the ground and took out his cell phone.

Bolan called Stony Man, and eventually reached Kurtzman. He laid out the details. "Give me time to clear the area, then call this mess in. But I need some feedback. Fingerprints from the guy in the trunk of the Ford. The shooter in the barn and the pair in the chopper. Might give me some connections."

"Okay, I'll call you when I get the data. You need anything else?"

"An explanation for the rental company for why their SUV looks like Swiss cheese.'

"Now that one will take some fast talking."

"Give it to Hal. Tell him I'm coming in."

Bolan broke the connection. He took a final look around, then crossed to his vehicle, dropping in the sniper rifle and ammunition bag, and got behind the wheel. He swung the vehicle around and headed down the track, away from the farm, picking up the narrow feeder road that would lead him back to the main highway.

CHAPTER FOURTEEN

Moscow

"I'm not imagining it," Yan Chenin insisted. "I'm being followed. Someone is watching me."

"Do you know who it is?" Federov asked.

"One of Berienko's men. I got a quick look at him yesterday afternoon. Gregor."

"Anton Gregor?"

Chenin was silent. All Federov could hear was his uneven breathing over the line.

"Anton Gregor, yes," he said finally. "You know him?"

"I know him," Federov said.

"What should I do?"

"Above everything, do not panic. If he suspects, he may well do something drastic."

"Drastic?"

"Yan, go home. Stay there until you hear from me. If anyone calls, you are ill."

"At least I won't be accused of lying then," Chenin said.

"Go home." Federov cut the connection, then dialed a new number. It was a direct, private line, answered by Leopold Bulanin. "That matter concerning Chenin we spoke of some time ago? It has become a nuisance. He's being watched by one of Berienko's people. Anton Gregor. Berienko must have become suspicious. If Chenin has been careless, he is no use to me any longer."

"I'll have the matter dealt with." Bulanin paused. "What about Gregor?"

"Who?"

"Consider it done."

ANTON GREGOR, HUDDLED for warmth in his car, banged his fist on the heater control. Even though the engine was running there was barely any warmth coming through the air vents. He glanced up at the windows of Yan Chenin's apartment in the dark concrete building, wondering peevishly whether the man was sitting in the cold. Unlikely, he decided. He would be warm, not freezing in a department car that should have been scrapped six months earlier. Gregor checked his watch. Almost midnight. He would give it another half hour, then he was going home himself. Chenin wasn't going anywhere this night. The weather was foul. Cold and raining. It seemed to be like that most of the time now. Gregor glanced up at the window again. He leaned over to rub condensation from the car window, sure he had seen movement in the apartment. Yes, there was a slight figure at the window. Chenin? He seemed to be staring directly at Gregor's parked car, as if he knew he was being watched.

Someone tapped on the opposite window. Gregor turned and could make out the distorted outline of a figure wrapped in a thick overcoat. Perhaps General Berienko had sent someone to relieve him. The thought evaporated quickly.

That would be most unlikely. Berienko was not the kind of man to consider the physical comfort of his staff.

So who was it?

Gregor stretched his cramped limbs, leaning across to wind down the squeaky window. It let in a blast of cold air and rain.

And the bulky suppressor attached to the muzzle of an automatic pistol.

There was no time for Gregor to react. His chilled body was slow to respond and he practically just sat there, staring into the black hole of the suppressor until the pistol fired. Twice. The bullets cored in through his forehead, into his brain and out through the back of his skull. Gregor flopped back, jammed up against the driver's door, skull fragments and brain matter sliding down the window glass.

YAN CHENIN KNEW WHAT WAS happening. The dark figure bent over the car door, remained there for a brief time, then stood upright and looked directly up at Chenin's window. The figure turned and walked around the parked car and started across the glistening street. There was a measured calmness in the walk, and the man paused as he reached the curb directly below Chenin's window. Though his face was a blur, Chenin saw clearly enough the outline of the object he carried in his right hand—a pistol, fitted with a sound suppressor.

Chenin knew he had to get out, to get away from the apartment. He pulled back from the window, turning in confusion. He snatched up his bulky coat and forced his arms through the sleeves, moving for the door, panic clawing at his insides. He fumbled with the door lock. He knew that trying to do it in a rush was causing his clumsiness, but the thought of imminent death filled him with uncontrollable fear. He dragged the door open and stumbled into the dimly lit hall. He had moved yards down it when he realized all he was doing was going to meet the man with the gun. A soft whimper escaped his lips as he turned back and hurried in the opposite direction. If he used the emergency exit he could take the stairs down to the rear exit. He pushed through the door and started down the concrete steps. His footsteps echoed loudly. Below him the floors were lost in the gloom. He had to cling to the iron railing to steady himself, forcing a slower pace.

The final two flights were all he had to negotiate now. Chenin felt clammy sweat on his face despite the chill. He could even see his own breath. The iron rail was icy beneath his hand. He stumbled as he made the turn on the small landing, the steps in front of him.

A dark, bulky figure stood at the bottom, waiting for him, the muzzle of the suppressed pistol already angled up at Chenin.

"Please...no..."

His final plea was ignored. Three rounds sliced into Chenin's heart, the impact kicking him back against the concrete wall. He slithered down, on his knees, then fell face forward.

The silence that followed was broken by the dry squeal of stiff hinges as the emergency door opened and closed.

OFFICER NIKOLAI DIMITRI crossed the OCD facility and stopped in front of Commander Seminov's cluttered desk. His superior officer was hunched over documents spread out before him, one big hand clamped around a mug of black coffee. He didn't appear to have noticed Dimitri's presence and carried on studying the detailed report, occasionally shaking his head. Dimitri waited. He was young, only recently promoted to the OCD, and was still eager and dedicated.

"Are you going to tell me what you want, Nikolai, or should I take up mind reading?" Seminov asked without looking up.

"Sorry, Commander, I thought you were…"

"Busy? Why would you think that, Officer Dimitri? Don't I spend my days fiddling with myself and dreaming about retiring somewhere warm and sunny?"

Embarrassed, Dimitri found himself lost for words. He thrust out the folder he was carrying. Now Seminov looked up and Dimitri saw his boss had a smile on his lips.

"Tell me what is so important, Dimitri."

Relieved, Dimitri cleared his throat.

"The Bulanin surveillance?"

The OCD had been running surveillance on Leopold Bulanin's organization for months. Bulanin was a clever, well-protected criminal, who was into every illegal operation in Moscow. He ran a tight ship and had the best lawyers in Moscow on his books. He considered himself untouchable and in many ways he was exactly that. Seminov was aching to get something on the man. He even had an undercover OCD officer in Bulanin's organization but couldn't get a damn thing he could use. The surveillance operation had produced nothing, but Seminov had no intention of giving up on the racketeer.

"I think we may have something," Dimitri said, his face flushed with excitement.

"Tell me you are not just trying to make my morning feel better."

"No, Commander." Dimitri waggled the folder. "This time we do have something."

Seminov held up his hands. "Sit down, Nikolai." The OCD chief stood and took his mug across to the stove where a steaming pot sat. He emptied his mug, refilled it and poured a second one. He placed them on the desk, one in front of Dimitri, then resumed his own seat. "Tell me."

Dimitri opened the folder and began to remove items as he spoke.

"Vash Karpachov. We knew he was one of Bulanin's enforcers." A photograph of the man was pushed across Seminov's desk.

"We have him down for at least six murders, but as usual he walked every time."

"Since yesterday it's gone up to eight," Dimitri said. "A call came in from our undercover operative. He said he had picked up on Karpachov being sent out on some contract work for Bulanin. Surveillance was switched to Karpachov, but the team lost him for a while. When they did pick up on his movements they were minutes late and he had already completed his night's work. But they caught him leaving an apartment building. Karpachov still had his gun in his hand. He tried to shoot his way out but the team took him down. He's dead."

Seminov absorbed the information, sensing there was more. He drank from his mug, watching Dimitri's smug expression.

"Spit it out, boy, I can see you want to."

"When the team checked out the building they found a dead man on the emergency stairs. Shot. It was found later the bullets came from Karpachov's weapon. The same as the bullet they found in a second body in a car across the street from the apartment building."

"Identification?"

"Yes, Commander," Dimitri said, sliding two more documents across the desk. "The man in the apartment building was Yan Chenin."

"The Chenin who worked in Lubyanka?"

"FSB. And the man in the car was Anton Gregor, another FSB agent who was directly linked to General Berienko.'"

Dimitri picked up his mug of coffee, sitting back in his seat with a satisfied look on his face.

Seminov read and reread the reports, his own face registering something close to ecstasy. He finally pushed the papers away from him, sitting back and letting out a long breath.

"If I was a religious man, I would now understand how miracles work. As I'm not, I'll put this down to plain good luck." He paused, sneaking a look at Dimitri's glum expression. "And some damn good police work. If I had a spare badge in my desk, I would promote you to sergeant."

"Commander, I am already that rank."

"What? Oh, yes, well that only goes to prove you earned it."

"What do we do about all this? Arrest anyone?"

Seminov shook his head. "No. Remember we were told to stay out of FSB business after Pieter Tchenko and his family were murdered. If they hear we are going after the FSB again, the top floor will shut us down and we'll lose any credibility."

"What do you think is going on, Commander?"

"Understand how this works, Nikolai. Do not believe

the world all black and white. Most of the time it's shades of gray. Things are never how they seem. That applies to people, as well. Here at OCD we exist within our own boundaries. If we step outside and crush sensitive toes, then our influence is restricted. If that happens, we can't do what we are paid to do."

"But, Commander…"

Seminov held up a big hand. "Don't be so eager to rush in headlong. Circumstances dictate we approach the problem from a different angle. You know and I know that there is something going on at FSB they don't want us looking into. Remember the FSB has influence. It has friends in very high places. Friends who would not be pleased if we hauled them into the daylight. And also, FSB has ways of reaching out to deal with anyone they decide is in their way."

"So we do nothing?"

"There is doing nothing and doing nothing unofficially. The only rule is not being caught."

Dimitri smiled. "I understand."

"Don't understand too quickly, Nikolai. If we continue to investigate, it has to be done very carefully. No paperwork. Nothing that can be traced back to us."

"Yes, Commander."

"Speak to no one in the unit. The more people we involve, the more likely the word will get out." Seminov checked his watch. "I need to go out. There is something I need to do. Carry on with your normal duties until you hear from me. No independent actions, Nikolai. Understand?"

Dimitri nodded. He watched as Seminov pulled on his coat and hat. He picked up his OCD car keys and walked out of the department.

IT TOOK HIM AN HOUR to locate the man he was looking for. He found him in a shabby café down a side street. Seminov was glad to close the door against the rain. The strong smell of hot soup mingled with tobacco smoke. Steam rose from a large urn behind the counter. The café was not busy, with just a few poorly dressed customers hunched over mugs of tea. Unshaved faces looked up as he entered then returned to their own business. In that part of the city it was wise to be invisible.

Seminov spotted his man at a corner table, concentrating on a crossword puzzle in a crumpled newspaper. Seminov ordered two mugs of tea and took them across to the table, setting one in front of the man. There was no reaction. Just the scratch of the pencil on the crossword grid. Seminov let the silence drag for a while, until a grubby, almost skeletal hand reached out to grasp the mug of tea.

"Pieter Tchenko was my good friend, too," Seminov said, his voice kept to almost a whisper.

"Then why has no one been arrested for his murder, Commander Seminov?"

The eyes that stared into Seminov's were set deep in a gaunt face that showed every year of Lem Topov's life. His features were creased with heavy wrinkles, each pore defined, his beard stubble gray and spiky. Over his thinning hair he wore a shapeless, grubby cloth cap.

"If I could do that, I would not need to ask for your help, Lem."

"What do *I* know?"

"You were his eyes and ears on the street. You gave him information. He looked after you. Now help me."

Topov rubbed a sleeve across his nose, sniffing noisily. "He is dead. That is all I can tell you."

"No. There's more. It came to me a little while ago why no one has been able to find the information Pieter had gathered, the information that got himself and his family slaughtered. Did you know what they did to him? To his wife and his son? I saw the photographs, Lem. They were terrible things to look at."

Topov raised his mug and drank as if the taste would wash away his thoughts. "You should not tell me such things. I'm an old man. Haven't I had enough misery in my life?"

Seminov had to smile. The old man constantly used his *sad* life to gain sympathy. True, he had not been blessed with life's riches, so he played on his misfortune to his own advantage. His true vocation was his insight into all things underhanded. He watched and listened, picking up gossip and information, mostly of a criminal nature, which he then bartered for food, clothing and money. If it was happening in and around Moscow, Lem Topov was more than likely to know about it.

"Lem, did Pieter ask you to look after something for him?"

Topov refused to meet his gaze, lowering his eyes to stare into the tea mug. That simple action told Seminov what he needed to know.

"I need that information, Lem. It will help me find the ones who murdered Pieter and his family. You know I will look after you. Just like he did."

"I have to go," Topov said.

He had picked up his pencil again and Seminov could hear it rasping against paper. The sound ended. The newspaper was pushed across the table as Topov stood, pulling his grubby coat around him. He shuffled out of the café and was gone.

Seminov glanced down at the newspaper and saw that

Topov had been writing in the white space above the cross-word section. He turned the newspaper around and read the surprisingly neat and legible message.

Time and place.

A meeting in a couple of hours.

Seminov folded the newspaper and pushed it into his pocket. He walked out of the café to where he had left his car. He returned to OCD and went directly to his desk.

He checked his handgun, then took a couple of extra clips from a drawer and made to put them in his pocket. The folded newspaper got in his way so he took it out and dropped it on his desk. As he stood he saw that Dimitri was watching him from his own workstation. Seminov paused on his way out.

"You came back very quickly," Dimitri said. "Extra magazines? Where are you going?"

"The firing range. I need to practice."

"No," Dimitri said defensively.

"Remember what we talked about? We keep this to ourselves. I will tell you about this later. For now you stay here. That's an order, Officer Dimitri."

He turned away before the younger man could reply, making his way back to where he had parked his car. He started the engine, deliberately pushing his foot down hard on the gas pedal and making the tires squeal as he drove out of the parking area. He had to switch on the wipers against the increasing rain as he headed through the city streets and to his meeting with Lem Topov.

Seminov felt foolish now, allowing his anger to affect him. Dimitri had only been showing concern. All he wanted to do was to stand by his superior officer, to make sure Seminov wasn't placing himself in unnecessary danger. So why had Seminov reacted the way he did? He found it difficult to answer that, so he concentrated on arriving at the meeting on time.

CHAPTER FIFTEEN

Seminov rolled his car into the gap between two of the derelict workshops. He cut the engine and stepped out, jamming his hat on and quickly turning up his collar against the rain. He looked in the direction of the warehouse Topov had identified. The deserted site was littered with debris and broken machinery. Seminov remembered the days when the place had been in full production, working day and night to meet its quotas, but never ever reaching the magic numbers that were always kept deliberately high. He recalled that one of his distant uncles had been a foreman in the foundry, a big man with huge hands that were always marked and scarred from handling the hot metal.

He approached the warehouse, a vast metal building. Windows were broken, sections missing from the sides. The large doors sagged open. Seminov reached inside his coat and drew his pistol, thrusting it into the large side pocket in his coat. At the entrance he stopped and looked around, seeing nothing but the silent, empty buildings, the scattered detritus of the former plant.

"Commander Seminov."

Lem Topov's voice reached him from inside the warehouse, echoing in the empty space. Seminov stepped inside, glad to be out of the rain. It seemed colder inside the building.

Seminov could not see the man until he stepped out from behind a mass of machinery. Here in this place Topov did not seem so out of place. He fitted in, a slight, bedraggled figure in grubby clothing. Seminov noticed for the first time that the old man wore a pair of oversize trainers on his feet. They might have once been white. Now they were stained and cracked, long laces trailing to the filthy floor of the warehouse.

"I think you need some new shoes, Lem," Seminov said.

Topov looked down at them. "Pieter Tchenko gave me these. They were new." He gave a little laugh. "That was a long time ago. They killed him. He was a good friend to me."

"A good friend to everyone who knew him," Seminov said. "So we have to find the ones who murdered him. Have you come to give me what he left with you? It will help me to flush them out."

Topov reached inside his tangled clothing and pulled out a thick envelope sealed with tape. He held it out to Seminov.

"He hid it in this place because we had used it before. No one knew."

Seminov took the envelope and pushed it into the deep inside pocket of his coat. "It's time we left, Lem."

They retraced their steps to the doors. Topov moved ahead of Seminov, sure of his way around the site. He took two steps from the opening, head down against the rain. His left shoulder blew apart in a gout of red, flesh and bone bursting from the exit wound. His thin body twisted under the impact. As the flat crack of the shot reached them, a second bullet hit Topov in the chest, then two more in rapid succession. Seminov saw the man roll back, limbs going from beneath him, the back of his coat suddenly glistening with bloody eruptions. Topov hit the concrete, his body arching in brief agony. The sound of the shots faded. Seminov was still framed in the open door. He dragged his handgun from his coat pocket, aware he had nothing to shoot back at. It was an automatic reaction, just as wrenching himself to one side of the warehouse door and flattening against the inner wall, the sick feeling he was caught alone in unknown surroundings. Only a few yards away Lem Topov's body sprawled on the ground. His blood was already being sluiced away by the rain.

As quickly as that, Seminov thought. One moment alive, the next everything gone, wiped out by some nameless, faceless bastard with a high-powered rifle. The thought crossed his mind that Topov most likely had been under surveillance himself. It had to have been common knowledge that he was the late Pieter Tchenko's informant. So the FSB had placed him in their sights as a possible means of tracking down the lost evidence. In this instance they had been right. That had placed Topov on their elimination list. Sooner or later they would have reached out and forced the man to talk. Seminov glanced again at the body. Hard as it was, Topov had suffered less by being shot than he would have in one of the FSB's interrogation cells.

He looked around. The vast warehouse stretched in the distance, cold and shadowed. He needed a way out other than the main door. He had no doubt that the sharpshooter would still be out there, waiting patiently, hoping his next target would show himself. As far as that went, he was going to have a long wait. There had to be more ways out of the warehouse. Seminov recalled the missing panels in the side of the building. They were, unfortunately, on the same section of the warehouse as the main doors. The shooter would have them covered, too. So he was going to have to check out other means of escape.

Seminov was about to move when he heard a rattle of sound. Someone moving around in the shadows. It stood to reason there might be more than one shooter, a backup sent to flush him out of the warehouse and into the cross-hairs of the waiting sniper. Another rattle of sound. It was closer, coming from somewhere within an untidy collection of metalwork and racks. Seminov eased away from his position and moved at an angle, approaching the place where the sound had come from. For his size he was light on his feet, and he was able to enter the area unheard and unseen.

The sound of footsteps reached his ears, then a pause when the stalker realized his quarry had vanished. Seminov heard the man muttering something to himself, then he hurried forward. Again the man cursed himself for being clumsy enough to advertise his presence. Seminov, standing still, caught a glimpse of the figure just ahead of him. The man was staring forward, his head moving back and forth as he tried to pick up Seminov again. Before he could turn around the commander stepped in close, swinging his pistol and slamming it hard across the side of the man's skull. The blow sent the shooter stumbling against the storage racks, clutching his head where he'd been struck. The hand holding his own gun hung at his side, forgotten about in the confusion that overtook him.

Seminov stepped around the man, reaching out with his left hand to relieve him of his pistol. Then he jammed the muzzle of his own weapon into the side of the stalker's neck and put on some pressure.

"I think you need to reconsider your work options, Leninov," he said. He had recognized the man as he had caught a glimpse of his face.

Rudolph Leninov worked for Leopold Bulanin. Bulanin the racketeer. It was an old title, but one that Seminov liked when referring to the likes of Bulanin. Prostitution, corruption, hard-core pornography. Contract work. Anything that could turn a profit. Bulanin would ally himself to anyone who might be useful. Even to the extent of doing business with the FSB. The man himself was coarse and flashy. He loved loud clothing and ostentatious cars. He flaunted his position, his wealth and the power he commanded. None of that impressed Seminov. He viewed men like Bulanin with contempt. Their breed was making life intolerable for those who simply wanted to walk a straight line. Greedy, with little regard for life or property, Bulanin was a menace, and Valentine Seminov wanted nothing more than to put him down. And now that he had discovered Bulanin was holding hands with the FSB, Seminov's need to stop the man had become nonnegotiable.

Seminov caught hold of Leninov's fur-collared coat and spun him, pushing him back against the racks. Leninov had a hand clutched to the side of his head where blood was running down his face. He was a lean, emaciated man with a boney face, thin lips and deep, hooded eyes. His dark hair, straight and wet from the rain, hung across his forehead.

"Still running errands for your boss? I'm surprised at you, Leninov. Didn't Bulanin explain the sentence you can get for threatening an OCD officer?"

Leninov's eyes sparked with anger. "*You* attacked me. Look at my fucking head."

"I was simply defending myself. You have a gun and were about to shoot me."

"No…all I was supposed to do was to see that you showed up so…"

The thought flashed through Seminov's mind. So I could be shot like poor old Topov after he handed over Tchenko's evidence.

What an idiot he had been. Bulanin had been watching Topov, and it had allowed him to draw Seminov into their trap. The commander reacted instantly, aware that time was probably running out for him.

He slammed his pistol across Leninov's skull, hitting him twice. The man groaned and slumped to his knees. Seminov caught hold of his coat and dragged the dazed man with him, back to the warehouse exit. He paused briefly, pulling Leninov upright.

"You need to clear your head," he said, and before the man could react the commander pushed him out though the open door.

The cold rain on his bloody face snapped Leninov back to reality. He stumbled to a halt, starting to yell, then his body jerked under the impact of rifle fire. He fell to his knees, twisting to look back at Seminov.

"This wasn't how…" he said an instant before a close pair of rifle shots slammed into the back of his skull and blew out the front of his face, the impact tossing him facedown.

So much for loyalty, Seminov thought. The hit had not gone down as planned, so the distant shooter was making sure there was no one left alive to talk.

Back on his feet Seminov moved down the length of the warehouse. There would be more exits from the building. All he had to do was find one. He stayed close to the wall, where the shadows were deeper. He stopped every so often, pressed against the wall and listened. Apart from his own labored breathing, the building was silent. His situation could have been better.

All in a day's work, Valentine, he told himself. Considering what had happened, sitting behind his desk back at the OCD headquarters was beginning to look extremely attractive.

He reached a narrow side exit, the metal door hanging from one hinge. Seminov checked outside and saw a forest of large, stacked metal drums. There seemed to be hundreds of them, in haphazard rows, some six high. The drum coatings were streaked and rusting, the concrete around them stained. Seminov realized they would provide him with cover while he worked his way back to where he had left his car. It seemed to be the only option open to him. He figured this was going to be his best chance. The longer he stayed inside the warehouse the more likely the sharpshooter might decide to come looking for him up close and personal.

Seminov felt his inside pocket and located his cell phone. When he checked, he saw there was no signal. He put it away and checked his handgun. Then he remembered the one he had taken from Leninov. He found it was loaded with a full clip. At least he had a little more firepower now. The thought didn't offer him all that much comfort. Two loaded handguns, with limited range, were no match against a distant man with a high-powered, probably scoped rifle. There was also something else to consider. Were there any other shooters around? Seminov knew about the rifleman. And Leninov. But were there others who might be out there somewhere? Just waiting for Seminov to show himself? He leaned against the wall, wondering, then decided whatever the odds he had to play them. If they surrounded the warehouse and closed in, he might find himself trapped inside the building, with no cover to speak of.

He waited a few seconds longer, then, pistol in each hand, he ducked out through the door and moved quickly along the closest rows of the stacked drums, hoping the cover they provided would allow him his chance to escape. Seminov felt the prevailing rain increase, the lighter fall turning heavy, slanting in across the area. The sudden downpour struck quickly, the sheeting rain bouncing off the stacked metal drums and sweeping down between the rows. Seminov was caught and soaked. He ignored the discomfort. As long as he could be uncomfortable he was still alive.

He had covered barely a quarter of the distance along his chosen path when he caught sight of a darting figure up ahead, someone crossing between rows. So he had been right and there was at least one more man looking for him. Even in the hurried moment Seminov caught a glimpse of a stubby SMG in the man's hand. The gunner was positioning himself. Seminov didn't have long to wait before the man reappeared, the SMG held forward, muzzle tracking in. The commander had been anticipating the move, and he was ready. The moment the man appeared, Seminov dropped to one knee, his right wrist braced across his left to steady his hand. The pistol settled, Seminov eased back on the trigger. The moment he fired, he triggered a second, then third and fourth shot. Two 9 mm slugs hit the target in the upper chest. One struck a metal drum just above the target's head.

Pale liquid began to spurt from the ragged bullet hole. It pooled on the concrete around the body of the man Seminov had shot. By the time he reached the corpse it was soaked in the liquid and the pooling had spread. Seminov could smell the liquid now. It had a gasoline odor. He wasn't sure what it was exactly, but it was giving off strong fumes. He walked around the pooling liquid, pausing to feel in his pocket for the disposable lighter he always carried. There were times when Seminov fell victim to the nicotine habit. He wanted to stop smoking, but on occasions of stress and frustration he gave in and had a cigarette or a cigar. He flicked the wheel and the flame showed, instantly doused by the falling rain. Seminov muttered, crouched close to the edge of the pool of liquid and flicked the lighter again, shielding it with his body. The flame held. He pushed the slide that increased the size of the flame to maximum, then reached out and held the lighter close to the liquid. The fumes rising from the liquid ignited. There was a soft whoosh of sound, rising to a greedy breath, and then the flame was racing across the pool of liquid, flames surging, growing, expanding at a terrifying speed. Seminov didn't stay to watch. He pushed to his feet and moved quickly away from the fire he had started, hoping the blaze might cause a distraction.

Whatever he had expected Seminov was caught unawares when the sucking roar of the flames became a solid and massive explosion that threw boiling heat in every direction. He felt the shock wave of the blast reach out along the rows of drums, pick him up and hurl him clear of the stacks. Helpless in the grip of the explosion Seminov saw the ground rushing up to meet him. He hit, bouncing, twisting, the breath slammed from his lungs. Dazed and hurt-

ing from his fall, he lay facedown. The surge of heat from
the blast washed over him. He was sure his clothing had
been scorched. His exposed skin tingled as the still falling
rain pounded him. Seminov wanted to climb to his feet. He
could barely move a finger, so he decided to let nature take
its course and gave in to the weary sensation that engulfed
his battered form.

IN HIS HEAD A SIREN WAS echoing its shrill sound. Seminov
blinked, opened his eyes and found he was looking up at
a white ceiling. He felt himself rocking slightly, then realized it was not a ceiling. It was a roof panel. The movement was because he was inside a vehicle. An ambulance?
It had to be. Why? Had he been hurt? Maybe shot? No. He
ached but there was no individual area of pain. Seminov
tried to sit up. The effort cost him and he sank back with
a groan.

"Commander? Are you all right?"

An anxious face swam into view. Someone was bending over him, eyes searching his face. Seminov recognized
Nikolai Dimitri.

"There is a sharpshooter around somewhere," Seminov
warned. "He has already killed Lem Topov and silenced
one of his own."

"Not any longer," Dimitri said. "He tried to run when
we showed up. He did not get very far."

The solemn face of a uniformed paramedic appeared.
The man checked Seminov's condition with bored patience. "He'll be fine. I told you it was only shock. A night
in the hospital will sort him out."

Dimitri returned to fill Seminov's field of vision. He
looked as if he was on the way to a funeral.

"I'm not dead yet, Dimitri," Seminov growled. "How did you find me?"

"It wasn't hard, Commander. The explosion could be seen for miles, and I was already on my way. When I saw it, I called for medical help and the paramedics arrived minutes after we did."

Seminov's mind was clearing slowly. "How did you know where I was? I didn't let on where I was going."

"The new cars, sir. They all have inbuilt tracking devices. All I had to do was to log on to your vehicle and it pinpointed your location. And the newspaper on your desk had a location written on it."

"What else do you read on my desk?" Seminov muttered. "All right, but *why* were you tracking me in the first place?"

Dimitri actually flushed with embarrassment. "I take full responsibility for that, Commander. I realized you were reluctant to discuss this matter. So I took it upon myself to follow you in order to provide backup in case you had a problem."

Seminov didn't say anything. He was still trying to absorb everything that had happened. His body ached. His head ached. Everything ached.

"Commander, I will understand if you take disciplinary action over my breach of your orders. But I stand by my actions."

"Officer Dimitri, what you did today was against my instructions. You took actions on your own, ignoring standing orders. You accept that?"

"Yes, sir."

"I hope you have learned something today that you will remember." Seminov paused long enough to see the dismayed expression on Dimitri's youthful face before he continued. "The lesson that a good cop must act on instinct as well as doing what he's told. You mistrusted the situation and felt you needed to do something. The signs of a good detective. If you do nothing else, Dimitri, stay with that attitude. A good call."

Dimitri slumped back, relief washing over him. He hadn't expected that. A reprimand, yes. Perhaps even demotion. Certainly not the praise that Seminov had just handed out.

"Commander, what else can I do to help?"

"Let's get back to the department. My car is over there."

"I'M TOO DAMNED OLD to be chasing around old factory sites," Seminov grumbled.

He was hunched behind his desk, nursing a large black coffee that Dimitri had laced with vodka. The department was quiet, the rest of his squad out on assignments. It allowed Seminov to inspect the information Pieter Tchenko had collated.

When he had opened the envelope he found CDs and printouts of text. While Dimitri scanned through the CDs Seminov read the report. Tchenko, as usual, had been thorough. His covert investigation had uncovered links between the FSB and Leopold Bulanin. Belonging to the criminal fraternity meant Bulanin's security was not as tight as that of the FSB. Tchenko had witnessed meetings between the racketeer and members of Krushen's department. He had photographs, on the CDs Dimitri was checking, of clandestine contacts between the two parties—Krushen, Bulanin, Yan Chenin and a number of Bulanin's bodyguards. According to Tchenko's notes, there had been a number of these meetings over a period of a month. Later the principals stopped showing, but intermediaries from the FSB and Bulanin's organization met on occasions.

Tchenko's investigation came to an end after he had handwritten a footnote at the bottom of his last printed report. It simply stated he felt he was being watched, that his investigation had been compromised and he would have to make sure his data was protected. Tchenko had signed and dated the note. Checking the date, Seminov saw that it was only five days before Tchenko and his family had died.

"Commander, what will we be able to do about this?" Dimitri asked. "If all this comes out, will you be ordered to drop it again? The investigation into Tchenko's death was suppressed."

"There are ways of getting around orders," Seminov said. "The CDs. Do they contain a transcript of these printed notes?"

"Of course. It's all there."

"Good."

Dimitri was puzzled but said no more.

Waiting until the younger man had returned to his own desk, Seminov used his cell phone to call Aaron Kurtzman at Stony Man. The commander told him he wanted information downloaded onto the Stony Man system.

"It's a safeguard in case I am compromised. Also it shows a connection between a Moscow criminal organization and Krushen's FSB section."

Kurtzman set up a link to Seminov's computer and downloaded the contents of the files.

"Tell Cooper that the names he sent me have checked out and are people who work for Krushen. There is no doubt that he is up to something in your country. Knowing Mischa Krushen, it will not be anything good."

"Thanks for your help, Valentine. You watch your back. If these people are as bad as you say, they won't hesitate to try to take you down."

"I'm prepared for that," he said. "After what happened today both sides understand the rules of the game."

CHAPTER SIXTEEN

The address, when Natasha Tchenko located it, turned out to be a two-story house on a quiet street on the south side of the city. The houses on either side had real-estate boards on the unkempt lawns. A plain four-door sedan was parked on the short driveway, so she parked farther down the street in front of yet another house up for sale. Stepping out of the car, Tchenko turned up her coat collar against the light rainfall, wondering if it ever stopped raining in Grand Rapids. Locking the rental car, she pushed her right hand deep into her pocket, closing her fingers around the butt of the pistol she was carrying. The Glock she had taken from Cooper was tucked beneath the driver's seat. The money she had "borrowed" was tucked into her pocket.

It was late afternoon, the air chilled. It suited Tchenko's mood. She had been torn between staying with Cooper and striking out on her own. That decision had been made for her when the room phone had rung. She had refrained from picking up and had allowed the call to be recorded on the answering service. When she had checked, the message had been just what she needed. It gave a location for the telephone number Cooper had found on one of the Russians who had abducted her.

She had reasoned that Cooper had his own trail to follow, so it was up to her to check out this fresh lead. If there was any possibility it might lead to Krushen, then she wanted to be there.

She took a taxi from the Amway Grand Plaza to her old hotel. She needed to get back into her room to pick up her belongings. She walked into the lobby, checking out the desk clerk. She breathed a sigh of relief when she saw it was a different one. A young woman. Tchenko crossed to the elevator and pressed the call button, nervously fingering the key still in her pocket. It had been in her jacket when she had been taken. When she emerged from the elevator she paused to check out the corridor. It was empty. She reached the door and unlocked it, pushing the door open and waiting as she scanned the room. Clear. The room appeared as it had been before she had been forcibly removed.

Tchenko spent a few minutes packing her belongings into her case, checking that her small purse was still there. Inside were her passport and credit cards. The cash she had brought with her. She switched on her cell phone. The power was low but there was enough to show she had a few messages. A couple from her relatives in London, checking to see if she was okay. There was one from Commander Seminov. He also wanted to know where she was and what she was playing at. It made her smile. She would speak to him later. She pulled on her long all-weather coat, transferring one of the handguns she was carrying to the side pocket. The second weapon she placed inside her case. Not wanting to risk staying too long, she closed the case and left the room, locking the door and making her way back down to the lobby.

She knew there was a small parking lot at the rear of the building so she avoided passing the desk by using the door that led to the rear exit. She walked across the lot, turning and making her way back to the street. She distanced herself from the hotel, then hailed a taxi and asked to be dropped off at the nearest car-rental agency. Ten minutes later she was negotiating for a budget vehicle. The young man behind the desk, who seemed fascinated by her accent, got her a good deal.

Tchenko realized he was flirting with her and took advantage. She left the office holding the keys for a late-model, two-door that had more features than any car she had driven back home in Moscow. Her young admirer had also furnished her with a map on which he had marked the route she would need to reach the address she was now approaching.

Tchenko turned off the sidewalk and walked to the rear of the empty house immediately next to her target. The backyard was badly overgrown, helping to conceal her approach. She trod through thick grass and weeds, over soaked cardboard and scattered cans. She stepped over the low fence between the properties, deciding to take out the handgun from her coat. She flicked off the safety. The weapon was already cocked. A sudden squall sent dancing rain across the back lot, slapping against the rear of the house and helping to cover Tchenko's final approach. She pressed up against the clapboard wall, edging along until she was just below the kitchen window. The window was partway open and she picked up a voice. A man talking in Russian, the conversation seeming one-sided until she realized the man was on a phone. She caught a few words. Then more as the man raised his voice, complaining because he had been left on his own to clean up everyone's mess.

That was welcome information. One man, more concerned with grumbling at his misfortune than keeping an eye out for visitors. Tchenko moved quickly on that information. She had to take advantage before it was lost. She headed to the small back porch, up the steps and to the kitchen door. Raising her foot, she slammed it hard just below the lock. The flimsy door burst open and she followed through, into the kitchen, her pistol tracking and locking on the startled man as he slid the cell phone into his pants' pocket.

"Hands where I can see them," Tchenko ordered. "Down on your knees. Hands back of your head."

If she had been on duty in Moscow she would have cuffed the man. Here all she could do was talk him into submission.

The kneeling man stared at her, his face tight with suppressed anger. Even she picked up on his stubborn attitude. This was no hired help. He lacked the demeanor of a contract hand. Tchenko realized he was one of Krushen's FSB agents.

"You should understand who I am," her captive said. "I am FSB. You know what that means?"

"I know it means you are one of Mischa Krushen's henchmen, running around doing his dirty work. Just like Ilya Malenkov in London. Did you hear how I dealt with him?"

The man's expression showed he understood. "You are Natasha Tchenko."

"Then you know I am not playing games. And you know why. Make it easy on yourself. Tell me where Krushen is and maybe I won't kill you."

"Malenkov was an asshole. I'm not that stupid."

Tchenko backed away from him, not wanting to be too close in case he attempted a sudden move. "No? Take a look at who has the gun and who is on his knees."

The words hit home. The kneeling man glanced around the kitchen, as if looking would suddenly provide him with an escape route. Tchenko watched him, seeing beads of sweat pop out on his forehead.

"No way out, *comrade*." She used the old word with a slight smile on her lips.

Her captive inclined his head, acknowledging the slight.

And in that brief moment his right hand dipped, slid beneath his shirt collar and came out holding a slim-bladed knife that he launched at the woman. The move caught her unprepared. His action had been so fast it went in a blur. She tried to move aside. Too slow. The slender blade penetrated her left shoulder just below the bone and sank in at least a couple of inches. Tchenko gasped at the sudden rip of pain, stepping back, her finger tightening against the trigger of her weapon. It fired, the recoil sending shock waves of pain through her impaled shoulder. As she bounced against the wall at her back, she caught a fractured image of the man jerking up off his knees as the 9 mm slug hit him over his ribs, right side. He spun, crashing to the floor, and Tchenko, forcing herself to ignore the pain in her shoulder, leveled her weapon again and put a second slug in his right thigh as he kicked out at her. The shot tore his flesh open, shattering the bone. White splinters showed through the torn flesh. A scream of agony burst from his lips as he squirmed across the kitchen floor, leaving a slick of blood.

With her weapon transferred to her left hand, still

trained on him, Tchenko closed her fingers around the hilt of the knife embedded in her shoulder. It moved when she put pressure on it and drew a soft cry of pain. She clamped her teeth together, knowing what she had to do and also knowing she was going to suffer. She recalled something from her training days, when one of the instructors had told the class that it was possible to eliminate pain by the power of the mind. All an individual had to do was to concentrate on the inner core of one's being and distance oneself from the source of the pain. Tchenko had never been fully convinced of that. She would have liked to have had that instructor with her right now, the knife buried in his damn shoulder while he told her there was no pain. Okay, she decided, there was no pain—and she drew the blade from her agonized flesh. She expressed her feelings in a low moan as the knife came out. Warm blood gushed down her body beneath her clothing. She fought the wave of nausea, trembling. The pain was strong enough to be almost exquisite, and the words that tumbled from her lips would have exactly told the instructor what she felt about his mind-over-matter philosophy. It was only leaning against the wall that kept her on her feet.

Tchenko stayed put until the nausea passed. Part of her mind willed herself to keep her wounded assailant covered with the pistol. He was curled up against the kitchen units, bloody and moaning softly. His earlier bravado had dissipated with the pain that had engulfed him.

The cold steel of the knife in Tchenko's bloody hand dictated her next move. On unsteady legs she crossed to kneel over the FSB man. Ignoring his pained protest, she pushed him on his back, leaning over to place the keen edge of the knife against his throat.

"You have very little choice in what happens next. I don't care whether you live or die. Understand that now. With the way you're bleeding you'll be dead soon enough unless you get medical help. I can call for that, or I can walk away and leave you here. Your decision."

"Bitch."

"Hurt my feelings and I *will* walk out." Tchenko thrust her hand in his pants' pocket and pulled out the cell phone he had been using. She dropped it in her own pocket. "I wouldn't want you using that," she said. "Unless you have a suicidal nature, you would start being helpful. Krushen won't have much use for a crippled agent. I suggest it's time for you to look out for yourself."

"By telling you where Krushen is?" His voice was getting weaker as blood loss started to drain his strength.

Tchenko moved the knife blade enough to remind him she still held his life in her hands. "Perhaps not," she said. "Most likely you will lie and send me on a fool's errand. I have your cell. There are ways of tracing where calls originate. I can find him that way. The FSB is not alone in having technology. Leaving you alive gives you the opportunity to warn him."

"Then you can double check. As you say, I have nothing to lose. Krushen has little patience with anyone who lets him down." He told her where Krushen and his team were, tracking down the final pair of sleepers in Chicago before moving on to the Black Judas facility in the small town of Singletree in the Cascade Mountains. A company called CoreM. The information included the cover names of the two Russians. "The area code of the call I made will show you I was not lying."

Tchenko watched his eyes glaze over. He lapsed into an

unconscious state. She pushed slowly to her feet. She dropped the knife into the kitchen sink, pressing her hand to her aching shoulder. She turned and walked out of the kitchen, conducting a search of the house. There was evidence a number of people had been occupying the place—discarded food containers; empty drink cans and bottles, stubbed-out cigarettes; old newspapers and magazines. There was nothing of a personal nature. When Krushen and his team had left, they had removed everything that might identify them. In the bathroom she did find a couple of small towels. She exposed her shoulder, grimacing at the deep gash the knife had left. She cleaned away much of the blood from her body, then wadded a torn piece of towel over the wound, promising herself she would tend to the wound properly once she had the opportunity. There was nothing else she could do at the moment.

Satisfied there was nothing to find in the house, she returned to the kitchen. She stood over the man on the floor. Blood had pooled under his shattered limb. He stirred, turning his head to stare up at her.

Tchenko felt the weight of the gun in her hand. The need to pull the trigger felt overwhelming and she angled the muzzle toward his head.

CHAPTER SEVENTEEN

"Lawrence Pennington," Brognola said. "Likely the guy is running. And just as likely he was working for the Russians, supplying information from his employment at the Pentagon. He worked at the Department of Defense and had access to sensitive information. The picture is slowly coming together. He lived on his own and had an eye for the ladies. Money to burn. His Washington apartment had been abandoned, the wall safe cleared. A dead man was found on the floor with half his head shot away. Pennington's car is missing from its parking spot, and earlier the same evening there was some kind of firefight in a Washington park. Looked like a couple of people were hit, but only one body left behind, which turned out to be a Russian named Navotney. The local P.D. checked his wallet and found his address. When they checked it, Pennington's address and telephone number were on the guy's laptop."

"Anything on the body in Pennington's apartment?"

"W.P.D. called in the FBI. They ran his prints through AFIS and it came up he had a long rap sheet. Bottom line, he was a hired gun who worked for a guy named Jake Waller. Waller has a checkered career. He had a brief stint in the military, with a couple of overseas postings, and was suspected of running minor rackets, but there was no solid proof. When he quit the military he ran with lowlives before he started his own outfit. He calls himself a mercenary, and if you come up with the cash, then he's on board."

"Hal, this gets more complicated every time a new player shows up."

"We're trying to pull some answers out of the mix back here, Striker. If we can kick-start the crystal ball, maybe we'll get lucky."

"If Pennington is running, maybe we can lock on to him. Get Aaron to check out his vehicle registration to see if there's a tracker on board. Or any security camera footage. And check his cell phone."

"His credit card usage is being looked at. That might give us a hint which way he's moving."

"Keep me updated," Bolan said.

He started the engine and turned the SUV around, then flicked on the wipers. A diner down the road caught his attention and he pulled in, sprinting through the rain to reach the entrance. Inside he moved to a booth and ordered a breakfast, with coffee. Bolan sat nursing his steaming mug, watching rain slide down the window's glass, his mind busy with the permutations of events revolving around Black Judas. Everything came back to that eventually. The name seemed to be attracting all kinds of attention.

The wrong kind.

The kind that was getting people killed.

He was well into his food when his cell phone rang.

It was Brognola.

"Your unknown from the farm turns out to be an FBI agent. The guy had been working inside a suspect group allied to the FSB, so it looks like the FBI had some idea about the Russians but were playing it in-house as usual. I can't get much sense out of the Bureau about this guy, but if he was taken out, it suggests he'd been compromised. They sent him along as bait to draw Carson into the meet then decided to deal with them both. Striker, these guys are playing a hard game. Sounds like a one-way street for anyone getting in their way. Aaron has picked up a trace on Pennington's movements. He's used his plastic twice. Got some gas off the interstate. Later he booked into a motel. Looks as if he's heading east. Akira is working on locating the tracker in his car. If he can get a signal we should be able to get you a tighter fix."

"Okay," Bolan said. "I'll head out in that direction. Call as soon as you pin him down."

"If we can locate Pennington, the opposition might be able to."

"I'll deal with that if it happens."

"Striker, we'll feed you updates as they come in."

Bolan cut the connection and put down the cell phone. He called for more coffee as he returned to his meal. He couldn't be sure when he might have the chance to get another.

Twenty minutes later he was pulling away after filling the SUV's gas tank, heading in the direction of the interstate and the vague trail he hoped would lead him to Lawrence Pennington.

He had been driving for an hour when Kurtzman called.

"Akira, bless that boy, worked on Pennington's profile. He hacked his way into the guy's life status and managed to locate his cell phone number. That, coupled with our lock on his car tracker, gives us a pretty tight fix on his position."

"Give me the details. I'll see if I can get him to talk to me."

BOLAN CALLED FIVE TIMES before the cell phone was answered. Even then it was just the message service. Bolan left a voice mail, asking Pennington to call him back using a land line. He identified himself and told the man he needed to contact him urgently. Bolan knew it was a pure gamble. If Pennington was running scared, there was no telling what he might do if he decided Bolan's call was just a trick to corner him. He carried on driving, knowing he was getting close to the man.

THE VOICE ON THE CELL phone was strained, telling Bolan that Lawrence Pennington was close to being whipped.

"Who are you?"

"Agent Matt Cooper, Justice Department. I understand your reluctance to talk, Pennington. I want you to realize the position you're in. We know about Navotney and the hit man at your apartment. There are men looking for you, and if they find you we both know what will happen."

"I suppose you're going to tell me I'd be wiser to give myself up."

"My job isn't to persuade you to do anything you don't want to. I tell you what I know and leave it to you. All I will say is, running isn't the answer. Looking over your shoulder, expecting the worst to happen. Not being sure who is friend, or who wants to slip a knife between your ribs. Pennington, you chose to do what you did. Payback can be rough. Call me in and I'll do my best to deliver you to safety. Nothing more."

"Cooper, you know how to make a guy feel wanted."

"This is no budding romance, Pennington. We're not about to take cozy walks holding hands and getting misty eyed.

Make your decision fast, because I have the feeling your Russian buddies have a team locked on to you right now."

"God, what a fucking mess."

"The choice is yours, Pennington. Work with me, or wait until your Russian buddies find you. If they do, I imagine you have an idea how they'll handle that meeting. They tried to kill you once already. It's why you're running."

Bolan could hear the guy's hard breathing over the phone.

"Jesus, some choice. *They* want to kill me. You'll help put me in a cell for the rest of my life."

"You put yourself into the situation. I'm not about to let you play the martyr. Not on my watch."

"You son of a bitch. All I am is a source of information to you."

"Isn't that what you've been to the Russians?"

"Bastard," Pennington yelled. Then he calmed down. "At least they paid me."

"Right now it's costing you. What's your life worth?"

"Can you guarantee I won't die?"

"No. I won't even promise I can get to you first. If you keep stalling, the odds on that are getting smaller."

This time the pause was longer. Bolan could sense the concern crowding Pennington's thoughts. The man would realize his position, become aware that one way or another his options were running out.

"Cavendish Motel. Off the interstate." He quoted Bolan a map reference.

"Keep out of sight."

Bolan checked his map, locating the place.

"How long?" Pennington asked.

"I'm closer than I figured. Forty minutes if I don't get any delays."

Bolan ended the call and pushed the SUV back into the traffic. As he rolled along the blacktop, he was working out the chances of his reaching Pennington and finding him still alive. He decided they were thin, and getting thinner by the minute.

"WE'VE GOT HIS LOCATION," Waller said. "He's holed up in a motel off the interstate."

"How long to reach him?" Kirov asked.

"Less than an hour."

"Try to make it less."

"Now we have a fix on his car, we'll know if he moves. And the lock on his cell phone is a bonus."

"I want to be informed."

"Will do, Mr. Kirov."

"Make sure of that, Waller. Your bonus depends on it."

"No problem. You just said the magic word."

BOLAN RAN INTO A HEAVY rainstorm a few miles from the motel. The windshield wipers were hard put keeping the glass clear. He was forced to lower his speed. The rain stayed with him and was still bouncing of the road when he braked and took the ramp off the interstate. It was late afternoon and the sky was thick with dropping gray cloud.

He found the sign for the motel easily enough. The neon display shimmered through the downpour as Bolan rolled into the motel lot, which held only a couple of cars. He spotted Pennington's car and cruised by the door to number three. At the far end of the lot Bolan turned the SUV around so he could cover the lot and see the exit clearly, then cut the engine.

Bolan picked up his cell phone and called Pennington.

"Cooper," Bolan announced.

"Where the hell are you?"

"Parked at the far end of the motel lot. I can see your room from here."

"You alone?"

"Looks clear. Pennington, the sooner we can get this done the better."

"You think so?" Pennington's voice had an edge to it.

"I'm coming in."

"Don't fuck with me, Cooper. I have a gun."

"So do I. Should keep us both happy."

Bolan opened the door and left the vehicle, leaving it unlocked. He crossed to the covered walk and approached Pennington's room. Pennington's window was the only one showing any light. At the door Bolan rapped on the panel.

"Cooper."

He waited, picking up the tread of footsteps inside. He took out the Beretta 93-R and held it at his side. The door opened, Pennington standing up close, his own handgun in plain sight. Bolan moved inside, closing the door and checking out the room.

"Do we hug, or is there a secret handshake?" Pennington asked, his tone betraying his nervous state.

"No," Bolan said. "And no passwords. Just you and me, Pennington."

The man nodded. He looked pale, was unshaved, and dark shadows were evident under his eyes as he fixed his gaze on Bolan. The man was scared, out of his depth in a situation created by his betrayal of his own country and the duplicity of the people he had been dealing with. The man would have no illusions where his position was concerned. His comparatively safe existence was gone, snatched away by the looming threat to his life. Survival would be paramount.

"Cooper, what happens now?"

"Convince me you're worth saving."

Pennington pointed to the leather satchel on the bed.

"My handler, Navotney, gave me that after we were ambushed in the park when the men chasing him showed up. He offered me the chance to get clear while he held them off."

"But they had someone waiting at your apartment?"

Pennington nodded. "Don't remind me. He wanted me to clear my safe. He couldn't have known I kept my pistol in there. I...I surprised him. Shot him. Then I got out of there. It wouldn't have been safe for me any longer in Washington. I decided to just drive. To get some distance..."

"Have you checked what's in the case?"

"Papers. Disks. Mostly in Russian, which isn't my first language, before you say anything. The only title I could translate said Black Judas."

"Time we moved out," Bolan said. "Grab the attaché case."

As Bolan turned, he caught the bright gleam of vehicle lights flash across the room's window. He took a swift look and saw the dark bulk of a black SUV swinging up in front of the room. The glare from the lights seared across his eyes.

Bolan realized what was happening, knew the seconds were falling away. He burst into action, crossing the room in long strides and slamming into Pennington, ignoring the man's protest. They tumbled against the far wall, losing their balance, and as they hit the carpet the front wall of the room imploded, filling the room with splintered wood and chunks of plaster. The leading edge of the ceiling dropped a couple of feet. Dust swirled in pale clouds as the SUV came to a jerky stop halfway inside the room.

The Executioner recovered fast, knowing that the backup crew would be closing in behind the vehicle. On one knee, he raised the 93-R and triggered a triburst through the windshield, saw the driver jerk as he took the 9 mm slugs. He used his left hand to haul Pennington to his feet. The man was almost sobbing. Bolan ignored that and pushed the man toward the bathroom door.

Glancing back Bolan saw an armed man clambering into the wrecked room over the splintered debris, another close behind. He double-fisted the Beretta and hit the lead guy in the chest with a 3-round burst. The man stumbled, dropping his weapon to clutch his body. He lolled against the side of the SUV, an easy target for Bolan's second burst, which cored in through the side of his skull. As the guy fell, Bolan switched his aim and put a burst into the second attacker that flattened the guy before he had a chance to raise his weapon.

Pennington was clinging to the frame of the bathroom door. He resisted when Bolan caught his arm to move him forward.

"Move your ass," Bolan growled, "or I'll shoot you myself."

He slammed his flat palm between Pennington's shoulders with full force, forcing the man forward.

The bathroom window shattered, the barrel of a shotgun sweeping back and forth to clear the glass from the frame.

Pennington gave a startled yell, throwing his hands in front of his face.

"Down," Bolan yelled, and saw Pennington drop below the level of the window. The shotgun boomed loudly, the full charge cleaving the air above their heads.

Bolan fired up at the dark bulk of the man framed in the

window. Three rounds slammed in under the guy's jaw, angling up to emerge out the top of his head, tearing off a sizable chunk of the skull. As the body slid away from the window, Bolan nudged Pennington back on his feet. He heard movement out front and realized there were more of them, and turned around, peering into the wrecked motel room. Bolan saw another shooter clambering in across the debris, his SMG swinging from its wrist strap. The soldier leaned out from the bathroom-door frame and hit the guy with a 3-round burst that kicked him off his feet. Bolan spaced out more bursts to keep the rest of the attacking crew away from the opening until the weapon locked on empty.

"Grab that attaché case," he told Pennington. "And stay low."

A shout from outside reached Bolan's ears as he dropped the spent magazine from the 93-R and snapped in a fresh one. With the Beretta cocked and ready, Bolan scanned the room. A shadow on the wall showed him the opposition was still active. He broke away from the bathroom door and crouched behind the overturned bed, waiting, conscious of the bathroom at his back. At least he would be able to spot anyone coming through from where he was now.

He picked up shouted orders, the sound of movement. Whoever the opposition was, they didn't appear to be in a hurry to quit.

A volley of bullets buzzed through the shattered frontage. Bolan felt the impact as they hammered the rear of the room, gouging out chunks of plaster. Then he heard someone yell "Go!" and he picked up the sound of boots on the pile of rubble around the 4x4. Bolan took a look over the edge of the bed. A dark figure was outlined by the light coming from the motel courtyard, an assault weapon in his hands. Bolan didn't hesitate. The Beretta tracked in and fired, the 3-round burst kicking the man off his feet. More return fire followed. Slugs burned through the air, chunking into the room's back wall. A lull in the firing followed as the strike team reassembled.

"Move up to the SUV," Bolan said. "Keep to the left."

He followed Pennington's scuttling figure, his eyes searching the floor of the room until he picked out the shape of an SMG, dropped by one of the shooters he had taken out. Bolan snatched up the weapon, tucking his Beretta into its shoulder rig, and saw that he had a 9 mm Heckler & Koch MP-5, double taped magazines in place. The weapon was already cocked.

"What the hell are we going to do?" Pennington asked. "Surround them?"

"My SUV is parked at the far side of the lot. Dark blue. Unlocked. When I say, go directly for it."

"What about them?"

"My problem."

Bolan reached up and opened the passenger door of the SUV. He leaned in and dragged the bloody body of the driver out. Then he slid inside himself, across the seat until he was behind the wheel. He dropped the lever into neutral and turned the key. The powerful engine caught. Bolan held down the brake pedal as he stamped on the gas. The SUV shuddered.

"Go," he yelled above the howl of the motor.

Bolan released the brake, knocked the lever into Reverse and felt the SUV rock. The wheels found traction and the heavy vehicle shot backward, out of the room and across the motel lot. Bolan yanking the wheel around. The SUV slid on the wet ground, gravel spinning up from beneath the wheels. Armed figures pulled away as the bulk of the SUV burst in among them. A yelling man was thrown aside. The rattle of autofire reached Bolan's ears above the howl of the engine and he felt the SUV vibrate as slugs tore into the bodywork. Others shattered side windows, showering the interior with glass fragments. Rain was blowing into the SUV through the shattered windows and the windshield gap.

A quick glance in the right-hand exterior mirror showed Pennington, concealed by the bulk of the SUV, heading in the direction of Bolan's own vehicle.

The rattle of autofire started up again, the SUV peppered with slugs. Window glass shattered as Bolan yanked the lever into Drive and hammered the gas pedal to the floor. He felt the SUV surge forward. He snatched up the MP-5, pushed open the driver's door and rolled out of the vehicle. He landed in a crouch, almost stumbling, pushing upright again.

He could almost hear a clock counting down the numbers. Time was running out.

CHAPTER EIGHTEEN

Off to Bolan's left a figure turned in his direction, weapon rising. The soldier hit him with a hard burst that cut his legs from under him, coming about and sprinting in the direction of his own vehicle. Behind him the runaway SUV slammed into one of the cars parked in the lot, tires spinning and throwing out the pungent odor of scorched rubber.

A rain-soaked man appeared in Bolan's path, his angry face glistening. The guy was raising his SMG when the soldier slammed into him. The impact hurled the man aside and he crashed to the ground, the breath bursting from his lips. Bolan ran on, reaching the SUV. He saw Pennington's white face staring at him through the windshield. The Executioner snatched open the door, key already in his hand. He slid it into the ignition slot and fired up the engine. High revs sent the SUV surging forward across the lot as Bolan released the brake. The guy he had bowled over was pushing up off the ground when the SUV hit him. He was thrown into the air, his broken body twisting helplessly.

The crackle of gunfire followed the SUV as it hurtled across the lot, up the slight incline, tilting as Bolan threw it into a left turn, rubber burning and smoking. The solid impact of a couple of slugs hitting their target came as Bolan took the SUV out of sight, cutting across an intersection to gain the lane he wanted.

He checked the mirror. Bolan had a feeling they hadn't seen the last of the strike team. His concern was answered when a black 4x4 spun into view from the motel lot, dropping into pursuit behind them. He stepped on the gas, hoping that exceeding the speed limit might attract a local police cruiser. His luck was off line, and no flashing lights showed as he led the pursuing 4x4 away from surrounding traffic.

Beside him Pennington remained still and silent. Bolan wondered if the man had caught a bullet during the melee in the motel lot. A glance across at the traitor showed he was pale faced but otherwise unharmed, soaked from the rain. He held the attaché case tight to his chest, his arms wrapped around it.

They cleared the urban area, open terrain on each side of the road. Bolan knew he had to deal with the crew in the vehicle following. He was aware they were out to stop Pennington, and Bolan would be on their list now. He had cut down the strike team, blocking its attempt to deal with Pennington. One way or another this was going to have a bloody end to it.

Bolan saw the pursuit vehicle closing in. It had picked up speed and was running dangerously close. The solid front of the 4x4 slammed into the rear of the SUV. Bolan felt the steering wheel jerk in his hands. The chase vehicle dropped back a few yards, then burned rubber again as it closed in fast. The second impact was harder than the first. Even though Bolan had been expecting it, the effect was drastic. He felt the SUV's back end slide, one rear wheel going off road and sinking into the soft mud edging the blacktop. It took Bolan long seconds to fight the vehicle back onto solid road.

Pennington came out of his daze, turning to look back at the chase truck.

"Are they trying to kill us?"

"Hell, Pennington, nothing gets by you."

Ignoring the rain-slick surface of the road Bolan put the gas pedal down hard, flooring the SUV. The powerful engine sent the vehicle hurtling along the strip, leaving the chase truck way behind.

He stared out through the rain-streaked windshield, scanning the landscape and searching for a way out. Outrunning his pursuers wasn't the answer. They weren't about to quit. Ditto for himself. So that left a basic solution. Rather than let them gain any advantage Bolan needed to draw them in and deal with them hard and fast. And he knew there was only one way to do that.

"Fasten your seat belt," he said.

Pennington realized it was an order, not a polite request. He also had the sense not to ask why, because he would not have liked the answer. From the corner of his eye he saw Bolan lock his own belt in place, then hang the MP-5 from his neck.

Watching the road ahead, Bolan spotted a feeder road on his left. It curved across the open land, with no cover, but he wasn't concerned with hiding, simply looking for a spot he could use to get off the main highway. The feeder road wasn't totally perfect, but it was going to have to do. He judged distance and speed, and knew he was going to have to be close with his timing.

The turn came up quickly. Bolan hit the brake, dropping his speed and working the wheel. He heard the tires squeal, felt the SUV swing, the rear end starting to lose its grip. He compensated, brake, gas, more brake, and clung onto the steering wheel to stay upright. The SUV's frame groaned against the pressure of the violent turn. As it reached the optimum swing, Bolan felt the wheels on his side lift off the ground and for a few, very long seconds the horizon hung at an angle. Bolan heard Pennington cursing loudly as he was slammed hard against the passenger door. He took his foot off the gas for a fraction and the SUV settled back on all four wheels, rocking heavily.

In his mirror Bolan saw the chase truck brake, smoke and spray erupting from the wheels as it shuddered to a stop. He hit his own brake, feeling the SUV skid and slide on the soft surface of the feeder road.

"Still got your gun?" he asked Pennington. "You might need it. Stay down."

Bolan opened his door. He freed the belt and dropped to the ground. He took the MP-5 from around his neck, lay flat on the ground and slid under the SUV. He could smell the hot metal of the exhaust system, could hear the clicks and pings. The earth beneath him was cold and waterlogged.

From where he lay he could see the chase truck rolling toward the SUV. It slowed while it was still out of range, then stopped. The black paint glistened beneath the downpour. The truck seemed to be waiting….

JAKE WALLER HADN'T LOST it for a long time. Being able to control his emotions was part of his professional makeup. But right now he was mad. The son of a bitch driving the SUV had taken down his crew, leaving Waller and one surviving member of his team. Waller still found it hard to take.

One fucking guy.

He had handled Waller's team as if they had been Salvation Army tambourine players. As angry as he was, Waller had to hand it to the guy. He knew combat. He had engaged without hesitation and had used his acquired SMG like a man who had been in the thick of action many times before.

Tennenbaum, sitting beside Waller, was showing signs of impatience. He was staring out through the streaming windshield at the SUV parked up ahead of them.

"What is that bastard doing?"

"He's waiting for us to make a move," Waller said. "That old boy knows we want Pennington and what he's carryin'. So he's sitting there just daring us to go for it."

"So why are we sitting here? Let's go get the sucker. Put him down for good and all."

"You figure?" Waller grinned. "Don't forget he's armed and he just cut down our team all on his ownsome."

"So we going to let him get away with that? That Russian, Kirov, is payin' us good bucks to handle this. I'd like to collect."

"So would I, Kyle. Catching a handful of slugs in the guts isn't going to help you spend it."

Tennenbaum ejected the magazine from his MP-5, checked the loads and snapped it back in place. He worked the slide to cock the weapon, reached out and opened his door.

"Time to get it done, Jake"

He was gone before Waller could protest, zigzagging across the open ground as he closed in on the waiting SUV.

Waller slipped the catch on his own door, waiting until

the shooting started before he moved. He didn't have to wait long. There was crackle of autofire from the SUV. Tennenbaum gave a screech of pain and slumped to his knees, jerked up his MP-5 and returned fire. He was firing wild, not sure where his target was. Waller spotted muzzle-flash from the SMG firing back at Tennenbaum. It was coming from underneath the vehicle.

Smart boy.

As Tennenbaum caught the second burst, his body arching around in a bloody mist, Waller eased his door open and slipped out. He moved to the rear of the 4x4, working his way around it, using it as cover as he headed for the front end. He leaned out and tracked in with his own MP-5, loosing a long burst that raked the sodden earth beneath the SUV's chassis.

He was ready to move forward, his intention to hit the target area again, when he caught movement out of the corner of his eye and saw the other guy…and knew he'd been outflanked.

THE MOMENT HE FIRED his second burst, driving Tennenbaum to the ground in a haze of bloody body shots, Bolan rolled out from under the SUV. He had seen the 4x4's driver's door ease open, saw the dark shape as Waller moved to the rear of the 4x4. On his feet, knowing he had only seconds to alter position, Bolan cut away from the SUV in a wide curve that placed him clear of the vehicle when Waller leaned out to fire.

Bolan brought up his SMG, Waller's head turning as he realized his adversary had already moved.

The burst was short, directly placed, and Waller fell away from the 4x4, a cluster of 9 mm slugs coring his skull.

As the bulk of Waller's body became exposed, Bolan fired again, a longer burst that ripped in through ribs and chest, turning him over on his back, rain slanting down to wash at the blood pumping from his wounds.

Bolan stepped up to clear weapons away from Tennenbaum, then Waller. He slung the MP-5 from his shoulder before he searched the bodies. Waller's cell phone had been shattered by Bolan's 9 mm fire. He stored it in a pocket. There was nothing in Tennenbaum's pockets apart from a fold of cash money. Bolan crossed to the 4x4 and checked it out. Clean except for a canvas bag of ordnance. Bolan took that and dropped it in the rear of the SUV along with the MP-5s.

Pennington, his pistol hanging loosely in his hand, watched Bolan climb back into the SUV and start the engine.

"Where to now?"

"A safehouse. I need an expert opinion on the contents of that attaché case."

Bolan contacted Stony Man and spoke with Barbara Price.

"Where are you?" she asked.

"My meeting with Pennington was interrupted. Someone tried to park an SUV inside his motel room."

"You okay?"

"Yeah. There was a firefight. I'm bringing in something that might provide us with some answers."

"What do you need?"

"The safehouse open. A translator on hand. A secure connection to Seminov."

CHAPTER NINETEEN

A two-story house standing in enclosed grounds, the safe-house was situated fifteen miles away from Stony Man. A three-man blacksuit team was already in place when Bolan and Pennington arrived. Aaron Kurtzman had arrived and taken his place at the conference table.

Bolan had asked for clean clothes to be dropped off at the safehouse. Once he had Pennington settled and under the watchful eye of the blacksuits he headed to the bathroom and had a shower. The streams of hot water helped him to relax and work the stiffness out of his joints. In clean, casual clothes Bolan went back downstairs and saw that the translator had arrived and was helping herself to coffee from the pot prepared by one of the blacksuits. The large-screen television monitor had been switched on, and Kurtzman sat facing it, impatiently pushing his files around the conference table. There was an audio connection with Valentine Seminov.

"Glad you could join us, Striker," Kurtzman said gruffly.

Bolan took a seat at the smaller conference table, motioning Pennington to sit on one side and Erika Dukas at the other.

"This young lady is our best translator," Bolan explained to Pennington. "She'll tell us what your Russian contact passed to you."

Bolan swung the attaché case onto the table, opened it and slid its contents across to Dukas. She immediately began to go through the files, head down, oblivious to the rest of the room. As she read, she jotted points of interest on a yellow legal pad.

"You want to bring everyone up to speed?" Bolan said to Pennington.

Lawrence Pennington cleared his throat. "For the past few years I've been providing information from my post at the Pentagon to a Russian named Sergei Navotney. He was my handler. He received what I collected, paid me and provided me with…with other benefits. As far as I was concerned, it was a good working relationship. I make no excuses for what I did. The thought I was selling out my country never actually crossed my mind. I must have been extremely naive. A few days ago everything changed. Navotney dropped out of sight. I was unable to make contact. I couldn't understand what was going wrong. Then he called and said we had to meet. It was clear something was wrong."

"This Navotney. He didn't give you any explanation?" Kurtzman asked.

"No. Just that we needed to meet. So we arranged a time and place. When Sergei did show, all hell broke loose. Suddenly there were men shooting at Sergei. He pushed the attaché case at me and told me to leave before I got shot, as well.

"I drove back to my apartment and there was someone waiting for me. He wanted me to open my safe. I was lucky I had a gun in there. After I shot him, I got in my car and drove. I wasn't even sure where to. It made no difference. I'd been followed. If Cooper hadn't made contact, I would probably be dead by now. I don't even know who those people were."

"There has to be a second team," Bolan said. "Working against Krushen. They show up and start to wipe out the sleepers. First Spokane, then Grand Rapids."

"Maybe Navotney's data will help," Pennington said. "I don't have any more information on any of this."

Bolan picked up one of the phones on the table and spoke into it. Moments later the door opened and a pair of blacksuits entered. They crossed to flank Pennington.

"It had to end this way," Bolan said. "You'll be taken to meet agents from the FBI and handed over."

Pennington stood. He offered no protest as he was handcuffed.

"No matter what you think about me, Cooper, I hope you catch them."

Bolan didn't answer the man. He waited until Pennington had left the room.

"Aaron?"

"We're getting a picture now," Kurtzman said. 'Still fuzzy 'round the edges, but the FSB seems to be at the head of the list, resurrecting Black Judas so they can put it into operation."

"Led by Mischa Krushen," Seminov said over the speaker, speaking for the first time. "He was behind the killing of Pieter Tchenko and his family. Tchenko had unearthed information that connected Krushen to Leopold Bulanin, a Moscow racketeer who aided Krushen."

"Valentine, any thoughts on who this other group might be?"

"If this Black Judas project is so secret, I would suggest this opposition comes from others within Lubyanka. Anything that involves the FSB comes from the FSB, if you understand what I mean. These people are paranoid when it comes to protecting their little schemes. They will go to any lengths to prevent information getting out. Look at what they did to the Tchenko family."

"Pennington's details are in here," Dukas said, glancing up from the Navotney files. "I also have names and a location for the last two sleepers. Nathan Parker and Jerome Kincaid. According to Navotney's records, they were located in Chicago and are still in that area."

"I'll have it checked out," Kurtzman said, picking up a phone to contact his cyberteam. "See if there's been any unusual activity."

"If they are the surviving pair, it's likely they'll be kept alive," Bolan said. "Krushen will need them if he intends activating the project."

"And the mystery group?" Seminov asked.

"It has to be one of two things," Bolan said. "The total elimination of the Black Judas project, or a takeover bid by someone who wants control of it for their own reasons. Whatever it is, there's too much collateral damage. And it isn't over yet."

Kurtzman, passing along his instructions to his team, paused, listening to someone giving him information. He put down his phone.

"That was Akira. That cell phone you brought back. He managed to extract the memory card and get some information off it. The last call Jake Waller made was to a Washington number. Akira looked at the contact list. That number is listed under the name Kirov, and he says he's part of the Russian diplomatic community. What do you think, Valentine?"

"I know that name. It means something. But let me run some checks at this end."

"Get back as soon as you can," Bolan said. "If you find anything, call me on my cell phone."

"Where are you going, my friend?"

"To try to locate those surviving sleepers."

Bolan clicked off the connection. "Erika, is there anything else about Black Judas?"

"A pretty extensive summary of the project. Our initial figuring was pretty well on the mark. Cut to the bone, Black Judas was designed to hack into U.S. financial databases and control the whole structure. There are descriptions here about taking down the infrastructure. Also the computer heart of government and banking. We are talking about wiping out the nation's finances. From high-yield private and government stocks right down to welfare benefits for the needy. If they got this working, the U.S. could end up penniless, unable to trade and with every ATM frozen. Now that's a basic breakdown. In reality it would be a lot more complicated."

"But it could be achieved?"

"With the right people pulling Black Judas's string…yes."

"Is there any information on where they would operate this project from? A base?"

"Only a reference to something they call the core."

"Where they have their command center?" Bolan suggested.

"Maybe a supercomputer system. That doesn't finally come online until a teamed pair are installed," Kurtzman said.

"Maybe that's the reason for those code numbers in the

tattoos." Bolan turned back to Erika. "A numerical key? That switches this system on?"

"Any details on where the core is located?" Kurtzman asked.

She shook her head. "Nothing specific. But there's still a lot I haven't got to yet."

"Then let's get more people on this," Bolan said. "Talk to Barbara and Hal. Get them to wave their big sticks. I'm getting the feeling time might be running out for us."

VALENTINE SEMINOV PUT DOWN his phone and leaned back in his seat.

Kirov.

He did know the name. If he could only place it and tie it in to whatever was going on in the U.S.

Kirov.

Mischa Krushen.

Was this man Kirov on the FSB team? Working for Krushen? He shook off the thought. Surely it was not Krushen who was trying to eliminate anyone connected to Black Judas. No, Krushen wanted Black Judas up and running. He would do all he could to keep members of the project alive. So that put Kirov in the camp of the people who seemed intent on wrecking the project.

But who were they?

Seminov crossed to the steaming pot of coffee and poured himself a large mug. He paced the floor, dredging the darker corners of his memory, trying to make some kind of sense out of the fluttering shadows of memory. The name kept floating into his consciousness, then away again before he could get a solid fix on it.

He failed to notice when Dimitri came back from some

errand. The younger man noticed Seminov's preoccupation, something in his commander's stance that suggested he was struggling to recall some elusive fact. Dimitri retreated to his desk and started to go through the documented details of Pieter Tchenko's investigation again. One of the pages listed photographic evidence, images that had been taken from the digital camera Tchenko used and transferred onto a CD. Dimitri picked up the CDs and found the one that held the images. He placed it into the drive on his computer and opened the disk. He ran through the thumbnails, viewing each image enlarged. Toward the end there were a few showing the late Yan Chenin with Krushen and Bulanin. At the bottom of the list were a few isolated shots of Chenin entering and leaving his apartment building. Dimitri sighed, leaning back to stare at the final image of Yan Chenin coming out of his apartment building. He reached out to click off the image.

And his hand froze. He touched the wheel on his mouse and enlarged the image, then swore softly to himself.

How could they have missed it?

Dimitri reached for a notepad and quickly wrote on it. He left the image on screen and reached for a telephone. He punched in a number, waiting impatiently until someone answered.

"Anna, this is Nikolai. Yes. And yourself? That's good. Of course I am looking forward to seeing you this weekend. Really? I hope no one is listening in, Anna. Will you do something for me? No, not that, young lady. Just behave. This is official OCD business. What? Oh, extremely official. Write down this address." Dimitri quoted the details he had taken from the plate fixed to the wall beside the entrance to the apartment building in the photograph.

"I need a list of all the occupants of that apartment building. You can do that, can't you? I know how dedicated you are, Anna, so this should not prove too hard. Will you send me an e-mail with the list? Thank you. Pardon? Yes, Anna, I will express my gratitude in any way you want. I said *any* way. Goodbye, Anna."

When Seminov happened to glance up he saw that Dimitri had a wide smile on his face. He decided that perhaps he was being too easy on the young officer.

TWENTY MINUTES LATER Dimitri heard his e-mail delivery ping, telling him he had a new message. He opened the service and saw that it had come from Anna's computer in the Department of Information. He printed out the list and deleted the e-mail. Then he placed the sheets of paper on his desk and began to read through the names and apartment numbers. There were more than two hundred occupants. None of the names rang any bells until he reached the third sheet of paper, halfway down. He picked up a pen and circled the name, then looked across at Seminov, who was re-reading Tchenko's report.

With the sheet of paper in his hand Dimitri crossed to Seminov's desk and placed it in front of his superior. There was no reaction immediately. Then Seminov snatched up the sheet and held it in front of his face.

"My God, Dimitri. Where did you get this?"

"Tchenko's photographs. The last few were of Yan Chenin coming out of his apartment building. I realized the last one had him coming out of a different building. Not his own. So I had the occupants of the building checked, and there he was."

"There he was, Dimitri. All the damn time and we didn't

connect it. Now it fits. Yan Chenin knows Karl Federov, and Karl Federov knows Kirov. Viktor Kirov. He is not working for Mischa Krushen. Kirov is with Federov."

"KARL FEDEROV AND VIKTOR KIROV go back a good few years," Seminov explained to Bolan. "Until I got Federov's name, I couldn't make the Kirov connection. It wasn't public knowledge when Kirov was accused of abusing his authority within the FSB. His conviction was part of an image-making ploy to show the FSB in a good light. They sent him to a prison that had a bad reputation. Federov was one of the few who stood by him, but even he could do nothing. Until a few weeks ago when he was surprisingly released. You see, my friend, I have my sources, too. My telephone has been very hot for the past hour. The man who paved the way for Kirov's release was Alekzander Mishkin, Federov's boss. He is the Security Directorate minister. Mishkin is very ambitious. He wants to reach the top of the political ladder. One of his main functions is the running of an oversight directorate, with Karl Federov as his operations director. The object of the Mishkin-Federov partnership is of course the FSB, specifically the section under Krushen and his immediate superior, General Berienko. The FSB is an easy target for someone like Mishkin. The Black Judas project would be a feather in Mishkin's cap if he could wrest control from the agency."

"So Mishkin has Federov heading the opposition against the FSB team here in the States? With this guy Kirov hands-on?"

"Kirov is ideal for that kind of work. It is what he was trained for. At best, Kirov is a hard man. At worst, a sociopath with little regard for human life."

"Something still isn't gelling here, Valentine. If Mishkin wants control of Black Judas, it doesn't explain why the sleepers are being killed off. There's no sense to that. The reason three teams were inserted was to be prepared in case some were lost. There were always so many in reserve. Cutting down the odds isn't the wisest thing to do."

"I agree. It defies logic."

"Thinking outside the box, maybe Mishkin and Federov are working this for themselves. Not Russia. From what we know about Black Judas it would enable those in control to strike at the very heart of the American financial setup, bring it down and destroy banking and the stock market. Flip the coin and it could also be used to create great wealth for whoever runs it. Instead of destroying markets, it manipulates them."

Seminov was silent for a time. "Cooper, that imaginative mind of yours may just have come up with something. I have one reservation. Alekzander Mishkin. This man is an unqualified patriot. Understand me, my friend, Mishkin would *never* betray Mother Russia. On the other hand, Federov is cut from different cloth. We know he consorts with a local racketeer. And he has managed to persuade Mishkin to free that crazy man Viktor Kirov. The first thing he does is send Kirov to America to hire men like himself to run around and terrorize. I think, Cooper, you may be correct and Federov is running his own little scheme to get his greedy hands on the project. For his own use, and Minister Mishkin is being played for a fool."

"A point, Valentine. Would Federov let Mishkin know he's in bed with Bulanin? If Mishkin is as straight as you say, he wouldn't want to be associated with a gangster. Not the kind of thing he'd have on his election manifesto."

"I do not believe Mishkin will know any more than

Federov wants him to." Seminov chuckled. "I will enjoy telling him. In the public interest, of course."

"Exactly. Make sure you cover your back, Valentine."

"Of course."

"And update me if you hear from Natasha."

"I promise. So tell me, Cooper, what are *you* going to do?"

"What I do best."

Moscow

"OUR PEOPLE WERE UNABLE to get close to the farm. It was swarming with police and FBI."

"Any feedback from our informant?"

"Carson is dead. There were also four other bodies at the scene. Two were in a downed helicopter."

"Kopek and Nabov. What about Kaminski?"

"Found in the barn. Hennessey was in the trunk of his car."

"At least we are rid of him. Kaminski completed his assignment. But who killed the others?"

"Our interfering unknown? I wonder about him. There is no doubting his expertise."

The silence following Krushen's last comment caused him concern. He sensed Berienko's mood. Aware of his own position, Krushen made the first move.

"I will deal with it, General. Everything is in hand."

"It had better be, Mischa. We cannot be seen to be weakening. Georgi Bella is becoming a damned nuisance. I know he has his spies in America. They will be watching how we perform. Remember that, Mischa. You may think of *me* as a bastard, but next to Bella I am Mother Teresa."

"General, I understand. Believe me, there is no one who wants a good result from this more than me."

"Call when you have that good result."

The line went dead. Krushen stared at the cell phone, the urge to smash it on the floor gripping him. He realized that the palms of his hands were sticky with sweat. Only General Berienko could make that happen. The man's strength of character and the power he wielded gave him that intimidating aura. A thought intruded on Krushen's consciousness, which brought a smile to his lips. The general had made it clear, intentionally or not, that Georgi Bella was using a similar threat against him. So Berienko was under pressure, too. It made Krushen feel a little better. Only a little and for a brief moment, but it was a good feeling while it lasted.

"EVERYTHING IS READY, sir," Leo Lipinski said. He was a lean, intense young man who took his responsibilities extremely seriously. "Shall I order the move?"

"Yes, do that."

Krushen glanced around the room. It had been comfortable here, even though their stay in Grand Rapids had been short. He hoped their upcoming accommodation would be as pleasant.

"Let's go," he said.

CHAPTER TWENTY

Chicago

Bolan's flight touched down midmorning. He made his way through the terminal building and went directly to the car rental agency where a vehicle had been booked for Matt Cooper. Bolan signed off, took the keys and located the sedan. He placed his bags in the trunk and rolled off the lot.

He had locations for both the sleepers. His main hope was that they hadn't yet been contacted. If all the assumptions were correct, the two survivors of the Black Judas project were unlikely to be killed outright. They were needed alive and able to kick-start the project. That didn't eliminate the chance of some kind of violent confrontation taking place if both groups looking for Parker and Kincaid came together. Bolan didn't want other innocent deaths to take place.

Megan Carson.

Steven Cross, the young detective from Grand Rapids.

He couldn't forget the other sleepers. Placed in America as part of Black Judas they had been killed needlessly.

Not in combat, but murdered to satisfy men's greed and a desire to create chaos.

The combatants Bolan had faced down were another matter. They had chosen to kill, had taken money to destroy the lives of people they didn't even know. Bolan knew the type. He had been battling their kind for years. They were always around. Available to anyone with the need and the money to pay for their loyalty. As long as the finance was there, those kinds of men would wear anyone's colors.

He turned onto the street where Jerome Kincaid lived. Old, well-maintained houses that had been converted into apartments for the executive classes. The cars parked along the street were new, shiny, late models. Bolan pulled in behind a gleaming yellow sports model that was so low slung it had to be near impossible to get in without dislocating something. He went up the steps to the house and checked the post boxes just inside the porch.

"Can I help you?" The young woman, leggy and impossibly tall, had the kind of looks that told Bolan she *had* to be the yellow car's owner.

"I'm looking for Jerome," Bolan said pleasantly. "I have a deal I need to discuss with him."

The woman smiled. "Who doesn't? I haven't seen him today. Come to think of it, this is his day down at the mission. It's over on the South Side. Pretty depressing area, but our boy Jerome just thrives on it."

"The South Side? Thanks."

BOLAN REACHED the South Side, following the route he had worked out on his street map. He found the locale where Jerome Kincaid's mission was located. The old tenement buildings in the area were partly deserted, partly occupied.

The neighborhood was crumbling, but the people who still lived there kept it alive. They existed in that forgotten place, where only human dignity gave them the strength to keep their heads high.

The mission was housed in what had been a general store in better times. The double-fronted establishment, long past needing a fresh coat of paint, stood with open doors. A steady stream of people, from youngsters to the elderly, came and went.

Bolan parked and crossed the street. He went inside, seeing the rows of trestle tables and benches. At the far end a table held steaming food trays, and behind a number of people were filling plates and handing them to the constant line of hungry people.

"Can I help you?"

The man who asked, in a black, creased suit and dog collar, was Hispanic. His black hair showed traces of gray. He stepped out from behind the serving table.

"I am Father Aguilar."

Bolan showed his Justice Department credentials. "Agent Cooper. I'm looking for Jerome Kincaid, Father. It is important that I find him."

"I am afraid you are too late, my son. Jerome left over three hours ago with some other men who came looking for him. Such a dedicated young man. So busy at work, yet he comes down here so often to help. Even when he's here his cell phone is always ringing. I don't think he goes anywhere without that thing. Always in his pocket."

"Father, can you tell me anything about these men who came to see Jerome?"

"They arrived just after we had opened. In one of those very large 4x4 vehicles. Black and shiny. Three of them got out. There were others who stayed inside. Two of the men stood with Jerome and spoke with him for some time. I thought he looked agitated for a time, but then one of the men spoke to him and he seemed to calm down. Then he came over with the man and said he was going to have to go for a while. A business emergency."

"These men," Bolan asked. "Did you speak with them?"

"Only briefly to the one who came over with Jerome. He apologized for the intrusion. He said Jerome would return as soon as possible."

"What did he sound like?"

"I'm sorry?"

"His accent? American? Foreign?"

The priest nodded. "Oh, yes. Certainly foreign. He had a strong accent." Father Aguilar gestured with his hands. "Russian, I think. At least from that region of Europe."

"Just one more thing. Did you by chance notice the license number on the 4x4?"

"I didn't myself, but I can go one better than that." The priest turned and called out to a tall, stooped figure. "George. George, come here."

The man, clad in faded military fatigues, oversize trainers on his feet, shuffled over. Though he seemed to be looking at Bolan he was seeing beyond him, into somewhere far away.

"George, this is Agent Cooper. I told him you could help. He wants to know about the big 4x4 that Jerome left in. You remember that, don't you?"

George's eyes flickered and suddenly he was focused.

"This year's Dodge Durango. Black paint job, with a 5.7 V-8 engine." He gave Bolan a gap-toothed smile then recited the vehicle license number. "I didn't miss anything, did I, Father?"

"Not a thing, George."

George nodded. Bolan held out a hand and took George's.

"Thanks, George, you've been a great help."

"I've been a great help," George repeated, moving back to his position outside the store.

"That was kind of you, Agent Cooper. He'll be a happy man now for a few days."

"Is that all it takes? A grateful word?"

"To be noticed is all George wants. He was in the military until he got wounded. It left him disoriented. People look at him and turn away because they are embarrassed. All George wants is human contact." Aguilar touched Bolan's arm. "You gave him that today, Agent Cooper. Any time you want, you will be welcome here."

"Thank you, Father. Would you excuse me?"

Bolan took out his cell phone and called Stony Man.

"Hal, I think we missed Kincaid. He's already been taken." He described the events Father Aguilar had explained. "If Parker has been picked up, too, the next step will be a trip to the Black Judas site. We don't know where that is. Has Erika come through with anything from the translations yet?"

"Still working. She's having problems with Navotney's notes. The guy wasn't the best at keeping his reports neat and tidy."

"I'm going to run down Parker's address. See if he's still around. I'm getting the feeling our Russian buddies are moving faster than we figured."

"Best shot is all we can give it, Striker."

"I need to talk to Aaron."

Kurtzman came on the phone.

"I'm here."

"Run down a vehicle for me." Bolan recited the information George had given him. "This is a late model. I'm guessing it will be fitted with GPS technology. Can we track it?"

"If it has that on board, no problem. Anything else?"

"We have Jerome Parker's details?"

"Anything in particular?"

"His cell phone number?"

"Uh-huh. You want me to run a trace on his cell phone? See if we can locate where he might be?"

"My contact here says he never goes anywhere without his cell phone. Always on it talking business."

"If his cell phone is switched on, I can triangulate from the test signals it kicks out every so often. Might take some time but it can be done."

Before he left the area Bolan gave Father Aguilar his cell phone number. "If anything happens I might need to know, Father, give me a call."

"I will."

"Others might come looking for Jerome. If they do, try not to upset them. Tell them whatever they want to know."

"Are they violent men?"

"They could turn that way if they believe you are lying to them. Father, be careful. Understand?"

Aguilar nodded. "Yes, I understand, and thank you for warning me."

TWO HOURS LATER Bolan had verified that Nathan Parker had not been seen that day. He had not shown up at his office, had not called in, which was unusual. Everyone Bolan spoke to said the same thing. If he hadn't shown up for work and failed to call in, something was wrong.

Bolan, sitting in his car outside Parker's work building in downtown Chicago's Loop, the financial heart of the city, had his cell phone in his hand. He was turning the phone over and over as he tried to figure his next move. The thought struck him at the same time the cell phone rang.

"Parker?" Brognola asked.

"Missing from work. He didn't call in sick."

"Okay, we may have something here for you. Aaron has tied down the Dodge. It does have GSP equipment on board, so he'll be able to work out where it's heading. Akira has located his cell phone signal, too. Once they run some comparisons, we'll know if Kincaid is still in the vehicle. And Erika says she should have a possible location on the base these guys are going to run Black Judas from."

"Let's start with the route that 4x4 is taking. I can top up the rest of the information once I'm tracking these people. And, Hal, see if you can get some help from the Chicago P.D. Someone needs to keep a watch over Father Aguilar's mission. I'd hate to think he might get a visit from our other Russian guests, looking for Kincaid."

"Leave it with me, Striker."

Kurtzman's voice broke through the call. "That Dodge is heading due south. Head in that direction They've got a good start on you. We'll stay on them. We ran a check on the GSP and the cell phone signal. Both tracking the same route, so I think we have them on the radar."

"Good work, Aaron. Keep me updated."

Bolan started the car and swung into the traffic.

At least now he had an objective, somewhere to go, a target to aim for.

An unbidden thought came into his mind. For the first time in a while he wondered where Natasha Tchenko was. And how she was.

CHAPTER TWENTY-ONE

Moscow

Federov received the news of the setback with surprising calm.

"It hasn't exactly been peaceful here," he said.

He related the events involving Yan Chenin and Anton Gregor, adding the incident with Lem Topov and Commander Seminov.

"That OCD bastard is becoming an irritant. He has the survival instincts of a damned cockroach."

"Karl, what is the problem then?" Kirov said. "Don't you remember what to do with cockroaches? You step on them and squash them into the ground."

"What is your next move?"

"Tracking down Kincaid and Parker. I have people checking Parker's workplace. I have a lead that may bring Kincaid into our hands. I'll get back to you when I have some news. Karl, don't worry."

KARL FEDEROV'S DAY was not getting any better. He had just finished his conversation with Kirov when an urgent summons to Minister Mishkin's office reached him. When Federov arrived at the ministry, he was shown directly into the office. Mishkin was not alone. He had a pair of grim-faced men with him who had the stamp of internal security all over them. They wore dark suits and darker expressions on their gaunt faces. They both turned to stare at Federov as he stepped into the chill room.

"Minister, I came the moment I received your message."

"Punctual at least." Mishkin's tone was icy. It held no trace of familiarity, and Federov experienced a twinge of unease.

"Minister?"

Mishkin spoke quietly to the two men. They nodded, saying nothing as they turned and left the room, closing the door behind them. Mishkin waited, then stood and went to stand in front of the room's single window to stare at the rain slanting out of the clouded sky.

"Is something wrong, Minister?" Federov asked, and immediately regretted speaking when Mishkin turned back to face him.

"I was hoping you could tell me, Karl."

"I am not sure I understand, sir."

Mishkin returned to sit behind his desk. He opened a file and rifled through a number of printed papers. Federov recognized it as part of the Black Judas documentation he had presented to the minister.

"Did you believe, Karl, that I would simply accept what you gave me without having it thoroughly examined? That I would take your word? Karl, do I look that gullible?"

Despite the discomfort he was experiencing, Karl Federov maintained his outward composure.

"I really do not understand, Minister. What am I being accused of?"

Mishkin leaned back. "I do not recall actually accusing you of anything, Karl. Yet. However, since you have raised the matter, perhaps we should pursued that line."

Federov failed to come up with a suitable comment this time.

"Lost for words, Karl? Maybe I can provide some. Betrayal? Deceit? An attempt to conceal all the details on Black Judas? That should suffice for a start."

Federov's mind exploded with fear and confusion. A rush of denial. A need to explain. He faltered, knowing from the look in Mishkin's eyes that nothing he said was going to get him off the hook.

"Bringing Viktor Kirov onto your team made me wonder. I allowed it at the time because I thought, wrongly it now appears, that you needed his help. Of course you did. But not because you were lacking in skilled people. Oh, Karl, we have experienced people by the score. No, you wanted Kirov as an ally. As a partner. You are very good friends. The only one to champion Kirov during his trial. He would give his life for you. And you needed someone in America to pursue your takeover of Black Judas. Not for me. Not for Russia. For yourself, Karl. So you could steal money. You and Kirov."

Mishkin opened a drawer in his desk and took out the data Federov had concealed in his apartment safe. Mishkin spread the material across his desk.

"No one has secrets, Karl. Not even you. Your precious little safe has been known to me for months. Your apartment had been swept a long time ago. As soon as I began to worry about you and Kirov, I had your safe opened and look what was found. Your CD has been checked against the one you gave me. Do you know what we found? Of course you do. A full version of the Black Judas files. Did you forget to provide me with all the information, Karl? How very remiss of you."

A silence descended and in that quiet Federov heard the door behind him open and close, and he knew that the two security agents had returned. They were standing close behind him.

"The strange thing is, Karl, that I'm not all that disappointed. You have acted just as I expected. My only regret is you did it out of sheer greed."

"As opposed to what? Why do you want to take control of Black Judas? For you it's nothing but another means of making your attempt to climb to the top of the ladder. Personal gain. No better or worse than what I wanted to do. You are no different than me, Minister."

Mishkin smiled, his eyes fixed on Federov.

"I'm different, Karl. In another hour it will be midday. I will still be alive then."

Mishkin nodded to the two silent figures behind Federov. As he moved from behind his desk, making for the door and locking it, strong hands gripped Federov's arms and pinned them to his sides. Mishkin returned to face his captive, reaching inside Federov's coat to remove his holstered pistol.

"You won't be needing this," he said. "Take him out. Deal with him in the basement garage."

An arm circled Federov's throat, drawing tight and restricting his breathing. He was dragged across the office to a door in the far corner. It led, he knew from past experience, down narrow steps, to the garage that served Mishkin's department. It was a separate enclosure, away from the main parking area for the ministry building. It was there to conceal exits from the building that were unusual business.

Federov understood the meaning. Individuals taking the narrow flight were starting a one-way journey. Once in the basement they would be dealt with efficiently, placed in the trunk of a car and driven to some out-of-the-way spot where they would be quietly buried and forgotten about.

It was with that knowledge in mind that he fought for his life. On the narrow stone steps he wrestled with his handlers, knowing he had no other choice. Mishkin had sent him to his death at the hands of the two security agents. Federov would not go down without a fight.

His frantic struggle, disregarding his own safety, threw the agents off balance. The flight of stone steps as well as being narrow, was steep. Halfway down, the agitated resistance paid off. Federov and his escorts fell, crashing down the remainder of the flight in a tangle of arms and legs. At the bottom their combined mass sprang the door open and they sprawled across the garage floor.

Ignoring the savage pain in his left arm and down his left side, Federov lurched to his feet. He could feel blood running down the side of his face from a ragged scrape over his right cheek. He slammed his fist against the button that opened the garage shutter. As the shutter began its grating rise, Federov turned to locate the car that would have been used to give him his final ride. He heard a sound behind him, turned and saw one of the agents pushing to his feet and reaching under his jacket for his weapon. The man had a deep gash in his head. Blood was streaming down his face and soaking into his shirt. His functions were slow, affected by his dazed condition, and Federov reached him before he had the pistol clear. He slammed into the agent, using his right shoulder to batter the man's chest. The man stumbled away from Federov, still clawing for his weapon.

Federov lashed out with his right fist, clubbing the agent across his mouth. He followed with another blow that pushed the man against the wall. With a surge of rage Federov kept hitting the man until he went down on his knees, head hanging, blood streaming from his mouth. When the pain in his hand was too much to bear, Federov stopped. The agent was slumped on the dirty floor. Federov could see the butt of the pistol poking out from the man's jacket. He reached down and snagged the pistol, wincing at the pain in his bloody hand.

Federov checked the other agent. The man lay in an awkward position at the base of the door, his head was twisted at an impossible angle. When Federov felt for a pulse, he found nothing.

He found he was staring up the stone steps to the door that led back into Mishkin's office. He felt the weight of the pistol in his bloody hand. Behind him stood the car he could use to get away from the ministry.

But for how long?

Mishkin would set more agents on him. Unless Federov could arrange a quick exit from the country, his life would become little more than a series of evasive actions. Mishkin would have him labeled a traitor and declare open season on him. And while this was going on Minister Mishkin would be reaping the benefits of Black Judas.

"No," Federov said. "Not that way."

He started for the steps.

MISHKIN HEARD A TAP ON HIS DOOR. He was seated behind his desk again. Not expecting anyone, he hesitated then quickly opened a drawer and scooped the Black Judas material out of sight.

"Come," commanded.

The door opened to admit the man he recognized as Commander Seminov from the Organized Crime Department. Behind Seminov was a younger man. He closed the door and stayed there as Seminov crossed the office.

"Commander Seminov. Unusual to see you here." Mishkin made no attempt to stand, or to offer Seminov a seat. The affront did not appear to bother the man.

"I don't see the point in wasting time," Seminov said, "so I'll get straight to the point. My investigations into certain matters have raised questions. I need answers."

"Seminov, I am aware of your bluntness. Your reputation is well-known. But I believe you were instructed to drop all investigations into the Pieter Tchenko case?"

A slow smile edged Seminov's lips. He turned to glance back at his partner, Dimitri.

"They all do it, Dimitri. It doesn't matter how smart they think they are. In the end they trip over their own stupidity."

"I'm warning you, Seminov. You do not come into my office and insult me…"

"Minister, I haven't even said why I'm here. So why would you imagine it has anything to do with Tchenko? Or is it Black Judas on your mind?"

Seminov saw the shock on Mishkin's face.

Mishkin had half risen from his seat when the door on the far side of the office slammed back against the wall.

A disheveled figure lurched through the door, blood streaming down his face, his clothing streaked with dust. The man held a pistol in his hand.

"Damn you, Mishkin, and damn Black Judas."

Karl Federov opened fire, triggering the pistol at Mishkin. He hit the man with at least five 9 mm slugs, knocking him away from the desk, his expensive suit and tailored shirt patched with blood. Mishkin toppled back, tripping against his seat and crashing to the floor in an untidy heap.

Seminov had stepped aside as Federov started shooting, reaching under his coat for his own weapon. He was still drawing it when Federov swung the pistol in his direction, his wild eyes staring, seeing Seminov as another target. The muzzle began to settle.

A weapon fired from behind Seminov, and Federov was thrown back and onto the floor, four slugs buried in his chest. He squirmed, pain showing on his face, an odd smile curling his lips as he died.

Seminov turned to face Dimitri.

"Your saving my life is becoming a habit, young man. People are going to start talking about us."

Dimitri shrugged. "I was only thinking who would sign my expenses if you were shot."

"Never mind expenses. Just tell me how we talk our way out of this mess."

CHAPTER TWENTY-TWO

Chicago

The information Natasha Tchenko had gained led her on a long drive to Chicago, where she hoped she would find Parker and Kincaid, the third Black Judas team. According to the man she had confronted, this was where Mischa Krushen and his people would show. They needed the two men desperately. With the other teams having been eliminated, Parker and Kincaid were the surviving pieces of the puzzle. If Krushen intended to activate Black Judas, the two-man team was needed to set it into motion.

Tchenko arrived in Chicago early afternoon, weary from her long drive. The journey had been made difficult by her lack of expertise with the American road system. She had forced herself to drive at a steady pace, aware of speed restrictions. The last thing she had wanted was to be pulled over for a traffic violation. She had stopped only to fill up with gas and to purchase cups of coffee. That and visits to rest rooms had been the only causes for delay.

She had regretted not having been able to fly to her destination. Flying would have meant ditching her weapons, something she refused to do.

Driving through the outskirts of the city she looked out for a motel. She had realized they were the most anonymous establishments available. Designed for a transient population, motels provided the basic needs for those on the move. She turned in at the first decent motel she saw. The parking lot held a few family-size cars and campers. In the office a young woman with a ready smile offered her a double room at the single rate.

"How long you figuring on staying?"

"I am not sure yet. It depends how my business goes."

"Well, you can decide later."

"Right now I need some sleep. I have been driving a long time."

"That's fine," the woman said. She stared at Tchenko's registration card. "Now that's an unusual name."

"Russian. I come from Moscow."

"Now isn't that interesting. Hey, you are a long way from home." The young woman leaned across the desk. "So what do you think of the U.S.?"

"You have a beautiful country. It is so big, too. And everyone is so friendly."

"Isn't that nice. You on vacation?"

"Vacation and a little business."

"Well, you just enjoy yourself. You need anything, give me a call. If you need to eat, there's a nice diner across the way."

"Thank you."

Tchenko took her key and returned to her car. She drove along the line of rooms and parked in the slot outside her own. She took her bag and went inside, locking the door behind her. She considered a shower but the wide bed beckoned. She got out of her clothes and slipped beneath the covers. Sleep came quickly and the next time she opened her eyes it was dark.

During her drive to Chicago Tchenko had tended to the knife wound regularly. At different locations she had purchased the items she needed. Bandage and antiseptic cream. Dressing and adhesive plaster. Now, in the bathroom, she removed the current dressing and inspected the wound in the mirror. It had started to heal. Because she had not had any stitches to close the wound, she would be left with a scar. That didn't worry her too much. More important was the lack of any infection. Beyond the gash itself, the flesh was bruised and slightly reddened, but there was no unexpected swelling. Movement still caused a little pain but even that was becoming less and less restricting.

Tchenko stepped into the shower and turned on the water, enjoying the relaxing sensation of the spray on her skin.

She left the shower reluctantly, put on clean clothes, tidied her hair and left the room. The bright lights of the diner beckoned. A good meal before more rest. In the morning she would start her search for Parker and Kincaid, and ultimately Mischa Krushen.

CHICAGO WAS A NIGHTMARE. The city spread out in all directions. It took Natasha Tchenko over two hours to locate Jerome Kincaid's address. When she did arrive, asking questions, she learned that Kincaid was away for the day. Eventually she managed to find out where he was. Some other news she learned concerned her greatly.

Kincaid's whereabouts seemed to be the interest of the day. Several people had inquired about his whereabouts. Krushen's name immediately sprang to mind.

But who else needed to know?

She could only guess that the separate group intent on reaching the sleepers would be one of them.

And when she learned that a lone man had been asking for Kincaid, his description matched Cooper's.

Tchenko stood beside her car, a map spread out as she attempted to work out her route to what was called the South Side. The district looked to be a long way from her current location. Frustration grew as she tried and failed to decide her way to what her informants had told her was called the mission. She had asked for it to be written down for her. She glanced up now as a taxi rolled to a stop just in front of her parked vehicle. She threw her map inside the rental and ran around to the driver's side of the taxi, waiting until the fare had climbed out and paid.

"I need to get to this address as quickly as possible," she said, offering the paper to the driver.

The driver, a broad-shouldered black man, read the address and gave a hearty laugh.

"Girl, you'd do better if you stayed away from this address."

"Is it that bad?"

"You have to be a stranger in this town to even ask that. I stop longer than three minutes in that 'hood and the mothers will have my wheels and my engine block stripped and up for sale. You understand?"

"I'll make a deal with you. Get me as close as you can and I'll pay you triple what's on the meter."

The driver considered. "Quadruple it and we got a deal.'

"Wait just one minute."

Tchenko returned to her car. She took the Glock and a couple of extra magazines, pushing them into her coat pocket. She locked the vehicle and returned to the taxi, climbing into the rear. As the taxi eased away from the curb, the driver glanced in his mirror.

"What's so important, girl, that you want to go down there?"

"A friend of mine does work at a place called the mission. I need to see him."

The driver laughed again.

"Hell, girl, if you want to do missionary work, it be safer if you go to the Congo."

Natasha leaned back in the worn seat cushions, asking herself if that wasn't probably the correct thing to do.

The drive was long and slow. Traffic was heavy on the beltway and didn't ease until the taxi rolled down the off-ramp and onto quieter streets. Tchenko noticed, too, that the gleaming high-rise buildings had vanished. Now the area they were in appeared less affluent. The buildings shabby. Many silent and empty. There were large industrial units, their yards empty. They looked deserted.

"What happened here?" she asked.

"Progress. Money went to other places. There used to be big business around here. Meat packing plants that worked day and night. Steel mills. Employed a lot of folk. But times changed and people moved out. The businesses closed. The area just collapsed. They starting to redevelop, build again, but there are still some rough areas and you chose one of them."

In the far distance off to her left Tchenko could see the tall structures of cranes. The steel skeletons of new buildings. But they were pushing farther into a depressed and silent area. The empty streets were littered. She saw a number of burned-out cars. Very few people.

She could hear the driver muttering to himself. "What?"

"Nothin'," he said.

"Tell me."

"I'm telling myself what a fool I am to take you all the way."

"You don't have to."

The taxi rounded a bend and she saw ahead of them a long street that had empty stores on either side. Except for one where weary figures shuffled in through the open doors.

"I think that's your place."

The taxi pulled up at the curb. Tchenko sat for a moment. At least she had got this far. She pulled money from her inside pocket, leaning forward to read the amount on the meter. She added the agreed percentage and passed it to the driver.

"If I don't take it, you'll feel insulted."

Tchenko smiled. She patted him on the shoulder. "We wouldn't want that, now, would we? Thanks for the ride. Now you go, please."

She watched as the taxi turned and rolled back along the street. Then she walked to the entrance to the former store.

Cooking smells wafted through the open room. People were lining up, others already eating. Tchenko looked around for the man she had been told ran the place. A priest named Father Aguilar. He saw her first, threading his way through the crowd. When she spotted him, he held up a hand before she could speak.

"Let me guess," he said. "You have come looking for Jerome Kincaid."

"Is that priestly foresight, Father?"

Aguilar shook his head. "No. It's just that Jerome seems to have become extremely popular today."

It was not what Natasha had wanted to hear.

"Is he here?"

"No. He went away earlier after some people came for him. They had accents similar to yours."

"I am Natasha Tchenko, a police officer from Moscow."

"This is all becoming very complicated. Some time ago I spoke with an agent from the Justice Department. He also wanted Jerome."

"Agent Cooper?"

"That was his name. He seemed most concerned that Jerome had left with the first group who came."

"I know Cooper. We have similar interests in this matter."

"Miss Tchenko, I imagined that Jerome had left with business associates. Since then Agent Cooper has been here, now yourself. I am starting to be concerned about Jerome. Is he in some kind of trouble?"

"That's what we are trying to avoid, Father."

"Agent Cooper was able to get some information on the vehicle Jerome left in. If you speak with him he may be able to tell you what he learned."

Yes, I'm sure Agent Cooper would love to speak to me, Tchenko thought.

As they walked toward the door, she picked up the squeal of tires as a vehicle came to a stop partway on the sidewalk. Stepping up to the door she saw armed figures emerging from the large SUV. A second vehicle pulled in close behind the first one.

The lead man, his shaved head glistening, swung his stubby machine pistol at Father Aguilar as the priest edged his way past Tchenko.

"Jerome Kincaid? Where is he?"

"What do you want him for?"

Viktor Kirov lashed out with the barrel of his pistol. It made a meaty sound as it struck the priest across the side of his face. Aguilar stumbled, grasping the door frame for support. Blood was already starting to stream down the side of his face from the ugly, deep gash.

"That is not the answer I'm expecting."

Tchenko pushed herself in between the two men, knocking Kirov's gun arm away. She made no attempt to reach for her own weapon. It would have been a futile gesture given the number of armed men backing Kirov. She swung a balled fist at his face, feeling it rake his jaw. She would have followed it up if Kirov hadn't countered, driving her to her knees with a solid blow that tore her lip. She gasped as his hand coiled into her dark hair, yanking her head back.

"Not the best way to introduce yourself, Officer Tchenko. Still, we'll get to know each other during our long drive."

"Leave the priest alone," Tchenko said, pushing to her feet. "I know who has Kincaid. And probably Parker by now."

Kirov motioned a pair of his men to search Tchenko. They carried out the procedure with unnecessary attention to her body. She ignored the groping hands, staring directly at Kirov as he watched with a sly grin on his face. His men took her gun and cell phone.

"I feel safer now," Kirov said. "It appears you have been a busy young woman. And very resourceful. Look how far you've gotten all by yourself. Perhaps I should have hired you alone."

"I don't do wet work."

"You can save some blood being spilled," Kirov said, indicating Father Aguilar. "Confirm who has Kincaid and Parker. Is it Mischa Krushen and those FSB idiots?"

"Who else?"

Kirov nodded. He lowered his weapon. "Get her in my vehicle. We need to move." He turned back to Aguilar. "I suggest you forget our visit here. No police. Unless you want to be the cause of this woman's death. Yes?"

The priest nodded. "I will say nothing to the police."

"No absolution for my sins?"

Aguilar raised his bloody head, defiantly staring at the gloating man. "I doubt my mortal powers are strong enough to clear away your transgressions."

"Priest, your insight is amazing. Pity you won't have the chance to make the attempt. It would have been challenging to say the least."

Kirov turned and climbed back inside his SUV. The pair of vehicles swung around and made their way back along the street. Aguilar waited until they had gone, then turned to George, who had remained in his usual position, appearing not to have seen anything.

"Did you get them, George?" he asked.

George, rocking gently, smiled and said, "Got them both, Father. Models and license plates. Tell Agent Cooper, Father?"

Aguilar slipped a cell phone from his pocket and dialed in the number Mack Bolan had given him. As he waited for the connection, Aguilar debated the morality of breaking his promise to Kirov. He didn't really see there was any problem.

Agent Cooper was not a police officer.

CHAPTER TWENTY-THREE

Bolan's cell phone became busy.

His first call was from Erika Dukas, Stony Man's translator.

"From my translation it looks as if the final destination will be in Singletree, a small town in the Northern Cascades. It's where what is referred to as the core will be located. It's a computer manufacturing facility called CoreM. Aaron is running some checks on ownership of the property. That should mark it for us. He'll call back when he has it verified. The rest of what I understand is near enough what we talked about at the start. A heavy-duty attack on U.S. financial centers. New York. Chicago. Basically they want to screw up our systems, bring the stock market crashing down and blow out all the federal banking databases. This is a hell of a plan. If they hit the red button, excuse my pun, we won't get paid next month, or the next six months. The whole nation goes bankrupt. It would spread. Affect our global solvency. The money-go-round would grind to a stop."

"Erika, you'll get next month's salary if I have to pay it myself."

"Shucks, Striker, a steak dinner will do."

"You're on."

CALL TWO, Father Aguilar.

"A young woman came to the mission. She was a Russian police officer."

"Natasha Tchenko?"

"Yes. She, too, was looking for Jerome. I told her you had been here and I had informed you how he had gone away with some Russians. Before we could do more, another group arrived. Very violent men who struck me when I refused to tell them anything. Miss Tchenko intervened and was treated the same. She is a very determined young woman."

"Tell me something I don't know, Father."

"She agreed to give them information if they left me alone. What she told them caused them to leave. Agent Cooper, they took Miss Tchenko with them. It appears that Jerome and another man named Parker have been taken by a man named Mischa Krushen. Does that mean anything to you?"

"It confirms suspicions as to the identity of a suspect group. Father, thanks for your help."

"That isn't all. George played his part by memorizing the makes and license plates of the two SUVs those men came in."

"Tell George he ought to get a medal."

"The sad thing, Agent Cooper, is that George already has medals. A Purple Heart and Silver Star. It's a sad reflection on a nation that lets its heroes down once they have fallen by the wayside." Aguilar cleared his throat. "Excuse the sermon. But it is the prerogative of a priest to prick the conscience."

"Father, consider me well and truly punctured."

"Agent Cooper, I wish you well. Go with God, my son."

CALL THREE came from Valentine Seminov.

"My friend, how do you say it…yes…the shit has hit the fan. Right now I'm not sure how I will end up. Either promoted or reduced to seeing children across the school crossings."

"What have you been up to?"

"Here in Moscow the Black Judas project is crumbling before my eyes. Minister Alekzander Mishkin is dead, shot by one of his subordinates, Karl Federov. He is dead, too. I had gone to question Mishkin and walked in on the deed. Naturally I established a homicide scene and dragged in my department. When we searched Mishkin's office we found documentation and CDs that revealed everything about Black Judas, the sleepers in the U.S. Their handler over there is a man named Sergei Navotney."

"He's dead, Valentine. The way this thing has unraveled it's like a ball of string run wild."

"When we searched Federov's office I found a connection between him and a recently assassinated man named Yan Chenin. He was playing both sides, working for Krushen at the FSB and reporting to Federov. We already had the racketeer, Bulanin, in the picture so we raided his club. Among his possessions we found a digital recorder. He had been saving all his telephone conversations with Krushen. For his old age pension." Seminov paused for a moment. "Sadly, my friend, one of the conversations was the agreement by Bulanin to take out Pieter Tchenko. Once Bulanin realized how much we had on him, he decided to try to save his own neck. He told us everything. After that the investigation reached the ears of my superiors. It got very hot. Some wanted it hushed up again, but by this time too many people knew the facts. So it was decided to make an example. The FSB tried to close ranks, but orders came from on high that there would be no hiding this time. General Berienko and his committee have been suspended. One of Berienko's cronies, Georgi Bella, was found dead in his dacha. Suicide."

"A pebble dropped in a pool, Valentine. The ripples start small but just keep getting bigger."

"*Da.* The other group chasing Black Judas is headed by Viktor Kirov."

"I know. They also have Natasha as a hostage at the moment. Right now I'm following Krushen, and I figure Kirov is moving in the same direction. We've located the base where Black Judas is supposed to be activated. That could still happen if Krushen persuades the surviving sleepers to follow their orders. Kirov wants the same thing but for a different reason."

"Cooper, I wish I was in America and by your side for this."

"Just take care of things at your end, and we'll call it quits."

"The one who tried to attack you on the plane we have identified as Laszlo Chernov. He was a career psychotic. It appears he went to the U.S. just before the first Black Judas sleepers were killed. Intel reveals he was hired through Federov to assist Viktor Kirov. He specialized in chemical assassinations. You were fortunate he did not get any closer."

"My own fault for flying tourist."

"We will speak later, Cooper."

BOLAN SAW DARK SWATHES of cloud sliding in to hang low on the horizon. Minutes later the first drops of rain smacked against his windshield. The storm hit fully soon after, a deluge that was intensified by the harsh wind blowing in from the north. The road ahead was awash with rolling streams of water. Bolan settled in for the long haul.

Later he picked up another call from Kurtzman at Stony Man.

"I traced the line of shell companies involved in the purchase of CoreM. This is one slippery deal, Striker. Bottom line is, we do have a name. Pennington wasn't the only American playing cozy with the Russians. We have a Hugo Trenchard in the loop. He likes playing around with undesirables apparently. Keeps his affiliations pretty close to his chest, but I linked him to the CoreM purchase. These idiots forget that property deals have paper and electronic trails. Somewhere there's always a link."

"If there is, Aaron, you'll sniff it out."

"No question, my man. Mr. Trenchard will be hearing the Feds knocking on his door once we have this cleared up. So how are you doing?"

"Still moving. In the middle of a storm. The only consolation is that it slows down all parties."

"Watch your butt, Striker."

THE STORM HAD CAUGHT UP with them, heavy rain and a scattering of wind that slashed the downpour across the road.

Kirov ignored Tchenko during the first leg of the road trip. He seemed more concerned with making contact with someone over his triband cell phone. Sitting silently, the woman watched and saw his increasing agitation. She resisted making any comments because after his performance back at the mission she realized he had a short fuse and might easily be provoked into further violence.

She sat, head down, making herself subservient in her manner. After some time the armed man sitting beside her relaxed. Tchenko listened to the conversation Kirov had with the driver of the SUV. This one was an American. Her observation of Kirov's crew told her that it comprised both Russians and Americans. As well as his own people, Kirov had hired local help. The Americans would know their way around the country, easing the way for Kirov.

After yet another round of making futile calls, Kirov threw his cell phone on the seat beside him. From the way he hunched his shoulders and kept running a hand over his shaved head, Tchenko decided he was becoming more frustrated as time passed.

He twisted in his seat suddenly, fixing her with an angry scowl on his face. Kirov didn't speak at first; he simply studied her. Despite her attempt to remain silent, Tchenko found his scrutiny irritating. She eventually raised her head to return his hard stare. She maintained her steady response, unflinching. It was Kirov who broke off, smiling at her defiance. He spoke in his accented English.

"Natasha Tchenko. A very tough cop. So are you the scourge of Moscow's criminal class?"

"You'll find out soon enough."

"Perhaps a bullet in that pretty head will soften you up."

"That would be too easy. Even for you. You could have shot me earlier."

"That would not have been wise. There were witnesses. If I shot you then, I would have been forced to kill the priest. Bad luck. I would probably have gone to hell for that."

"You might still go."

Kirov laughed out loud. The sound cut off just as quickly and his hard stare returned.

"So, Natasha Tchenko, why are you so determined to involve yourself in all this? Because your father and your family were killed? Is this one of those revenge things? Like those cheap American Western movies, where you follow the killers until you have a showdown? How touching."

"I don't expect you to understand."

"You are doing me an injustice, Natasha Tchenko. I know exactly what you are going through. But your plans do not fit in with mine, so I need to keep you restrained for the moment."

"Or kill me to get me out of the way."

"The thought has crossed my mind. You *may* come in useful, so I will let you stay alive for now. Just answer me a question. Who is this American who has proved himself such a nuisance? Another cop? Or an agent working for the U.S. government?"

Tchenko smiled. "You will find out soon enough, Kirov. He will be on your trail, and when he shows up he'll be able to answer all your questions."

"Is this the one who took down Waller?" the SUV driver asked.

"The same. Mr. Waller was not as smart as he led me to believe."

"Waller had a fucking good reputation."

"This time he met someone better," Kirov's voice filled the SUV. "Someone check to see if those extra men are on their way. Hopefully they will not be related to the late Mr. Waller."

One of the men sitting behind Tchenko punched a number into his cell phone and began to speak to whomever had picked up.

"And you'll rendezvous with us? How long? Okay." He finished his call. "They're on the road, Mr. Kirov, and will join up with us down the road."

Kirov tried his own cell phone again. It was evident from the stiff set of his shoulders that there was no pick-up.

"No one home, Kirov?" Tchenko asked. "Maybe you should be worried."

He glanced at her, forcing a smile. "It is you who should worry. Whatever happens in the coming hours, one thing is certain. You will be dead at the end."

In the parking lot of an isolated diner where massive trucks overshadowed the SUVs, Kirov met his reinforcements. Six more men. There was a short stop while his crew went into the diner for food and coffee. Kirov stayed with Tchenko. He joined her in the center block of seats, saying nothing, his gaze fixed on the rain streaming down the windshield. After ten minutes the SUV driver ran out of the diner. He was carrying paper cups and plastic containers of food. He climbed into the SUV and handed the food and drink across to Kirov and Tchenko. As much as she would have enjoyed throwing the food in Kirov's face, she accepted it. There was no point starving herself and allowing her bodily resources to fade away. Kirov dropped down the trays fitted to the rear of the front seats.

"You see how civilized the Americans are. Nothing is too much trouble to equip their vehicles with. Don't you think so, Natasha Tchenko?"

"I *think* you believe this is all a game," she said. "It

doesn't matter how many people suffer and die, just as long as you get what you want."

Kirov bit into the thick steak burger. "This is quite tasty. Go ahead and try it."

The SUV driver grinned. "They say your last meal should be a good one."

"Very funny, Benton." Kirov drank from his steaming coffee cup. "As for your opinion of me, Natasha Tchenko, no, I do not care how many die if they get in my way. Those who do are simply casualties of war."

Fighting back her rising anger, Tchenko concentrated on eating her own food.

"The necessities of life make it inevitable that those who want to succeed will ignore the damage they create. If they paused along the way, reaching their destination would be delayed. And delay can cost more than most are willing to pay."

"Very pretty speech. It still leaves you nothing but a criminal."

Kirov did not rise to her taunt. He continued with his meal, watching her, smiling, confident he had all angles covered.

THEY HAD STOPPED FOR GAS. Ahead of them the mountain peaks were misted in the heavy cloud formations that delivered heavy rain. While the vehicles were being tanked up Krushen stood beneath the awning outside the station listening to Berienko. What the general told him brought a growl of anger from his throat.

"Suspended? I don't understand, General. What has happened?"

"Mischa, we have been shut down. Black Judas has

been brought into the open and everyone involved discredited. Federov and Mishkin are both dead. The OCD forced the government's hand. With all the evidence they exposed, it was a face-saving exercise. The accusations started to come thick and fast. The committee has been disbanded. Georgi Bella shot himself."

Krushen found the information hard to digest. After all they had planned. All they had put into the project. He glanced across to where the vehicles stood. They had the means to make Black Judas work. The sleepers. Ahead was the base where everything sat waiting. He was too close now to quit.

"General, I refuse to give in now. We are too close."

"I was hoping you would say that, Mischa. Are you willing to do this?"

"Yes. I'm too far from Moscow for them to do anything. If Black Judas succeeds, we still gain our victory. America will suffer and the Kremlin will no doubt make the best of it. We may yet get you reinstated."

"Mischa, don't concern yourself with me. Look after yourself and do whatever you can to put the project into operation. Just be aware that Federov's pet dog is still in America. The one thing you both have in common is the determination to see your missions through."

"Yes, General."

Minutes later they were back on the road, pushing on into the rising slopes of the Cascade Mountains. Timbered hills gave way to the higher peaks, lost at the moment in the glowering storm clouds. Krushen gave the order for the drivers to increase speed. His awareness of the situation forced his hand. He needed to get his team to the base before the one led by Viktor Kirov. He needed to gain and hold control, determined not to let the events back in Moscow stop his plans to initiate Black Judas.

PUSHING INTO THE FOOTHILLS Bolan decided it was time to gear up. He pulled off the road and shed his outer clothing, revealing the blacksuit beneath. He didn't have full details of how many he might be going up against, or how well equipped they might be. The wisest move would be to go in expecting the worst.

He had his Beretta 93-R and the powerful Desert Eagle, and had chosen his longtime favorite, the 9 mm Uzi as his lead weapon. The Israeli machine pistol might have been considered outdated by some, but from Bolan's perspective the subgun still delivered a lethal load and he knew its capabilities. He also had an M-4 carbine, a weapon he had faith in. Bolan chose his ordnance for guaranteed performance and reliability. New gimmicks and fancy hardware made no difference in the middle of a firefight. Bolan's weapons were the tools of his trade. They were not shiny, customized items for hanging from hooks in a hobby room. They delivered death and there was no room for glorifying them in Mack Bolan's world. He slid a sheathed Cold Steel Tanto combat knife onto his belt and loaded his combat vest with extra magazines for his weapons, adding an assortment of stun and fragmentation grenades. The vest was placed on the passenger seat, ready to be donned when the time came for him to exit his vehicle. Bolan added a compact set of binoculars.

He put his car back on the road, snapping his safety belt into position and keeping a close watch on the weather. The heavy rain was making driving difficult. Water runoff was coming down the slopes, and more than once Bolan had to negotiate deep pools that had built up on the undulating road. He felt the buffeting power of the wind against the side of the car.

If the weather hadn't been taking up part of his attention, Bolan might have spotted the black SUV coming up behind him. It was only the reflection in his rearview mirror that alerted him. The SUV loomed large as the driver pushed close, hitting his horn. Bolan pulled over as far as he could to let the other driver pass, and as it pulled out he noted another pair of vehicles following the first. The urgency of their travel alerted him. Bolan eased off the gas pedal to allow the SUVs to pass.

THE THICK BLACK HAIR and the strong profile hit Natasha Tchenko like a dash of cold water in the face. She had been sitting with her face close to the window as the SUV had swung over to pass the lone car, and the recognition drew a surprised gasp from her lips. It was part surprise, part relief at seeing a friendly face. Before she could stop herself she spoke his name. Only in a whisper, but enough so that Kirov heard. He immediately leaned over, staring through the glass at the man behind the wheel of the Ford.

"Your gallant rescuer?"

Tchenko shook her head. "No. I was—"

Kirov placed a hand at the back of her head and slammed her forcibly against the window.

"You lie," he roared. "See? He has recognized you." Kirov snatched at the transceiver clipped to his belt and ordered the other SUVs to block the car. "I want that bastard off our backs. Do it."

CHAPTER TWENTY-FOUR

The sight of Tchenko's face pressed cruelly against the window of the SUV snapped Bolan out of any complacency his long drive had created. He saw the SUV surge ahead, swinging in front of him, broad tires throwing up deluges of dirty water that obscured his vision. The second and third SUVs fell into formation, one alongside, the third crowding his back end.

There was nowhere to go.

Bolan was hemmed in by the menacing bulks of the SUVs. His ability to see ahead was marred by the spray being kicked up by the vehicle in front, his avenue of escape blocked by SUVs at his side and rear. To his right the open side of the road dropped away in a series of undulating slopes and dips. No way out there. He stayed calm. The only thing he could do was to keep the Ford running steady. His vehicle didn't have the solid bulk of the larger SUVs, so there was no way he could batter them out of the way.

He felt a hard nudge as the rear SUV closed in and rammed him. He felt the Ford rock under the impact. His vehicle slid to the left, scraping the side of the SUV run-

ning parallel with him. It was like hitting a stone wall. The
SUV stayed on course.

The impact generated a thought in the mind of the SUV
driver and he began to edge his vehicle in closer, making
contact with the Ford, pushing it to the edge of the road.
Bolan countered, turning his wheel to keep his vehicle sta-
ble. It was not a maneuver likely to work with the solid bulk
of the SUV forcing the issue. Bolan felt the outer wheels
of the Ford hit the ragged edge of the road. At the same
time the rear SUV hit again, the impact bouncing Bolan
closer to the edge. Working in tandem, the pair of heavy
SUVs drove Bolan into the side of the road and nothing he
could do would prevent the inevitable. The parallel SUV
made a final, full-powered swing. The impact swept
Bolan's vehicle off course. Hitting the brake had no effect.
He was rammed again from the rear, full-on, and lost it.
The Ford spun and leaped off the road, dropped, bounced
and tilted. The solid series of impacts threw Bolan against
the safety harness, and if he hadn't been wearing it he
would have been tossed around the interior like a rag doll.
He clung on to the wheel, his vision of the world outside
a fragmented, jerky image. The landscape blurred, rolled,
leaned at crazy angles as the Ford charged out of control
across the uneven terrain. It reared up on its back wheels,
then dropped into a deep trough half filled with water and
came to an abrupt and savage stop.

BOLAN GASPED at the final impact, the forward motion
throwing him against the safety harness. The only sound
he could hear now was the hard drum of rain on the Ford's
battered body and the trickle of water leaking into the car.
He could feel the safety belt digging into his chest, and his

abused body was starting to ache from the pounding it had received. Bolan released the belt and pushed it aside. Apart from the superficial aches from the crash, he felt no signs of anything serious. No broken ribs or damaged limbs. He looked for his combat vest, which had been thrown into the foot well, and retrieved it, along with the binoculars and his weapons.

He pulled on the vest, closing the zipper. Leaning over into the rear, he found the duffel that held the rest of his gear. He found a black baseball cap to wear against the rain and a pair of insulated thermal gloves. He debated whether to include the backpack so he could take along more ammunition, discarding the idea. He was going to have a long slog across hard terrain, so the less weight he had to carry the better. He figured he had ample ammo. If he couldn't do what was needed with what he had, then he would have to improvise.

Bolan had to use his booted foot to open the driver's door. The impact from bouncing down the rough slopes had knocked the Ford's bodywork out of shape. When the door finally swung open, rain hurled inside the vehicle. The soldier dragged himself out, reaching back to take the Uzi and the M-4. He looped them over his shoulders, hung the binoculars around his neck, easing the Uzi around so it hung close to his hands. The treated surface of his blacksuit rejected the rain, keeping him dry. He knew that eventually that rain would work its way through the weave of the fabric. Until then it was his exposed face that took the brunt of the downpour. If nothing else it helped clear his head.

Taking a long sweep around the landscape Bolan picked up the dark ribbon of the road winding its way up into the hills. His destination lay in that direction. He picked up dark objects moving away from his position. He utilized the binoculars and focused on the three SUVs.

Bolan settled the baseball cap, tugging the long peak to shield his eyes, and took the first steps of his walk into the Cascades.

MOVING TO A HIGHER ELEVATION exposed Bolan to heavier weather. He could feel the wind tugging at him as he negotiated the hilly terrain, the rain sweeping across the slopes. It was getting more rocky now. He stayed close to the narrow, winding road, but avoided walking on it. He didn't want to be spotted by anyone using the road in case they were hostiles. It wasn't paranoia, simply a concern that other parties might appear who conceivably might see him as a potential threat.

He checked his watch at intervals, wanting to know how much time had passed. By his estimate he had a few miles to go before he sighted the base. Bolan needed to reach it before dark. He wanted to reconnoiter the place before going in. Blundering around in the dark not knowing the strength of the opposition wasn't part of his plan.

NATASHA TCHENKO KNEW she was becoming a burden, and that Kirov would dispose of her given the slightest provocation. That left her with a single option.

She had to get away from Kirov and his men. If death was what he had in mind for her, she was not simply going to lie back and accept that.

Her chance came minutes later when Kirov moved from the middle seats to his position beside the driver. He was discussing their approach to the base, a map in his hands. She remained where she was as he maneuvered between the seats. That left a single man to watch her. He was on the far side of the SUV, and during Kirov's climb into the front there was a moment when her watcher was blocked from her view. Tchenko reached out to grasp the door handle and jerk it open. The door sprang wide, rain gusting in, and she lunged for the opening. Her watcher yelled and made a grab for her. Braced against the door frame, Tchenko kicked out, her foot hitting the man full in the face, driving him away from her. Swinging herself around, she took a breath and launched herself through the door. She curled into a ball, arms up to protect her head, thrusting hard with her legs. Her momentum took her over the edge of the road and she hit the rain-softened earth beyond. The impact was hard enough to stun her as she rolled and slithered out of control down the slope, bouncing over outcrops and grassy knolls before she came to a stop.

She lay gasping for breath, aching from head to foot, soaked by the rain and chilled by the wind.

And inside her head a voice was telling her to get on her feet and move before they came looking for her.

Or would Kirov decide to drive on and leave her?

"YOU LOST HER, KIRK. You find her," Kirov yelled.

Bleeding from the kick to his face, the man called Kirk snatched up his submachine gun and exited the SUV as it slithered to a stop. He dragged his thick parka around him, scanning the spot where Tchenko had jumped, and picked up her distant form.

Kirov leaned out the SUV. "Find her. Kill her. I don't need her turning up at the wrong fucking moment. I'll send someone back to pick you up."

Before Kirk could protest, the SUV convoy moved off,

leaving him on his own. He pulled the hood of his parka over his head and stepped off the road, moving at an angle that would lead him to the woman. His boots splashed in pooled water, soaking his pants. His still bleeding face hurt, and he cursed in the vilest way he knew how.

TCHENKO HAD SEEN the SUVs stop for a few seconds before moving on. She also saw the lone figure left behind. Perhaps it hadn't been her best move exiting the SUV. She had put herself at more risk now. She had no weapons, she was out in the open, not exactly dressed for the weather, and now she had an armed man coming after her.

She could imagine the look on Cooper's face if he could see her now. And then an image filled her mind—of Cooper's car being forced off the road, crashing out of sight as the SUVs had sped off.

For all she knew he might be dead, lying cold and still in the wreckage of his car. Or worse, injured and helpless. She found that the word helpless didn't sit right with Cooper's image. He wasn't the helpless kind. If he was still alive and able to move, he wouldn't be standing around feeling sorry for himself.

She pushed forward, closing her mind to the discomfort of the rain and the wind, the unforgiving terrain.

She still had a mission to complete, still needed to confront Mischa Krushen.

Tchenko stumbled. The ground had given way to ankle-deep water, the earth sodden and muddy. It clung to her boots and slowed her progress. She dragged herself from the mire, moving around the area until she came to solid rock, pausing briefly to locate her position. Ahead of her the ground rose in layers of glistening rock. It was going to be an uphill struggle to reach the curving strip of road. There was no other way for her to go. She walked on, risking a look back over her shoulder, and saw her stalker closing in. A brief moment of alarm jolted her. He was not so far behind. Still out of range for his SMG, but that could easily change if she didn't keep moving.

Slipping on the rain-slick surface of the rocks, she pushed on. More than once she had to resort to almost crawling, using her hands to help her along. She was shocked to see they were reddened from exposure to the cold and wet. She needed somewhere to rest. To get warm. That was not about to happen while Kirov's man was still on her trail.

Somehow, soon, she was going to have to deal with him. The question was how.

KIRK CLUTCHED HIS SMG tight against his chest as he tramped across the rain-swept slope. His anger had not subsided, nor had the pain from his damaged face. The kick from that Russian woman had split his upper and lower lip on the left side. Although the bleeding had stopped, the lash of the cold rain was not helping. Every time he moved his mouth the ragged splits made him suffer. He was sure a couple of teeth had been loosened. When he did get his hands on her she was going to suffer. It would be too easy to simply shoot her and end it. Kirk wasn't made that way. He held grudges.

We'll see how you like to be hurt, bitch, he thought.

And Kirov. He wasn't going to forget how the Russian had sent him out here onto this mountain. In the wet and the cold. Just because Kirk had made one mistake. He stared around at the inhospitable landscape. He hated this kind of country. Kirk was no outdoorsman. He was a city boy. Give him tall buildings and streets full of cars. Bars and restaurants where everything was close to hand. Not these slopes. Cold rain and wind. His legs ached from struggling across the harsh terrain. He reached down to check the lock knife nestled in his pants' pocket. Wait until he showed her that. Then he would see how tough she really was. Kirk had a way with a knife. There was something about the way it cut into soft flesh that gave him a deep-down thrill. Made him feel real warm.

Oh, yes, bitch, I'm coming to get you, he vowed.

SHE WAS TIRED OF RUNNING, tired of the cold and having to constantly check the position of her stalker. Tchenko would have given anything to find some warmth and comfort, but she knew that wasn't going to happen for some time yet. She also knew, with growing desperation, that if something didn't happen soon she would be too weak to make any kind of fight if that was what it came to.

It was her circumstances that forced her to her next decision. It was risky. If she had been in a stronger frame of mind she would never have contemplated such an overtly reckless act. The cold was lowering her resistance, and that reduced her capacity to think logically.

But dammit, I need to do something before I freeze to death out here, her mind screamed.

She found herself at the top of a long slope of rock. The extreme edge of the slope abruptly fell away in a sheer drop of twenty or so feet. Tchenko realized if she had been moving any faster she might have stepped over the edge and fallen. It would have been a quick finish to her situation. Standing with her feet set firmly on the solid slope, she turned to face the oncoming armed man and then let herself slump to the ground, leaning forward to brace herself against the rock. Head down, slightly turned, she was able to watch his progress. He stopped first, watching her, then when he saw she was making no moves, he advanced a little at a time until he was well within range of his autoweapon. He didn't raise it, simply covered the woman as he closed in on her position.

Tchenko knew she was gambling on his male curiosity as to why she had stopped. He knew from her time in the SUV that she was unarmed. She had been thoroughly searched when they had taken her, so there was no possibility she had any kind of weapon. Convinced, he moved closer, the SMG held solidly on her motionless form. She could see the lower portion of his legs. His pants were muddy, soaked like her own. She could hear his harsh breathing as he moved up the rock face.

"I hope you're suffering, bitch," she heard him say. "If you ain't, I'm about to ensure you do. A bullet is too quick."

His words were slow, slurred, because his badly bruised and bloodied lips made speaking painful. Kirk slid a hand into his coat and pulled out his lock knife. He opened the blade, clicking it into position.

Tchenko still didn't move, despite an overwhelming desire to move away from Kirk. She needed to wait for the right moment.

"Ever imagine what one of these could do to that face of yours?" Kirk said. He was relishing his apparent victory over the exhausted woman slumped on the ground. For the moment even the chill bite of the rain went away as he savored what he intended to do to her.

Tchenko sensed him leaning closer. Out the corner of

her eye she saw the muzzle of the SMG swing away from her, and knew she had to make her move.

She pushed herself to a sitting position, her left hand striking for his knife wrist. She gripped, yanking hard so that he rocked off balance, then thrust out with her right foot, slamming the heel of her boot against Kirk's knee. He gave a yell, feeling himself dragged forward, his right foot coming off the ground. Tchenko continued her action, drawing him closer, bringing up her right fist and punching him across the side of the jaw. Her combined actions toppled Kirk and he rolled over her, going over the edge of the lip. It happened too fast for him to realize his position until there was nothing in front of him, nowhere to plant his feet on solid ground. Tchenko let go of his wrist and sensed his bulk going over the edge. He gave a startled scream as he fell, turning once and then landing on the rocky ground below.

She climbed to her feet. peering over the lip. Kirk lay in a broken sprawl, making no sound, no movement. The Russian police officer stared at his body, then looked for the SMG. It lay a few feet from him. Like it or not she was going to have to work her way down there. She needed to see if the weapon had been damaged. If not, it at least put her back in business ordnancewise.

She had to skirt the lip and work her way around until the rocky slope leveled out. Then she retraced the distance along the base until she reached where Kirk lay. It took only a quick glance at his misshapen skull to know he wasn't going to recover from the fall. The first thing she took note of was the fact he still had the lock knife gripped in his right hand. She pried the knife free, closed the blade and dropped it in a pocket. She picked up the MP-5 and inspected it. The SMG had to have landed on its metal stock. There was a slight abrasive mark on that, but the rest of the weapon seemed in order. She ejected the magazine, ran through the breech check, removing the single cartridge and satisfied herself that the operating mechanism was working freely. She thumbed the cartridge into the magazine, snapped it back into place and cocked the weapon. Bending over Kirk, she went through his clothing. There was a second magazine inside his parka, and a 9 mm Glock was tucked in his waistband. She took the MP-5 magazine and the pistol. Her instincts told her not to be too squeamish, so she tugged the parka from Kirk's body and dragged it on over her own coat. Her cold fingers struggling with the zip, she ignored the bloodstains on the jacket. She pulled the hood over her head for further protection. With the strap for the MP-5 looped around her neck Tchenko struck out for the distant strip of road, watching the shadows start to lengthen.

CHAPTER TWENTY-FIVE

They had driven by the CoreM compound, following the main road for a quarter mile before pulling off the road onto the wooded slope. Kirov ordered that they conceal the SUVs well out of sight before leaving them. The timber and foliage helped to hide the vehicles. As well as their weapons, each man carried a transceiver for personal contact. For the benefit of the American team members Kirov instructed everyone to speak English.

"We keep this low-key. If Krushen has already arrived and has his people installed, we need to take control quickly. Remember he has the Black Judas team with him. They have to be kept alive to activate the project. Without them Black Judas is just another computer program."

"If they have already activated the program?" someone asked.

"Then Pushkin steps in. That's why he's with us. Let me remind you that his survival is as important as those sleepers'."

Pushkin stared around him, his thin face flushed with embarrassment. He was a loose-limbed young man with a shock of dark hair continually falling over his eyes. He had a reclusive nature and hardly ever spoke. His presence among the gun-wielding team had been a curiosity until Kirov had told them that Pushkin's talents would come to the fore when he was confronted by the Black Judas computer system.

"Pushkin is going to make us all extremely wealthy. But he can't do it if he's dead. So protect him. Do not expose him to any risks. Keep him close."

In silence they worked their way back through the timber, mindful of the sleeting rain and wind. They were to a man looking forward to getting inside the facility. The prospect of some form of violence didn't bother them. They were all experienced, both the Russians and the Americans. The lives they led were punctuated by bouts of violent action. If they survived, they walked away rich. If the reverse happened and they did not walk away, nothing else mattered. It was not that they had a death wish, but that they accepted their business had a high risk factor.

The perimeter fence blocking their path posed no problem. It was a standard chain-link barrier. An inspection showed there were no motion sensors and no electric current. Too much external security would have aroused suspicion in a peaceful community like Singletree. The high security would be inside the building. Around the core. That would be a secure place deep inside the facility. A restricted area where the day-to-day employees would never go. It would most likely be designated as a sensitive research area, manned by Black Judas specialists. Familiar with the regime of their employers, the workers would have eventually accepted the need to stay away from the research area and would concentrate on their own tasks.

Kirov ordered two of the team to go over the fence and

carry out a recon. He watched the pair drop into the facility and slip into the shadowed dusk.

"Sooner we can get our butts inside, the better," one of the team muttered. "I'm freezing my ass off out here."

The Russian next to him grinned. "Back home this would be considered a warm spring day."

The American glanced at him. "I just knew you were going to say that.'

"If we pull this off, you can both buy a section of beach in Hawaii and lie in the sun all day."

"Then we had better pull it off," the American said.

Minutes later Kirov's transceiver clicked. He unclipped it from his belt.

"Speak to me."

"Krushen must already be inside. Two SUVs are parked at the rear of the building. They're rentals with out-of-state plates. And there was an armed guy watching over them."

"Was?"

A second voice came over the transceiver. It was one of Kirov's Russians. "He stopped breathing when we dealt with him. And he was Russian. So I believe we have confirmation our targets are inside."

"Any others on watch?"

"We haven't seen any yet. That doesn't mean they aren't around, so take care."

"Can you disable the vehicles to prevent anyone leaving?"

"Our dead guy had the keys on him. Makes it easier for us if we need them."

"Fine. Go and check if we can get inside without setting off any alarms. We will come over the fence and join you."

Kirov's team scaled the fence, dropping to the compound inside. They filed silently toward the building. Kirov left a couple of his people to stand watch, issuing them with roving patrol instructions.

"If you cross any other sentries, deal with them using the suppressed pistols. Less chance of noise attracting others."

"What about Kirk?" someone asked. "The poor bastard is still out there searching for that Russian cop."

"That is his mission," Kirov said. "He created the mess. He cleans it up. We have more important issues to work out. When we have control, someone can go back and pick him up."

"Yeah. Pick him up with ice tongs," came the unsympathetic reply.

"Let's move," Kirov said. "We can't waste time."

He led his team along the side of the building, eventually rounding the rear corner where the recon team waited. They were crouching in the lee of a wide loading ramp. A rolling shutter door and a smaller personnel-access door were the means of getting inside.

"You checked them out?" Kirov asked.

"Yeah. Roller door is a no-go. The personnel door is the one we can use."

"Is it a problem?"

"Only if it's alarmed. Soon as we go through we'll know."

Kirov nodded. "Do it."

The team followed the American up onto the loading bay where they grouped near the door. Kirov told two of the men to remain outside as added security, then turned his attention back to the American. He had removed a lock-picking tool from his small backpack and was examining the door's lock mechanism. Satisfied with his appraisal, he made his selection, swinging out a pick and an L-shaped tension tool. He inserted the tools into the heavy brass lock, leaning in close as he gently maneuvered the instruments. It took him less than ten seconds before he nodded, reached for the door handle and turned it. The door opened without protest.

"Baby lock," the American said derisively. He returned the tools to his backpack and stood. "Let's rock and roll, Mr. Kirov."

The door opened to reveal the loading area inside. Low security lights illuminated the interior.

"Just because we haven't heard any clanging bells doesn't mean an alarm hasn't been activated. Could be a silent alarm. We won't know until they come at us with guns."

The team spread out, concentrating on the two open doorways that gave access to and from the loading area. Kirov, Glock pistol in his hand, led the way.

It was, he decided, time to show how to lead.

They proceeded through the loading area and into the main building, a low-ceilinged, large room with boxed goods waiting for distribution. A glass-partitioned office was situated against one wall. Kirov crossed to the double door that would give them access to the next area. He checked through the glass window to a production area and saw workbenches and equipment, partly assembled computer units.

No human presence.

Kirov used his transceiver to alert his roving sentries that they were going inside. The reply came back to confirm his people had spotted and taken down two of Krushen's men and the site appeared clear now.

Swing doors let them through into a long corridor where doors led off into smaller work labs. The interior was climate-controlled, the air dry and cool. The overall silence was broken by discreet electronic hums from unseen pieces of equipment.

As Kirov neared an intersecting corridor, he sensed movement. A thin shadow extended out from the passage. He signaled his team to freeze, holstered his weapon, then flattened himself against the wall close to the passage. He waited and spotted the dark muzzle of an autoweapon. A heartbeat later a dark-clad figure stepped into view.

Kirov moved faster than any of his own men could have imagined, hands reaching for the startled newcomer. He pulled, twisted, took the guy off balance. A brutal elbow smash hammered into the man's face. Blood flew in a red spray, spotting the neutral wall coloring. Kirov slammed a knee into his adversary's groin. Before the guy could respond Kirov had the SMG out of his hands, dropping it to the floor. He swung the man around and pinned him face-first to the wall. A knife appeared in Kirov's free hand. The tip pierced the flesh close to the main artery in the man's neck.

"Listen, my friend. I move this blade a fraction and your blood will be squirting all over this wall. You want that? Huh? You want that?"

A frantic shake of the head.

"Makes no difference to me. You can die right now."

Another movement of the head.

"How do we get to the core?"

Emphasis was made by a gentle pressure on the knife. It brought an instant response. An arm lifted, a finger pointed.

"The elevator takes you to the basement. It's down there."

Kirov sent one of his team to check.

"He's right."

"Any special operating needs?"

"No. Just press the button. Coding has been deactivated, and it only goes down."

"Does it open onto the main area?"

"Access passage. Leads to a kind of airlock doors that seal the place off."

"How many guarding the elevator below?"

"Two."

"That wasn't so hard."

Kirov's hand made a slight gesture and the keen edge of the knife blade sliced through flesh and artery. Blood began to jet from the wound, spattering the wall. Kirov held on to the man until blood loss weakened him. Then he let the corpse slump to the floor.

Kirov signaled for two men to stay and watch the immediate area, then led the rest of the team into the large elevator. As the car began to descend, he ordered that sound suppressors be fitted to weapons for dealing with the guards below.

"Make the shots count. We need to get inside the core fast."

When the car stopped, the doors opened silently. A pair of armed guards, weapons slung from their shoulders, turned too slowly. Suppressed weapons coughed out bursts of rounds that put the pair down instantly. Bullet-riddled, they sprawled inelegantly on the floor. Kirov checked out the passage stretching to the left and right of the elevator. To the left were a number of doors. Glancing right, he saw that twenty feet along, the blank wall of the passage became glass panels that stretched from ceiling to waist height. Another fifteen feet and there was the airlock. It stood out from the main wall. Kirov waved his men out and they moved along the passage until they were able to peer in through the sealed glass windows fronting the computer facility.

The core.

The home of Black Judas.

Kirov stood against the wall, out of view from the men on the other side of the core's sealed glass windows.

Kirov estimated at least a dozen men in the room, clustered around two of their number who were seated at workstations, keyboards in front of them. Each station had a large flat-screen monitor. What they could see was duplicated on the even larger wall-mounted monitors that took up most of the wall about ten feet in front of their positions. The section of the lab in front of the workstations was filled with electronic equipment. It was a computer buff's dream assembly. In layman's language it would be termed a supercomputer. Far more powerful than any home or office setup, it was capable of operating at high speed and absorbing vast amounts of information. Its ability to send out intricate programming data would have a similar capacity. Kirov knew no more about computers than the average person. He left the intricacies to the experts. Glancing again at the wall-mounted monitors, all Kirov could see were streams of data flowing down the monitors. None of the information meant a thing to him, and he wondered just how far Krushen had got with the activation process.

Kirov turned and beckoned Pushkin, his own computer expert. "What does all that mean?"

Pushkin stared at the data streams, his lips moving as he read the information.

"Well?"

"In simple terms they are firing up the computer. It will

probably take time. This is no ordinary machine. And now that the two sleepers have entered their codes, it will be installing coded program input. Before it can actually be operated it will conduct a series of self-tests to initiate the programs. The sleepers would have been given detailed instructions on how to bring Black Judas to operating status."

"How long will all this take?"

"Without knowing exactly the kind of input they had fed into the system, I can't tell you. If I was sitting with them, I would be able to assess better. Without that, I can take a guess and say it will take a couple of hours."

"We don't know just how long they have been in there," Kirov said. "The sooner we break into that room the better."

Pushkin cleared his throat as a way of attracting Kirov's attention.

"What is it?"

"When you go in," Pushkin said, "try to avoid any gunfire. If a stray bullet hits any of that equipment, you could lose Black Judas before you even gain control."

"Good thought."

Kirov spoke to his team. "You hear that? Do not damage the computer setup. Fuck it up, and we might as well go home."

They crouched below the level of the windows and moved toward the airlock. Through the window Kirov could see that the airlock protruded into the lab. There would be a set of solid-steel doors identical to the outer ones. Only one set could be opened at any one time to maintain the pressure and temperature within the core.

Kirov inspected the keypad set in the frame of the outer doors. There was nothing more complicated than a single button to open the doors.

"Gentlemen, let's do this," Kirov said, reaching for the airlock button.

The outer doors opened smoothly, with no more than a gentle rush of air. Pushkin, Kirov and six of his team entered the airlock. The remainder stayed in the passage. Set inside the frame was a button to close the outer doors. As soon as they had closed, there was a soft rush of cool air entering the airlock chamber. It would stabilize once it reached the air temperature and pressure inside the main lab. Until that happened the other set of doors would not open. Kirov moved himself and Pushkin to one side so that his armed team could exit the airlock once the doors opened. A green light winked on and a small display panel confirmed that temperature and pressure were equal and that the inner doors could be opened.

"Go," Kirov said, and one of his team touched the button.

The inner doors slid open and, the second the gap was large enough, Kirov's team eased out, weapons up and ready, spreading to cover Krushen and his people. It turned out to be easier than even Kirov had imagined. Krushen's team was absorbed in what was happening on the monitors. By the time someone became aware of their visitors, Kirov's men had the advantage.

Krushen stepped in between his own team and Kirov's. He was holding back the anger he obviously felt, composing himself before he spoke.

"If we start shooting at one another we all lose," he said. "One stray bullet is all it will take to destroy Black Judas."

"Then perhaps you should all put down your weapons," Kirov said.

"Viktor Kirov," Krushen said. "I remember your trial."

"You were one of those who spoke against me."

"Yes. But this is a different time. And your champion Karl Federov must have powerful friends to get your release. Minister Mishkin will be somewhere in the background I'm sure."

"Now we have that resolved, where do we go from here? Both of us have been involved in difficult situations to get this far. Does it end in a bloodbath?"

"I'm aware how you have been interfering in FSB operations, removing our sleeper teams one by one." Krushen smiled. "You missed your final chance to take control of the survivors. I got them here alive."

"Of course. You don't think I would eliminate the last team, do you? They were vital in activating the project."

Behind Krushen one of his team moved forward, impatient. Krushen gestured for him to step back.

"How did Federov find out about Black Judas?"

"Soviet efficiency. He found the original project files in some buried archive. He came across it by accident. Someone had misfiled the dossier, so he read it and uncovered your secret."

"And took it to Mishkin? The one man who was desperate to have something he could threaten the FSB with."

Kirov smiled. "So he thought. Only Karl forgot to show him the whole file. Just enough to get his interest. So that he would back Karl's play."

Krushen thought about that for a moment. "Federov wanted Black Judas for his own. To have control so he could…" Knowledge dawned, brightening Krushen's eyes. "He doesn't want to use Black Judas as it was intended. Then what? Not for something as crude as making money for himself?"

"As you just said, Mischa, this is a different time. It means we have different priorities."

"Perhaps I should let my team start shooting," Krushen said. "Do you expect me to accept your reasoning?"

"I expect you to think about your position right now. Neither of us will stand down. What do we do? Spend the rest of our lives staring at each other?"

"Ideology versus individual gratification," Krushen said. "Something of a moral dilemma."

Behind Kirov, where he had been watching the on-screen data, Pushkin spoke. "I think we should check that out."

He was pointing at the main monitor where the data streams had ceased, clearing the screen and replacing it with a blinking cursor. One of the men seated at the workstation glanced up at Krushen.

"Online, sir. Do we proceed?"

Krushen found himself transfixed. Here, now, Black Judas sat waiting for its instructions, ready to invade and corrupt America's financial heart and deliver a paralyzing blow. Once the instruction was given and the protocols set, the electronic signals would be released. The financial centers in New York and Chicago would be bombarded with viruses and safety overrides. The design of the Black Judas program would swamp the computer systems, rapidly expanding as the invasion self-perpetuated, multiplying on a constant loop, so that attempts to stop the tide would be overwhelmed.

Operators in control centers would see their screens stripped of information. The giant display boards, showing stocks and shares, would become filled with undecipherable lines of data, wiping away share values in seconds. Rebooting systems would achieve nothing, because the Black Judas plague was designed to dig to the root of everything stored in memory. Program restore points would have nothing to restore. Within a couple of hours the American financial world would be reduced to point zero. The malevolent spread of the Black Judas virus would encompass banking, business and private accounts being wiped. Government systems were also within the intrusion, their vast databases being corrupted. Shutdowns, system locks, financial chaos would be the orders of the day. America would be returned to the days of bean counters and the abacus.

Krushen caught Kirov's eye. What he saw reminded him that Kirov wanted something else. He was not interested in perpetuating the decades-old conflict of political and military posturing. He was a man from the New Russia, the have-it-now generation who wanted material gain over Soviet solidarity. Kirov, jaundiced by his old masters' treatment, had decided to take a different path. Behind Kirov stood his team, weapons still in place, as determined in *their* mission as were Krushen and his people. He wanted, at one and the same time, to rid himself of Kirov and to continue his own task. He also realized that right now the two were bound together. If Kirov could not achieve what he had come for, he would do his utmost to prevent Krushen's expectations.

"If I granted what you want?"

"Then I would take my team and leave. What you do with Black Judas is not my concern."

Krushen reasoned that Kirov's request would not interfere with his plan. If he allowed the man his moment of glory, Kirov could move on, happy with his success and leave Krushen to carry out his work. The thought occurred to Krushen that once he had crippled the American economy and returned to Moscow, it would not be outside the realm of possibility to move against Mishkin and Federov. And Viktor Kirov would also be swept up in the net. A small capitulation now. A sweeter victory later.

"Very well, Kirov. You can have your time. Do you want my people to assist?"

Kirov guided Pushkin toward the workstation. "I have my own man."

Pushkin pulled a flat case from his inside pocket and took out a CD. One of Krushen's sleepers vacated his seat and let Pushkin take it. The computer expert uploaded the CD's contents. He began to work on the keyboard, his finger sure and swift. On the screen lines of code appeared. Pushkin began to feed them into the central Black Judas banks.

"How long will this take?" Krushen asked.

"An hour or so," Pushkin said. "There is a substantial amount to be moved around. It can't be rushed. I would be embarrassed if you caused me to crash your beautiful program."

CHAPTER TWENTY-SIX

The flakes of snow, mixed in with the rain, touched Bolan's face as he crouched in thick brush. The small town of Singletree lay below him, encircled by high peaks that sheltered it from the worst vagaries of the mountain climate. It had the look of a nice town. Main street, with branch streets snaking off on either side. Lights were starting to show in stores and homes as daylight began to fade. It was a quiet little town an eternity away from the urban frustrations of larger cities.

His destination lay a mile or so on the far side of Singletree, where the highway started a long, slow climb toward the higher slopes of the Cascade Range. That's where the research facility stood. In its own right, it was an employer of a small number of local residents. They worked the public face of the company, but somewhere inside the facility was what the Black Judas files labeled the core, the secure area where the computer heart of the project sat.

Black Judas's heart.

He was there to shut it down. And anyone connected to it would go down with it, as well.

DARKNESS HAD DESCENDED. The chill wind soughing down from the high peaks brought more snow. Not enough to settle to any degree, but threatening to increase as the night wore on.

Bolan had circled the town, skirting the business section and the outlying homes. He bypassed Singletree as a silent, fast-moving shadow, unseen and unheard.

The manufacturing facility CoreM stood in its own fenced-off grounds, with a short stretch of tarmac road branching off from the main strip. Bolan had no idea of the odds he would face once he broached the perimeter fence, but he was primed for whatever he came up against. His only concern was whether there were any Singletree citizens still on site. He hoped not. Krushen, Kirov and their combined teams would want privacy, and would dispose of anyone who got in their way.

He stayed off the road, keeping in cover. The short approach road showed him the bulk of the building inside the secured gates. Security lights on high pylons threw illumination across the compound. Bolan moved up to the fencing, observing the compound. He saw nothing until a single figure appeared, moving out of the shadow at the side of the building into the light. Clad in dark civilian clothing and armed with a stubby SMG, the man was no uniformed security guard, who would have carried a holstered pistol. It told Bolan that one of the teams had breached the fence and was in place.

Krushen or Kirov?

There was no way of knowing. Both groups presented a threat. Whichever one took control and used Black Judas, America's financial power base would be threatened. It made him consider how far they might have penetrated the facility. Or how advanced the operation to activate Black Judas was. He could only answer those questions by getting inside himself.

Bolan watched the armed guard patrol the area. He waited until the dark figure moved back along the edge of the building, out of sight as he retraced his steps toward the rear. Working his way along the frontage, the Executioner eventually reached the far corner. He took this direction, moving along the perimeter fence, stopping when he saw the patch of disturbed ground. A group had stopped here. The wet earth had been trampled heavily, telling him there was a fair number in the team. On the other side of the fence Bolan saw where they had dropped down after scaling the fence. Glancing back, he spotted the footprints leading in from the trees.

He checked for security measures and, finding none, he scaled the barrier, dropping down and easing into the shadows away from the lights. He melded with the darkness, at home in this half-light world where stealth and the ability to conceal were paramount. His passing made no sound. The gentle hiss of the ever present rain only aided his infiltration.

He moved along the length of the building, aware that somewhere the armed guard would present himself. There was cover in the form of the usual detritus of a manufacturing site—empty packing cases, metal drums, a parked pair of forklift trucks.

It was there Bolan located his quarry and found that there were two guards, both carrying SMGs, which now hung from their shoulders as the men shared cigarettes, talking in low voices.

In Russian. Bolan picked up a few of their muttered phrases. They were, as men on guard duty did, bemoaning their bad luck at being chosen to remain outside in the poor weather while their comrades were inside and under cover. The name Kirov cropped up a few times.

Bolan waited them out, wedged into the gap between large wooden packing crates. The pair separated, moving in opposite directions, hunched in the parkas they wore against the inclement weather. The guard coming toward Bolan's hiding place was making a big play out of relighting his damp cigarette, cupping his hand over it as he tried to get his lighter to stay aflame. Lighter and cigarette fell to the ground as Bolan stepped up behind the Russian. The Executioner's powerful forearm snaked around the guy's neck, his other hand clamped against the back of the man's skull, pushing hard to close the lock, shutting off oxygen. The Russian struggled, reaching up to claw at his attacker's arms, but he was already losing the struggle as his brain was denied its vital element. Bolan increased the pressure, pulling the guy to the ground, ignoring the frantic wriggling. The motion ended quickly as the Russian sank into oblivion and became a deadweight. Bolan slid him to the ground, rolling him into the darkness. He took the guy's SMG and disarmed it.

Back on his feet Bolan tracked the second guard. He found him almost at the far end of the facility, turning to cross an open stretch of the compound. This man had a sharper sixth sense than his partner and despite Bolan's quiet approach the Russian swiveled without warning, his SMG angling up at Bolan's shadowy outline. The big American launched himself forward in a powerful body slam, knocking the Russian's weapon off track and driving the guy back. He followed up with a swinging kick that crunched into his opponent's ribs, drawing a pained grunt from the man. As the Russian doubled over, Bolan sledged a hard fist across the back of his neck. He struck a second time and the guy went down on his knees, attempting to draw on any reserves of strength he had. Bolan didn't give him the opportunity. He hit him again, a ferocious blow that dislodged the Russian's jaw. He toppled to the ground, unable to even offer any resistance against the hard-delivered boot that slammed his head against the concrete. The Russian convulsed, eyes wide with shock, then collapsed without a sound.

Bolan rounded the rear corner of the building and saw the loading ramp and the personnel door standing ajar. If that was the way Kirov's team had entered the facility, it would provide similar entry for Bolan.

He was moving in the direction of the ramp when he picked up a slight sound behind him. Bolan swung around, his Uzi rising. He sensed a dark shape coming at him out of the shadows. Someone slammed into him, catching him off balance.

Bolan went down.

TCHENKO HEARD THE TRUCK before she saw it. The light was fading fast. She had reached the road a half hour earlier, grateful at least that she was on firm ground. The continuing bad weather had stayed the course. Turning, she saw the vehicle laboring along the black strip of road. It was moving slowly along the gradient. She stepped off the road, crouching, and watched the vehicle. Even its headlights only cast a sickly yellow glow. She heard the gears grinding as the driver downshifted. As the slow-moving vehicle drew level, then passed her at walking pace, Tchenko saw that wooden slats formed the box section on a flat bed.

She moved quickly and fell in behind the truck. Grasping the tailgate, the police officer hauled herself up and over, dropping lightly inside. Apart from untidily rolled canvas sheets, the truck was empty. She crouched and dragged a section of the canvas around her. She was still cold but at least she could protect herself from the sleet.

The journey seemed endless. Tchenko stayed alert, ready to climb out if the truck detoured from the main road leading to Singletree. Recalling the information she had gained from the FSB man in Grand Rapids, which seemed an eternity ago, she knew she needed to be on the far side of the town, on the road that continued up into the higher country. CoreM was the only manufacturing facility in the vicinity. Set up as a supplier of computer systems, the facility was a cover for the Black Judas project.

The truck shuddered, the old engine groaning. It seemed to be slowing almost to a stop. Tchenko rolled out of her cover and peered through a gap between the slats and saw they were entering the town. Some stores lined either side of the street. Most were closed for the night, but she saw lights on in a restaurant, then farther along in a diner. A few cars and trucks were parked at the curb. She felt the truck swing into a slot just outside the diner. It rattled to a stop. She heard a door open and someone climbed out. A stooped old man moved slowly to the sidewalk and went inside the diner.

She pushed the MP-5 under her bulky coat. Moving to the rear of the truck, Tchenko saw the street was deserted. She climbed down, walking to the sidewalk and down the alley beside the diner. As she walked by the kitchen, her senses were assailed by the odors of cooking meat and coffee. Her empty stomach growled in protest. She carried on to the end of the alley, turning in the direction that would lead her out of town. She stayed in the shadows as she bypassed the rear of stores, then houses as she reached the town limits. Only when she was clear did she venture onto the road, following its winding course as it rose in a gradual slope.

Beyond the protection of the town she found herself back in the bad weather. The sleet seemed to be coming straight down off the dark peaks towering over the area. It stung her face, and she was glad she could at least thrust her hands deep into the pockets of the parka. She wondered if she would ever be warm again.

When she came on the facility with its chain-link fence and secured gates, the woman stared at it for some time, in disbelief almost, that she had made it finally. And if everything had gone as planned, Mischa Krushen would be inside the large building. All she had to do was get to him.

In her weary state the possibility of the fence being alarmed, even electrified, didn't even cross her mind. She moved away from the gate and dragged herself up and over the fence, dropping clumsily on the far side. She remained crouched while she struggled to pull the MP-5 from her coat. She looped the webbing strap over her shoulder, holding the weapon snug against the side of her body while she checked out the area for any movement. If Krushen was already here, he would have men out keeping watch over the compound.

Sleet buffeted her as she crossed the compound, staying away from the front entrance. A safer way inside would be through the rear. Tchenko accepted that there might even be someone on watch there. She took her time working her way down the side of the long building. The falling sleet obscured her vision at times. Shifting falls made shadows appear to be moving. She erred on the side of caution. When she reached the rear corner, Tchenko froze.

What she had just seen was no shadow.

It was a moving figure, back to her as it walked in the direction of the loading ramp area. As the figure turned partly, she saw the configuration of a weapon in the man's hands. She felt adrenaline surge through her. She had made contact at last. She had raised the MP-5 before realizing she couldn't use the weapon.

The sound of a shot could easily alert more of Krushen's men. She couldn't risk that. She needed to get inside the building without alerting anyone. She swung the MP-5. She was going to need to depend on surprise to reach the figure ahead before he had a chance to defend himself. It was a risk but it was one she had to take.

She lunged forward, using her strong legs to propel herself at the figure, launching herself at his back, arms reaching out to encircle his throat.

At the last moment he turned, alerted by something. Then Tchenko slammed into him and her force and momentum drove them to the ground. In the fall he twisted his body and she felt herself hitting the ground with her would-be victim on top of her.

THE FORM PINNED UNDERNEATH Mack Bolan wriggled furiously, and he realized it wasn't a male. Something flashed in his conscious stream of thought as he held back his fist from striking. At that moment his assailant's head turned and Bolan stared into the flushed face of Natasha Tchenko.

"Isn't this where you make some discouraging remark, Agent Cooper?"

"What the hell are you doing here?" Bolan growled, moving off her and standing. He extended a hand, pulling Tchenko to her feet. Taking her arm, he hustled into cover at the base of the loading dock, ignoring her resistance.

"At least you're not mad at me," she said sharply. "Or are you?"

"That'll depend on your answer."

Her eyes flashed with anger. "I'm doing my job."

"This isn't Moscow, Detective. I think your territory ends well before the Atlantic starts."

"From what I can see, Agent Cooper, territorial boundaries don't stop you."

He couldn't argue that, Bolan admitted to himself.

"You want to swap intel?"

"How could a girl resist a line like that?"

"Commander Seminov would be proud of you."

"So how are we going to do this?"

Bolan had a partner whether he liked it or not. Natasha Tchenko was with him for the duration, and considering how she had made her way this far, she had earned the right. She was driven by her desire to exact some kind of justice for her slaughtered family, but he sensed she would follow procedures if he laid them out for her.

"I think you know the answer to that. I'm not here working by the rule book. When we go in, it's to destroy whatever they have that controls Black Judas. If there's resistance, we deal with it. From either side. Krushen and Kirov might be on opposing sides. In my book they're both the opposition. The fact they're Russian doesn't come into the equation. Is that a problem for you?"

"I'm a cop, Cooper. They are criminals, here illegally." She paused, considering what she had just said. "Does my entry visa cover my intentions? Technically, I'm illegal, too."

"We'll worry about that later." Bolan indicated the MP-5. "You got anything else?"

She nodded her head. "Glock handgun and knife. Extra magazine for the MP-5. It will be enough." She glanced at Bolan's ordnance. "Cooper, I think you have enough for both of us."

"I wasn't anticipating a partner on this," Bolan said, "so I don't have any communication equipment."

Tchenko smiled. "If you want me, just whistle, Agent Cooper. You do know how to whistle, don't you? Just put your lips to—"

"Bogart and Bacall have a lot to answer for." Bolan put a firm hand on her shoulder. "Are you ready for this?"

"Cooper, I didn't come all this way for the weather."

Bolan ran a final check on his Uzi. "They'll do their best to stop us. Krushen or Kirov. They both want Black Judas up and running. They don't have any love for this country and what they want to do is going to cripple it. I can't let that happen."

"At least we agree on something."

"Let's do it."

Tchenko followed Bolan up onto the loading dock. They breached the door, separating as they moved inside, quickly crossing to the access doors that took them into the packing area. Bolan indicated the far doors. They moved over and peered through the window to see the corridor stretching before them. Once through it, they eased their way past the closed-off work labs, searching for any indication of the intruder teams.

Bolan saw the sprawled body first. The dead man's artery had been cut and had bled out. There was a wide, dark pool that spread from the body. His face also showed he had been struck forcibly before death claimed him.

Tchenko indicated the distant door that most likely led through to the front of the building.

"I will check there."

Bolan nodded. "Be careful."

He watched her moving quickly and silently along the corridor. When she reached the double doors, she spent time checking what lay beyond before she eased one of the doors open and went through.

That left Bolan to check out the immediate area. He came to the elevator doors, an out-of-bounds area where sensitive development could take place would be ideally suited to a closed-off section of the building. And a basement area would provide such an environment. Bolan figured he had nothing to lose checking it out. When he scanned the elevator keypad, his suspicions were given a boost. A coded keypad meant only certain personnel could use the elevator. The possibility that what he was looking for lay somewhere below was becoming even more likely. Bolan studied the keypad.

The sequence?

He could spend the rest of the night trying to figure it out. He jabbed at the main button in frustration and was rewarded with the soft hum of the car moving. Whoever had recently used the elevator had disabled the code. The car came to a smooth stop. The doors opened to reveal that it was empty. Bolan stepped inside. The control panel had three buttons. Up, Down, Emergency Stop. He pushed the Down button. The doors slid shut and the car started its descent. Bolan moved to the side where he would be concealed when the doors opened again. He held the Uzi across his chest, his finger close to the trigger. The car slowed and settled.

From his position Bolan could see a featureless passage with an anti-static floor covering.

He also heard the sound of cautious movement.

Someone was outside the elevator, waiting....

TCHENKO EMERGED IN THE FRONT entrance area. To her left was a wide reception desk. Doors led off to rest rooms, others to offices. The main entrance doors, glass, revealed that sleet was still falling. She was about to start checking out some of the offices when she picked up a reflection in the glass doors. An armed man was moving up behind her, the pistol in his right hand starting to rise.

The police officer remained where she was until the last moment. Her instinct for survival kicked in and the hard training she had undergone automatically took over. She let herself drop onto her back, spinning as she hit the floor, using her legs in a powerful sweep. She caught the gunman just above the ankles and he was hammered off his feet. Tchenko heard his startled cry as he went down, landing hard. The pistol flew from his grasp. Not allowing him any time to recover, the woman raised her right leg, bringing the heel of her boot down across his exposed throat. A spray of blood erupted from his gaping mouth, as the guy clutched at his ruined throat, desperately trying to suck air in through his damaged windpipe. Tchenko rolled to her feet, breathing hard, and closed her ears to the guy's death rattle.

The sound of the body falling to the floor had to have been enough to alert his companions. One of the doors across the lobby burst open and a gunner rushed into view. He saw the downed man and Tchenko as she rose to her full height. He swung his SMG at her. She triggered her MP-5, feeling the weapon vibrate in her hands as it jacked out a heavy burst. Enough slugs hit the target, spinning him off his feet in a bloody spray. Even as the brass shell casings hit the floor, Tchenko spotted movement at the door the first hardman had come through. With only seconds to spare before they opened fire she turned and launched herself up and over the reception desk, crashing to the floor on the far side with enough force to shake her.

She rolled close to the base of the desk as autofire riddled the desk with slugs. They burst through the wood, showering her with splinters. Tchenko scrambled to the rear of the desk, peering around an edge, and saw men spreading out as they crossed the reception area in her direction. She pushed the H&K into position, tripping the trigger and sent a scything burst of 9 mm rounds in the direction of the shooters. She kept her aim low, enabling her to remain on her knees. Flesh and bone disintegrated as the slugs ripped into lower limbs. Her targets took hard tumbles as their legs collapsed under them, leaving bloody trails across the floor. Tchenko hit the two shooters again, placing deliberate bursts into their upper bodies, rendering them immobile.

In the lull that followed, the woman scrambled to her feet. She saw that both the downed men had been carrying MP-5s. She frisked the bodies for extra magazines and came away with two. Crossing the reception area, she reached the door the shooters had come through and pushed it open, staying clear of the opening until she was certain the room beyond was clear.

Ready to move farther into the building she allowed her thoughts to stray, wondering how Cooper was faring.

CHAPTER TWENTY-SEVEN

The distant sound of autofire reached Bolan's ears. Faint as it was, the crackling noise alerted the unseen figure waiting outside the elevator. He picked up the rustle of clothing and the metallic sound of a weapon being cocked. Bolan decided he couldn't wait any longer. He fisted one of the stun grenades clipped to his webbing, pulled the pin and let the lever spring free. He counted down the numbers, then tossed the canister out of the elevator. The instant the grenade left his hand Bolan turned to face the corner of the car, hands clasped tight over his ears, eyes shut tight. Even so the harsh crack of the grenade left him with aching eardrums. Head down, with his eyes clamped tight, he avoided the brilliant burst of searing light. As soon as the reverberations had ceased, Bolan swung around, his Uzi up, and stepped out of the elevator car. Thin wreaths of smoke still drifted across the corridor, already swirling up into the vents of a recycling system.

Yards away an armed man staggered back and forth. His SMG, slung around his neck on a lanyard, was clutched in his hands and he pulled the trigger even though he was practically sightless. A spray of slugs passed harmlessly over Bolan's head, drilling into the wall behind him. Mindful that even errant gunfire could still find a target, Bolan brought the Uzi into position and hit the blind-firing shooter with a hard burst that punched him to the floor.

Bolan headed out. To his right the distant passage wall gave way to a wide glass window that looked in on what he figured had to be the core, the inner sanctum where life would be breathed into Black Judas.

The area, filled with computer monitor screens, wall- as well as desk-mounted, was occupied by a number of people. The majority appeared to be holding weapons. Hardly anyone seemed to be moving, and on his first look Bolan got the impression that one group of the armed men was holding guns on the other, who were responding likewise. The length of the passage and a soundproofed window had obscured Bolan's activity from the people inside the chamber, their concentration on the computer monitors. From photo images he had seen he recognized two of the men: Mischa Krushen and Viktor Kirov, the principal players in the Black Judas project. Both men wanted control, each for his own agenda.

The large monitor screen was alive with scrolling data. Bolan was unable to read much from it at his distance, but it appeared that whatever the Russians had come for was almost within their grasp. He reasoned that once the Black Judas program was activated it would be difficult to shut down, so any action he took had to be now.

Bolan backed across the passage, raised the Uzi and triggered a long burst at the sealed window. The glass shattered into a thousand fragments, registering the startled expressions on the faces of the gathered men. Some dived for cover while others, plainly combat experienced, swung in the direction of the shattered window and returned fire. Before the enemy got off a shot, Bolan had dropped to the floor. He heard the sharp rattle of autofire, heard, too, the solid thuds as slugs hammered the wall above his head. He was about to follow up with a stun grenade when a concentrated rush of booted feet warned him the opposition was recovering fast. He pushed to his feet, realizing that a retreat would be wise at this particular moment. His decision was to prove correct when armed figures appeared in the window frame, and autoweapons raked the corridor, slugs barely missing as Bolan sprinted along the corridor. He heard angry yells as more gunfire erupted.

The soldier flattened against the inner wall, presenting a reduced target to the shooters. Impatient with their lack of success some of them vaulted the window frame and spread across the hallway. It was an ill-considered strategy, as they offered themselves as full-on targets. Bolan, crouching, raised his Uzi and laid down a sustained burst. Two of his targets went down immediately, bodies devastated by the 9 mm slugs. Bolan caught a third as the man turned to take cover back inside the chamber. His burst hit the guy in the left side, chewing at his ribs and fragmenting into his organs. The guy slumped over the window frame.

With a degree of combat maneuverability others moved back to the cover of the airlock door as it opened. They crowded into the space, joining the team members who had chosen the door as a means of exiting the chamber. While they argued their strategy Bolan took stock of his situation, albeit a temporary one.

He had few choices: take the elevator back up to the main floor or use one of the doors behind him. He decided against that. All he would have achieved would be to box himself in.

Taking that a step further, he considered the situation within the core. As far as he had been able to figure, the airlock was the only way in and out. His quarry was still in there. Their presence was less of a threat than their ability to activate Black Judas. Bolan needed to access the chamber. His main objective was to disable the computer system. If he could destroy it, then the system program would crash and Black Judas would cease to function.

He needed to make that happen now. Delay only gave the opposition its chance.

Bolan switched weapons, bringing the M-4 into play and laying down a solid volley of single shots that hammered the airlock. He kept up the firing as he advanced back along the corridor until he could arm and lob the stun grenade in through the broken window.

He assumed the duck and cover position, waited until the sound had diminished, then pushed upright and vaulted the window frame. Bolan landed in a crouch, his eyes searching the misty confines of the computer lab. He heard angry mumbling as stunned figures moved around. He snapped up the M-4, targeting an armed man and taking him down with a couple of fast shots. He was not about to cut the opposition any slack.

Bolan heard the airlock door hum as it opened behind him. He turned and retreated to the far end of the computer lab, finding the best cover he could behind a metal cabinet. The moment the first armed man stepped out of the airlock Bolan leveled his M-4 and fired. The target stumbled back, cursing as slugs burned into his chest. The weight of the other team members pushed him aside. They came out firing. Bolan felt the burning sting of a round tear across his right arm. One guy was halfway across the floor when Bolan returned fire, the slugs from his M-4 shattering bone and tearing out chunks of flesh at the knees. The guy screamed, suddenly finding that his limbs refused to support him. He tumbled to the floor, his cursing changed to shrieks of pain. His riddled legs had turned to blood-spurting ruins. He made brief eye contact with his adversary a moment before Bolan's final burst drove into his face, turning it into a shattered mess. He hit the floor with a heavy crash, the back of his skull blown out.

Bolan plucked a fragmentation grenade from his harness, pulled the pin and let the lever spring free. In the scant seconds before the opposition's weapons began to fire he launched the grenade in an overhand throw. The spherical bomb arced over heads, curving down to land just beyond the workstations. It struck the floor, bouncing on the sound-deadening covering, detonating with a hard sound that filled the computer lab, the blast reaching out to encompass the workstations and the wall-mounted monitors. The concentrated effect reduced the computer setup to a smoking ruin of plastic and shattered circuit boards. Debris was thrown across the lab, deadly missiles that ravaged any human flesh it encountered.

Bolan was on the periphery of the blast. He had stayed at floor level, so the effects of the grenade blast failed to touch him, but the concussion from the explosion toppled the metal cabinet. It slammed down across his shoulders, pinning him to the floor. Smoke was billowing across the lab and the crackling of electrical circuits could be heard above the other sounds. Sparks arced in brilliant sprays.

Men were shouting to each other, a mix of English and Russian.

Bolan pushed against the cabinet, using his back muscles to raise it. Any delay would give his enemies time to regain their senses and rejoin the fight. Finding him pinned to the floor would have suited them well. He felt the cabinet shift, and pushed again. It slid away from him, coming to rest against the wall at his back. Bolan dragged himself free and pushed to his feet. As he glanced around, a lean, shock-haired figure smeared with blood and dust rushed at him, waving a handgun. He swung the weapon into play as he closed in. There was little time to fire, so Bolan savagely swiped him across the jaw with the M-4 and the guy's jaw burst with spraying red as he crashed to the floor, the autopistol bouncing from his limp fingers. The guy defiantly went after the weapon. Bolan put a burst into the back of his adversary's skull, which put a stop to any further resistance.

Figures were scrambling across the debris-littered floor, heading for the exit. Some were more concerned with getting out rather than engaging with Bolan, while hard-core shooters searched the rising smoke for the elusive black-clad intruder.

Overhead the sprinkler system came online, drenching the wrecked lab with water. The downpour began to dissipate the smoke, and Bolan found his evasive moves were no longer invisible.

He triggered the M-4, picking his targets with the deadly efficiency honed through countless combat situations. There was ruthless and methodical purpose behind his actions. It placed him marginally ahead of his enemies, and that thin advantage was the means by which he was able to overcome greater odds. His opponents saw that tall figure as a fleeting image, Bolan constantly changing position. The figure in black, a living embodiment of Death, made even the hardened shooters hesitate. That pause was their undoing. By the time they had wiped the specter from their minds Bolan's slugs had been delivered and the images of death became reality.

Bolan picked up on firing from outside the computer lab, the steady crackle of an MP-5.

He kept moving across the lab, reloading his M-4 and jacking out a steady stream of shots. He faced the airlock entrance and saw that the outer door had been breached, as well. A couple of bloody bodies were on the floor. Ahead of him a surviving shooter was engaging with the MP-5. Bolan hit him with a burst that tossed him out the door and across the passage.

And the firing ceased.

Bolan knew before he saw her that Natasha Tchenko was there.

"Natasha. Hold fire. It's Cooper."

He stepped out to meet her.

"Where is he? Krushen?" she demanded.

Bolan jerked a thumb toward the lab. "He was in there along with Viktor Kirov."

She pushed past him, striding back inside, searching among the bodies. As he walked up behind her Bolan heard her angered yell.

"He is not here. Where is he?"

Bolan moved into the room. He knew Krushen had not exited the area. So if he had stayed inside the lab, where was he?

He pushed by the wrecked workstations, past dangling

wiring and parts of the ceiling that had collapsed, into the far corner, where banks of servers had lined the wall.

And found a dark rectangle, an opening that had been obscured by the close-ranked metal cabinets. A slim door had been artfully constructed to blend in with the rest of the wall. He saw the black edges, ragged holes along one side. Explosive bolts had been fired to break the seal on the emergency exit. The sound had been missed among the gunfire.

He sensed Tchenko beside him. Her face was taut with anger, her eyes blazing with rage as she realized her quarry had eluded her again.

"No," she said. "No damn way."

She pushed by Bolan and stepped through the opening and was swallowed by the blackness.

CHAPTER TWENTY-EIGHT

Krushen led the way, with Viktor Kirov and a pair of their hardmen close behind. The tunnel was barely wide enough to accommodate a single person. The top was at least six feet high. Every twenty feet a low light gave some illumination. As they progressed, the floor began to rise. According to the Black Judas files, the emergency exit would terminate at the rear of the site, close to the perimeter fence. The exit was in the form of an inspection cover, set among actual covers for water and sewage.

In the confusion that had engulfed the computer lab, in smoke and autofire, Krushen had begun to see his mission crumbling before his eyes. The damage from the fragmentation grenade had spelled the end of Black Judas, and despite the overwhelming disappointment, his training as an FSB agent had taken over. Any setbacks had to be accepted and if they became absolute, the order was to withdraw. Remaining on site and attempting to resurrect something dead and gone would have been futile. Krushen had been wounded by the blast, and his mind turned to escape. He was a combatant engaged in battle, and it was his duty to evade the enemy. A combatant who gave his life for no good reason was of no use to his superiors. It was Krushen's obligation to the FSB and to Russia that he move on so that he could rejoin the battle in another place at another time.

Black Judas had been lost in this engagement. That did not mean it couldn't be resurrected at some point. The project had potential. As long as the files were intact, then the core of the plan could be brought into focus and set in motion once more.

He stumbled, scraping against the rough concrete wall. Pain from his lacerated shoulder brought a groan from his lips. Since the grenade, he had not had the chance to see how badly he had been wounded. In the chaos that had followed the blast, with gunfire all around him, Krushen had located the switch mounted on the wall, activating it so that the small explosive bolts had opened the secret panel. As he made for the opening, he was not surprised to see Kirov close by, followed by two of the armed team members. They had all filed into the tunnel, the noise of combat fading as they negotiated the narrow passageway.

Viktor Kirov was still coming to terms with the destruction of Black Judas. Pushkin had been so close to completing his computations when the computer lab became a raging fire zone. First the stun grenade that had caused so much confusion, then the place had been alive with gunfire. Kirov had maintained his close watch on Krushen. Despite the uneasy alliance with the FSB agent, Kirov had not fully trusted him. He suspected that Krushen would take advantage of any change in the situation, so he'd refused to relax fully. When the fragmentation grenade exploded, sending vicious pieces of shrapnel across the room, the worst casualties were the two sleepers and Pushkin. They had been closest to the blast center. Bloody and shredded, clothing smoking and torn, Kirov had been one of the lucky ones. Shielded by team members, he had caught nothing more than peripheral damage. Some fragments had peppered one side of his face, leaving it bleeding. Even as he recovered from the blast he had seen Krushen moving through the wreckage toward the far side of the room. There was a definite purpose in his actions, and when Kirov saw him activate the emergency exit he followed, gesturing for any of his team to follow. Only two did. They plunged into the shadowed tunnel, leaving the devastation and the gunfire behind.

Kirov understood that the Black Judas option was gone. His long trek across America had come to nothing. Anger rose. It was a bitter defeat, but in his mind was only a single thought. Survival.

He still lived, and a living man could achieve other victories.

He moved through the tunnel close behind Krushen. Once clear of the facility they could work on getting out of America. Kirov had contacts, the ability to obtain money from secure accounts. And in America money could buy you anything.

Up ahead he heard Krushen call out.

"Help me."

Kirov pushed forward. They had reached the end of the tunnel. It widened into a square box. Overhead was an iron cover. Metal clamps held it secure and Kirov took one of them, Krushen the other. The threaded screws had rusted with age. They moved reluctantly, but gradually the clamps loosened, showering them with gritty rust flakes. It took them some time to release them completely. With the clamps out of the way, they pushed at the iron cover. The seal gave and the cover lifted. As they pushed it to one side, sleet fell inside the tunnel. Krushen grasped the edge of the opening and hauled himself out, rolling clear. Kirov followed. He moved aside so the two team members could follow.

"My vehicles are over on the far side of the compound," Krushen said. "Let's go."

IN THE GLOOM OF THE TUNNEL Bolan could hear Tchenko's hard breathing as she forced herself along. The confines of the tunnel would not allow him to do anything but stay on her heels. In her determination to confront Mischa Krushen she was ignoring caution. It was only when they reached the end of the tunnel, finding the cover open, that he placed a firm hand on her shoulder.

"You wait," he said. "Ease off before you go out there with all guns blazing. Think with your head, not your heart."

"I won't let him walk away."

"I'm not suggesting that. But remember those men have just had their mission blown apart. Everything they came here for has gone. Right now they're alone in what they consider enemy territory, and cornered men can turn desperate. We need to be the opposite. Let me go out first to check things."

His tone was steady, firm and without panic. It was almost soothing. Tchenko knew he was right. If she blundered around in the dark, she might simply expose herself to harm.

"You are right, Cooper. Commander Seminov is always telling me the same thing. To consider the situation before I act. Sometimes I do listen to him."

"Really?"

Bolan slung his weapons across his back and grasped the edge of the cover. He raised his head slowly, peering around the immediate area. Security lights illuminated it clearly. This section of the compound was open, with the main building yards away. Over to his right was the loading dock where he and Tchenko had come together before entering the building. He didn't figure that their quarry would have reentered the building. Their purpose would be to get clear of the site so they could vanish.

He pulled himself clear, reaching back down to help Tchenko out. They crouched, weapons back online, and decided on their next move.

"There were a couple of SUVs over in that area," she said. "I saw them when I came in. Behind that storage shed. If they want transport, that would be the place they would go."

"We'll check it out." Bolan touched her arm. "Be careful."

"Cooper, did you know you are bleeding?" She indicated his arm. "And your head, too."

He hadn't even been aware of the head wound. Now Bolan felt the stinging sensation he had been ignoring. "Time for those later."

"Tough guy, huh?"

"Tough lady, huh?"

They broke position, using whatever cover they could find as they crossed the wide compound. The driving sleet helped to partially conceal them as they approached the storage shed. Easing around the structure, they were able to see the pair of SUVs. The driver's door of one stood open. Someone was inside the vehicle, leaning over the steering column. In the security light's glare Bolan recognized both Mischa Krushen and Viktor Kirov. The third man, armed with an autoweapon, looked like one of their team members. He was on alert, checking the immediate area. Bolan was about to move when he heard the SUV's engine burst into life, and he realized the man inside had been hot-wiring the vehicle, most probably because the keys had been lost. As soon as the SUV fired up there was a flurry of movement as the group headed for the vehicle.

"Cooper," Tchenko said.

"Go for the tires."

Bolan pushed away from the shed, angling across the compound, his M-4 tracking ahead. Out of the corner of his eye he saw Tchenko circling away from him, her approach taking her to the far side of the SUV.

The vehicle lurched forward, tires skidding on the wet ground as the driver hit the gas pedal hard. Bolan began to fire, driving his shots at the wheels. Sparks flew as his slugs hit the metal rims. He adjusted, fired again, and was rewarded with a rear tire blowing apart. He heard Tchenko's MP-5 crackling. She had dropped to one knee, steadying the SMG against her shoulder to determine her aim. She took out the front tire, then raised her weapon and laid a burst into the windshield. Glass imploded. The driver took it full in the face. The SUV swerved out of control, faltering as the engine stalled and coming to a jerky halt.

Doors flew open as the three remaining passengers scrambled out. The surviving shooter opened up with his SMG, Tchenko his target. She held her ground as slugs picked at the concrete, returning fire at the same time as Bolan. Neither of them knew who actually hit the guy. He fell back against the SUV, dropped and stayed there.

There was a split second lull in the exchange, then two

sharp pistol shots. Bolan saw Tchenko go down. He brought his M-4 around and settled it on Kirov as the man moved forward, his pistol still on the woman. Bolan stroked the trigger, emptying the magazine into Kirov's body. The Russian defied gravity and stayed on his feet until Bolan's final shot blew the back of his skull out. He went down then, spilling a mess of bloody debris across the concrete.

Mischa Krushen moved away from the SUV, his Glock held in a steady two-handed grip. He had the American firmly in his sights. He had seized the moment when Bolan had let go the empty M-4 and had reached for the Uzi. Even now he could save the day. Kill the American, then effect his escape. It would make—

The first shot blew his right knee to mush. Krushen screamed at the pain. He stumbled off balance, trying to overcome the agony. That was when the next slug shattered his left knee and he fell, pain sweeping over him. He braced himself on his hands, staring down at the bloody mess where his knees had been.

"It hurts, doesn't it, Mischa Krushen?"

Krushen knew the voice. He looked up and saw Natasha Tchenko standing feet away, her MP-5 leveled at him. Her left side was bloody where Kirov had shot her, and her face was sickly white. The color made her dark eyes stand out, eyes that were fixed on him and showing hatred he hadn't seen in a long time.

He pushed his pistol aside. "I am unarmed. I surrender."

"You think that will make a difference? My family was unarmed when you had them slaughtered. My father, mother and brother. You know what your animals did to him?"

"Face reality, Tchenko. I was doing my duty for the state. For the good of Russia. Sacrifice is necessary."

"You bastards always fall back on that. To justify your actions you lean on the state. People suffer. People die. And all you can say is 'I was doing my duty.' Good. It will ease my conscience if I can tell myself I was also doing my duty. By taking criminals off the streets."

The MP-5 moved a fraction before Tchenko pulled the trigger and held it back until the magazine had exhausted itself. The sustained burst hit Krushen in his midsection, tearing at flesh, bones and organs. Close-range rounds pulverized everything in their path, blood spraying out in glistening arcs. The shock on Krushen's face was still there even after he dropped back to the concrete, quietly coughing up frothed blood.

The MP-5 clicked empty. Tchenko's finger was still holding back the trigger. She turned in Bolan's direction, her face showing the pain she was feeling. He took a step toward her and she folded, slumping to the wet ground, blood starting to spread out from beneath her slack body.

In the distance Bolan heard the rising wail of sirens. He figured that triggering the sprinkler system had to have set off an alarm in Singletree. He just hoped there was an ambulance in with the response.

He knelt beside Tchenko. He raised her head, brushing at the wet flakes of snow that had settled. She opened her eyes.

"It hurts, Cooper. Dammit, it hurts."

"For a lady, you certainly cuss a lot."

"Is that not done in America? Not by real ladies?"

"In some circles maybe. But cussing or not, you are still one hell of a lady, Natasha Tchenko."

"Now you are cussing, Cooper."

"Yeah? Well, it's been that kind of a day."

She began to cry then, sobs that came from deep inside. Bolan held her, knowing that she wasn't crying for herself. It was her family. For the ones who were gone, taken from her in a moment of madness. She had tracked down and settled her grievance with the man responsible. It would go a long way to bring her closure, but it would never replace what she had lost.

Bolan knew that only too well. Whatever he had done in the past. No matter how final, it would never bring his family back. Let him look into their faces again. Hold them in his arms. Nothing could ever do that. It was the cruelest fact of all.

He was still cradling Tchenko in his arms when the convoy of vehicles swept into view, filling the night with their noise and flashing lights. He refused to surrender to the armed officers from the Singletree sheriff's department until Tchenko had been attended to and placed in the ambulance. His quiet determination and commanding presence held the cops back, and it was only after he had seen the ambulance on its way that he handed over his weapons and allowed himself to be taken into custody. After he had been searched and his Justice Department credentials found, there was an easing of tension. He asked to be allowed to make a call and finally got through to Brognola. The inevitable conversation with the local sheriff set up parameters of jurisdiction, and Bolan was handed back the phone. Brognola told him he would be flying up himself immediately. The Executioner could stand down.

It took days before the dust settled.

Bolan and Brognola were involved at the site for several hours. There was a great deal to sort out. Even after the dead were taken away and the wounded transported to hospital, the Black Judas computer lab was gone through a number of times. The grenade blast had wiped out the system. Bolan had set out to destroy it, and he had succeeded. Cyberexperts had been flown in to sift through the debris. They had wandered around the room clad in white coveralls, wearing latex gloves, bagging and tagging anything they thought might give them a clue as to how the Black Judas program worked.

"These guys would pick over a damned corpse to find something," Brognola growled.

"Maybe they won't be lucky."

"Those Russians put some thought into this place," Brognola said. "The way they maintained the lab for the day that might never have come. Hell, even down to that escape tunnel. Do they still hate us that much?"

"From what Valentine told me it was down to a cadre of hard-liners who refused to accept the end of the cold war.

General Berienko and company. Thing is, they were running Black Judas off the wall."

"We got lucky. Because this was a nonsanctioned operation it's given the Russians a get-out-of-jail-free card. Deniability. They're throwing it all at the feet of the FSB, making them the bad guys. We have them dead to rights, caught conducting an aggressive operation on foreign soil. Hell, Striker, relations with them are strained as it is right now. Fallout could have been heavy. But we have the proof, we have the bodies and we have emerging data on the way they financed CoreM. Names are being named. Accounts traced. I spoke to the President a little earlier. He's already laid down the law to the Russian premier and this will be kept out of the public eye as much as possible."

"What about CoreM? If this place is shut down, people here in Singletree are going lose jobs."

"The President has decided that ownership will be taken over by a strictly U.S. management team. The site will close for a couple of weeks while everything is cleared up. After that it's back to normal production."

"So what happened here?"

"Oh, a foiled attempt to hijack goods from the warehouse. Seems an organized gang tried to run off with expensive electronic equipment but it was prevented by undercover agents from the Justice Department."

Bolan nodded. "A cover-up."

"You could call it that. Better than telling the public we had Russian teams working on U.S. soil, attempting to wipe out the entire American financial system and plunge us into bankruptcy."

"Hal, the dead undercover FBI agent?"

"The President has had another session with the agencies. He used this incident to try to make them understand the need for cooperation and openness. He did point the finger at the Bureau and placed responsibility for the agent's death entirely on them."

"Will it do any good? It's not the first time and it won't be the last."

"Being cynical, Striker?"

"Being a realist."

Brognola huddled into his thick coat as they crossed the compound to the car he had hired. The weather was still wintry, snow dropping from the high peaks. Behind the wheel the big Fed asked, "What's the latest on Miss Tchenko?"

"She's going to be hospitalized for a while. She lost a lot of blood before they dug those bullets out. It'll be a couple of weeks before she can fly back to Moscow," Bolan said.

"At least she's going back to a friendly welcome."

"You can thank Valentine for that. He had her down as on special assignment for the OCD. So her being AWOL has been covered. I'm not sure his superiors were fully convinced, but he reminded them they were vindicated following all the detail that he came through with after the Krushen-Mishkin situation."

"Striker, this was a tangle from day one."

"Don't I know it. Tell Aaron next time he picks up something suspicious to iron out all the kinks before he drags us all in."

Brognola grinned. "I'll tell him. Do you think he'll take any notice?"

"Hell, no," Bolan said.

JAMES AXLER

DEATH LANDS

Plague Lords

In a ruined world, past and future clash with terrifying force...

The sulfur-teeming Gulf of Mexico is the poisoned end of earth, but here, Ryan and the others glean rumors of whole cities deep in South America that survived the blast intact. But as the companions contemplate a course of action, a new horror approaches on the horizon. The Lords of Death are Mexican pirates raiding stockpiles with a grim vengeance. When civilization hits rock bottom, a new stone age will emerge, with its own personal day of blood reckoning.

In the Deathlands, the future could always be worse. Now it is...

Available December wherever you buy books.

ROGUE ANGEL™

SWORDSMAN'S LEGACY
by AleX Archer

For Annja Creed, finding a Musketeer's sword is a dream come true. Until it becomes a nightmare.

In need of a break from work, archaeologist Annja Creed visits France to indulge one of her greatest fantasies: finding D'Artagnan's lost sword. The rapier has been missing since the seventeenth century, and Ascher Vallois, one of Annja's treasure-hunting friends, believes he has located the site of the relic. But Annja learns Vallois has made a huge sacrifice to protect the sword and its secret from a relic hunter. And the man won't stop until he gets everything he wants— including Annja.

Available November wherever books are sold.

GOLD EAGLE®

ROOM 59

THE HARDEST CHOICES
ARE THE MOST PERSONAL....

New recruit Jason Siku is ex-CIA, a cold, calculating
agent with black ops skills and a brilliant mind—a
loner perfect for deep espionage work. Using his Inuit
heritage and a search for his lost family as cover, he
tracks intelligence reports of a new Russian Oscar-class
submarine capable of reigniting the Cold War. But when
Jason discovers weapons smugglers and an idealistic yet
dangerous brother he never knew existed, his mission
and a secret hope collide with deadly consequences.

Look for

THE ties THAT BIND

by

cliff RYDER

GOLD
EAGLE
®

Available October 2008
wherever books are sold.

www.readgoldeagle.blogspot.com   GRM594

James Axler
Outlanders®

PANTHEON OF VENGEANCE

War machines and rebels clash in ancient Greece…

In his human skin, Baron Cobalt nearly destroyed Cerberus with his quest for power. Now evolved into his godly Annunaki form as Overlord Marduk, he's reconsolidating his power and claiming the Mediterranean. As Marduk's Nephilim-led forces challenge the ruling Hera Olympiad and her legion of cybernetic demigods to a death dance, Kane and the Cerberus warriors harness the power of a cyberarmy eager to bring retribution and justice to the real monsters of antiquity.

Available in August 2008 wherever you buy books.

If you are looking for spine-tingling
action and adventure, be sure to check out
all that Gold Eagle books has to offer...

Rogue Angel by **Alex Archer**
Deathlands by **James Axler**
Outlanders by **James Axler**
The Executioner by **Don Pendleton**
Mack Bolan by **Don Pendleton**
Stony Man by **Don Pendleton**
^{NEW} **Room 59** by **Cliff Ryder**

Journey to lost worlds, experience the heat of a fierce
firefight, survive in a postapocalyptic future or go
deep undercover with clandestine operatives.

Look for these books wherever books are sold.

**GOLD
EAGLE** ®

**Fiction that surprises,
gratifies and entertains.
Real Heroes.
Real Adventure.**

www.readgoldeagle.blogspot.com